Also By Colin Mustful,

Thy Eternal Summer: The U.S. – Dakota Conflict of 1862

A Welcome Tragedy: Factors That Led to the U.S. – Dakota Conflict of 1862

Unwarranted Expulsion: The Removal of the Winnebago Indians

The Generation of 1837: Attitudes, Policies and Actions Toward Indian Populations of Argentina

The Battle of Point Pleasant: A Critical Event at the Onset of a Revolution

The Tobacco Controversy of 1857: An Early Debate and Its Delayed Results

The American Tobacco Controversy: The Tobacco Controversy of 1857 Revisited

Unabashed Hypocrisy: A Dichotomy of Values

Grace
at
Spirit Lake

Colin Mustful

Illustrated by Bennett Berning
Edited by Jennifer Quinlan

ISBN: 978-1-4834-1265-8 (sc)
ISBN: 978-1-4834-1264-1 (e)

Lulu Publishing Services rev. date: 6/17/2014

Dedication

To my friend and former co-worker Dan Snyder;
a history major, just like me.

Acknowledgements

Rachelle Kuehl

Brandon Mustful

Sean Beggin

Ryan Parsons

Jessica Mustful

Jennifer Quinlan

AUTHOR'S NOTE

Let me try and explain myself. This is neither a historical fiction novel nor a work of narrative nonfiction. It is both. Throughout the book there are elements of historical fiction and narrative nonfiction. If you begin with the expectation that it is one or the other, you will be disappointed. Historical fiction and narrative nonfiction are both effective means of conveying history, but I have sought to capture and utilize the best qualities of both forms in order to tell this story. Using these means, both fiction and nonfiction, I have placed myself within the history as I observed it through primary and secondary source materials. But in order to do this I needed a vehicle. That vehicle is Antoine Joseph Campbell, the main character and narrator. Antoine Joseph Campbell was a central figure of the events which followed the Spirit Lake Massacre of 1857. At the time of the events he was 31 years old, which also happens to be my own age (at the time of writing this). It is conceivable that his views would not be much unlike my own. Therefore, I used Antoine Joseph Campbell as my own eyes and ears. I did not much embellish his involvement in the history, but utilized his participation as a means to insert not just his thoughts and emotions, but also my own thoughts, feelings, and observations regarding this part of our history. I did not do this in a selfish and self-serving manner, but rather as an objective means to provoke thoughtful discussion and reaction.

I don't know what can be gleaned from this part of our history. But I think it is important that we know. I think it is important that we become educated to the whole story, to each perspective, and to the entire context. Every character in this book is real and the majority of events are historically accurate. This story is an introduction to your history, what you do with it is up to you.

You don't know me. We've never met. You have not read about me. My name is on no one's lips. Even if you happened to come across my name it was insignificant enough that you did not notice or remember. But that does not mean I was not important. It does not mean that I do not have a story to tell. Rather, it is quite the opposite. That is why I am here today. That is why I have transcended time to be here. Because I do have a story to tell. A story you've never heard. It is a story that occurred years before your time. This story left an indelible stamp on your past and a permanent mark on your future. You don't see it; you can't hear it; you've never even thought about it. I wish I could say you forgot, but the fact is you were never told. It's history—it's *your* history. I want to share that history with you. I want to tell you a story.

Before I begin I suppose it would be prudent to introduce myself. My name is Antoine Joseph Campbell. Most people refer to me as Joseph, some refer to me as A.J., after my grandfather, but no one refers to me as Antoine, except perhaps my father. I was born in 1826 at Mendota, which lay just across the river from Fort Snelling. I am the eldest of four sons. I also have two older sisters and two younger sisters. My grandfather came to this territory in the mid-18th century. Archibald John Campbell was his name. He was a Scottish-born, French-speaking trader who settled at Prairie du Chien. He married a Dakota woman named Ninse, my grandmother. The relationship between my grandparents forged the necessary kinship ties that were essential for trade between the Europeans and the Natives. At the time, Prairie du Chien was the center of the northwest frontier. For my grandfather and the surrounding Natives, it was the center of the world. It was a meeting place where Indians brought their furs and Europeans brought their goods. Each spring the area was teeming with activity as traders tried to woo Indians and Indians sought to woo traders, each for access to more and higher-quality goods. Neither sought to change the other, they simply wanted what the other had to offer.

My grandparents had five children together. My father, Scott, was the second eldest. He grew up between two distinct and rich cultures. He learned the value of a good pelt from his father and how to become useful in the fur trade. But he also learned the ways of his Dakota mother. He spoke Dakota well and he knew how to hunt for goods and for food. My father's knowledge and expertise of both cultures earned him a position with the U.S. Government. In 1819 my father left Prairie du Chien. The fur trade was declining and the frontier was moving west. My father took a job at Fort St. Anthony (which later became Fort Snelling) as the interpreter for the newly appointed Indian agent Lawrence Taliaferro. Taliaferro was a major in the U.S. military and a veteran of the War of 1812. He was a cunning, intelligent man who sought to establish a government presence in the northwest. Taliaferro was a young man from Virginia and he knew very little of Indian affairs. Thusly, Taliaferro leaned heavily on my father's advice and knowledge. My father was instrumental in establishing and sustaining the credibility of the agency with the Dakota. In 1825, my father played a crucial role in the signing of the Treaty of Prairie du Chien, which identified specific tribal areas for living and for hunting. He drew on tribal connections and he understood the negotiations needed in order to reach an agreement.

But before long, things changed as they were apt to do in this part of the world and at this junction in history. By the mid-1830s, eastern missionaries began to settle in the area. This started with Samuel and Gideon Pond, who settled along the shores of Mde Maka Ska (otherwise known as Lake Calhoun) and founded a school. They were followed post haste by missionaries Thomas S. Williamson and Stephen R. Riggs. My father assisted these men with necessary language instruction so that they could translate scripture. The missionaries were devout people who gave their lives to the service of God and the Dakota, but they also ushered in a new era to the territory. They ushered in an era of conflict and change; one of cultural misunderstanding. This cultural collision was then aggravated by men like Henry Hastings Sibley who arrived in the territory in 1834. Sibley was a young, ambitious fur trader from Detroit. He immediately inserted himself into the political, economic, and social structure of the area. He made certain that things would never be as they once were. But I digress.

Like the treaty of Prairie du Chien in 1825, my father played a vital role in the 1837 treaty of St. Peter. In this treaty, the Dakota agreed to sell their lands east of the Mississippi River thereby opening the land to white settlement. This treaty set Indian removal into law and was a precursor for things to come. Taliaferro left his post at Fort Snelling in 1839, which gave way for Sibley and other traders to establish their own devices and methods. My father stayed on with the new agent Amos J. Bruce, but things were never quite the same. Corruption and neglect increasingly found their way into the territory and my father started drinking. In 1843 he was dismissed. He was unhappy and intemperate until he passed away in 1850.

My mother was a mixed-blood, just as my father. She was the daughter of a Menominee mother and a French-Ojibwe trader named Louis Menagre. In life she became a trusted companion and advisor to the great Indian Chief Little Crow. The two were related by blood. My mother lived well into old age, not passing away until 1900.

I lived a rich childhood. I had the advantage of growing up in two worlds. I admired my father and partook in all dealings which he allowed. I had a formal education and discovered a deep faith in God through Catholicism. When I was not mimicking my father or when I was not delved in study I was frolicking with the Indian boys at Kaposia. Kaposia was Little Crow's Indian village. All of my fondest memories originate from this place. The village was set among the pristine waters of the bending Mississippi and lay just below the white cliffs of Imnejah-skah, otherwise known as Pig's Eye. It was a beautiful landscape filled with activity. Every spring, traders announced their arrival with the chanting of French melodies. For weeks they turned Kaposia into a bustling marketplace dealing goods such as blankets, kettles, beads, needles, bolts of cloth, silk handkerchiefs, steel awls, thread, and whatever else you can imagine. The summers were a warm, happy time. Games were played continually while boys challenged each other with countless feats of strength and bravery. Feats with the bow and arrow, foot and pony races, wrestling and swimming. I came to envy the full-blooded Indian boys for their care-free nature. It seemed that when circumstances were favorable, the Indians were the happiest people in the world. I admired them also for their skill and knowledge and dedication toward learning. Their knowledge was passed down from generation to generation. Boys practiced daily the skills of their fathers and learned to listen and recite the stories of their elders. They even studied the animals to acknowledge their sensible habits and to discover how they might outwit them. The Indian way of life was indeed remarkable to me.

I was fortunate to grow up as I did among two distinct and rich cultures. Almost without realizing I learned to speak English, French, Dakota, Menominee, and even some Ojibwe. I was adaptable in a world that was constantly adapting. As soon as I was old enough I took a job as a clerk in St. Paul. I married at age nineteen a beautiful woman named Mary Ann Dalton. Mary was from Indiana and she traveled in Yankee social circles. I never met anyone quite like Mary; I think that is what drew me to her. We lived in a house right next door to my parents and family who were dear to us. We spent five years in this way. But after the death of my father in 1850, dramatic changes followed. In 1851, the Mdewakanton and Wahpekute signed the treaty of Mendota in which they relinquished their lands west of the Mississippi and with it my beloved Kaposia. The Dakota agreed to settle onto a reservation ten miles wide along either side of the Minnesota River. This of course meant rapid settlement for the areas surrounding St. Paul and St. Anthony. It also signified a major loss for the culture and way of life of the Dakota Indians. The Indians viewed life on a government reservation as physical and moral degradation. For a people who were once as free as the birds around them, a change to reservation life caused great suffering. But such was the case for the Dakota who, just since the time of my birth, were relegated onto smaller and smaller tracts of land. And with it came increased government intervention, dwindling game, and religious and cultural scrutiny.

I chose to take my family and move with my Dakota kin to the new reservation. Two of my brothers and I took work at the agency trading post run by Nathan and Andrew Myrick. My wife ran a boarding house while we sent our two daughters to receive a formal education in St. Paul.

Life on the Agency was never perfect. It was nothing like my days as a boy when surrounded by wilderness and when Indians vastly outnumbered whites. Frame houses replaced dwellings made of bark and hide and farming replaced the hunt. But we managed to make a living and the whites and Indians lived relatively peaceably side by side. I worked alongside the whites but I maintained strong kinship ties with my native friends and relatives. With my knowledge of languages I was found to be quite useful around the agency. Following in the footsteps of my father, I took work as the Government Interpreter.

But I have said enough. Now that we have met my story can begin. I know this story because I lived it. The year was 1857.

Forming an Expedition

July 12, 1857 - - "Gentlemen! Please!" shouted Major Cullen with hands raised.

I repeated his words in Dakota, but surely no one heard me over the commotion.

Major Cullen lowered his hands to his hips, tilted his head and scowled in an impatient manner.

"Gentlemen I beg of you, please settle yourselves," he hollered once more. "It is upon your own benefit that we reach a peaceful accord."

Major Cullen was the newly appointed Superintendent of Indian Affairs. His physical appearance was not imposing. He was short and thin and he often behaved in a smug and pretentious way. He spared no manner of eloquence either in diction or in dress no matter whether it was the Indians of the frontier or the President of these United States. He continued to stand in a pompous and impatient fashion in front of the thousands of Mdewakanton and Wahpekute Indians of the Lower Agency. He wore an elaborate overcoat, a distinct and colorful sash and he had garishly well-groomed facial hair. All of it seemed quite unnecessary. Major Cullen was a military man. Though diminutive in size he was brash in character. He knew how to take orders and how to give them out. He lacked no courage. What he did lack was tact. He was direct in a rather distasteful manner. He had little or no knowledge of the Dakota Indians or their way of life. His position was a political appointment no doubt acquired through the friend of a friend who never once considered the unique social climate of the northwestern frontier. I did not disrespect the Superintendent; for his job was an unenviable one, but I doubt if he could sit down and give a succinct, logical and intelligent description of the difference between the habits, manners, customs, and peculiarities of a Dakota Indian and a snapping turtle.

"Sirs, calm yourselves!" shouted Major Cullen.

At this point I was no longer translating the Major word for word. I was pleading with the Dakota men just as he was. But the Indian commotion was assiduous and unrelenting.

Suddenly there was a hush; an immediate and absolute silence fell over the crowd of hungry and frustrated Dakota Indians.

I searched the new setting with stunned curiosity over this abrupt development. And then I saw him and my curiosity turned to realization. *Of course*, I thought to myself, *who else could have such a profound impact on the men of the Lower Agency?* It was Little Crow.

Little Crow was the undisputed Chief of the Mdewakanton Dakota Indians. He was the third in a line of Crows who led his people. He had a strong posture, a distinct face, and a calm demeanor. On this occasion he wore traditional Dakota dress with moccasins, leggings wrapped with long-hanging weasel skin, and a buckskin shirt garnished with extremely long fringes. His hair was parted down the middle and hung down over his shoulders and held tight to his head by a woven sash that had three large eagle feathers tied into the back. Although his age was unknown to me, I considered him to be in his forties. He is a blood relative to my family, though the exact relation is difficult to determine. We called each other cousin.

"In your reluctance you gain nothing," Little Crow said assuredly from where he now stood in front of the crowd. "This wasichu chief was sent here by our Great Father," Little Crow continued as he turned just slightly toward Major Cullen. "I have traveled many moons and seen our Great Father. He has great wealth and will provide for us much like the buffalo provided for our fathers. But we must listen to his white children or like the buffalo we too will fade away. This is all I have to say."

The crowd was silent as Little Crow slipped back into the sea of Indians as quickly and quietly as he had appeared. Reverence for the great Dakota leader now hovered over the massive assembly.

"I will proceed then," said Major Cullen in the same poised manner as he always spoke. "I believe you know why you have been called here today. One of your own, the insidious Inkpaduta and his band of renegade Wahpekute are loose on the frontier and wreaking much havoc upon the settlers of the area. He and his small band have perpetrated the Spirit Lake Massacre, killing some forty settlers along the frontier."

He paused to let his words take effect. It took only moments for shouts of discontent to rise once more out of the great multitude before me.

"This band belongs to your people," continued Major Cullen as he raised his voice to quell the shouts. "As long as Inkpaduta roams free the citizens of the United States are not safe. As such, he and his band must be captured and summarily punished," he stated with one fist held forward. I translated his words as directly as I could although I felt uneasy doing so. Despite their discontent Major Cullen had their attention.

"Now, I have been instructed by my superiors in Washington City," Major Cullen said in a more explanatory tone, "to withhold your annuities . . ." and with that the crowd erupted in anger.

The shouts came from men, women, and children alike who together vehemently protested this unfortunate information. Major Cullen could do nothing but wait as the crowd expelled its acrimony on the man in front of them. Major Cullen showed no fear, but only annoyance. I cringed at the deafening volume and only wished it would stop.

After what seemed like several minutes, the crowd began to quiet even though they appeared in no way bankrupt of discontent.

"Gentlemen, I can hear your protests, but you have no choice in the matter," Major Cullen shouted with his first display of any real human quality. "I too have no choice in the matter. I am helpless toward you and therefore your shouts are useless. I have been instructed to withhold your annuities until you yourselves have apprehended the villain Inkpaduta and his men."

Shouts continued to spew from the crowd but this time they were quickly silenced by the Wahpeton chief Mazaomani who raised his hands to speak.

"You say Inkpaduta is one of ours, but he is not."

The crowd was attentive and listened.

"He lives south. He battles with the Sac and Fox. We have not seen the Scarlet Point for many seasons. Why does the Great Father punish us for his deeds?"

The crowd hooted and hollered in agreement. Their calls were shrill and loud.

"It is true Inkpaduta did not take part in the treaty of 1851," replied Major Cullen forthrightly, "but he did receive annuities in 1855 and 1856. Furthermore, and more importantly, the agent was reluctant to pay, but you Dakota spoke up for Inkpaduta. You argued that his blood ties and marriage ties entitled him to the payment. Do you now alter your position out of personal prejudice?"

"Those who backed Inkpaduta only did so because they feared Inkpaduta's revenge if they did not," answered Mazaomani forcefully.

"It matters . . ." Major Cullen paused while he waited for the commotion to recede. "It matters not why. You must be held responsible for the lawless characters of your nation. In view of this responsibility I would advise you to formulate some means by which you can apprehend Inkpaduta." Major Cullen again spoke in a manner both plain and straightforward. He appeared unmoved by the shouts of indignation directly in front of him.

Mazaomani gave no reply but just disappeared into the crowd. For several moments the Dakota raised their protest, this time less commanding than before but bullish all the same.

Next to raise his hand and quiet the crowd was Sleepy Eye, the old chief from Swan Lake. Sleepy Eye was once well respected and like Little Crow he too visited Washington, but that was many years ago. Now, due to age, he had stiffened limbs, a weathered face, and he had impaired mental faculties. However, he remained good humored and seemed impossible to offend.

"You have given us no choice," called out Sleepy Eye in a surprisingly audible tone. "Your traders have handed us great debt. Your chiefs have taken our hunting grounds. The numberless whites have made us dependent on your gifts. We are like fawn who cry out to their mother. If you say we must go, we must go. But your warriors are strong. They have many guns. They are paid to fight. We will go, but you must send your warriors with us."

Shouts of approval echoed over the assembly. Men raised their guns and bow strings. Many of them sounded more like wild animals than men.

"Impossible," returned the superintendent, but few heard him say this. "This is a council," pleaded the superintendent in an attempt to quiet the crowd. "This is a council and your cooperation is necessary."

Again Little Crow quieted the energetic Dakota men and women. "Sir," said Little Crow calmly, "we fear to go after hostile men. We only ask a few white soldiers."

"This cannot be granted," replied the superintendent as he shook his head. "Firstly, there are now very few soldiers at Fort Ridgely. Major Sherman has already informed me that there are not sufficient numbers at the post to make it advisable to spare any. Furthermore, it is the policy of not sending soldiers to cooperate with Indians. This policy exists in order that the soldiers do not become exposed to treachery on the part of the Indians."

This received an obvious negative reaction, but Major Cullen continued.

"Finally . . . finally," he shouted in a perturbed manner, "an expedition of that kind would rely on troops to do the work of capturing and killing."

A negative reaction again came from the crowd, but not nearly as harsh as the ones before. Major Cullen gave a rational response and I think the Dakota knew it.

Major Cullen then effectively raised his hands to calm the crowd and continue speaking. "Unless you Dakota Indians decide to undertake such an expedition alone and unaided, other measures than those already taken would be resorted to from necessity."

It was clear that Major Cullen was determined to withhold the annuity funds from all Dakota tribes regardless of their protests.

"May we council with each other over this matter?" asked Mahpiya, an Indian of Sleepy Eye's band.

"Yes," answered the superintendent, "you shall have one hour to confer."

Major Cullen then turned and walked briskly in the direction of his tent. He made no indication for me to follow. The Indians quickly organized themselves in a large circle and I could see they were already deep in conference. Although I could not hear, I could see the speaker gesticulate each word in a wild fashion. I could only wait and watch.

I was a half-breed. I grew up with the Dakota Indians. I played their games, spoke their language, and learned their customs. But I also grew up as a white. I had a formal education, I lived in a wood-frame house, I wore white man's clothes and I worked for the white man's trading post. I was well known and well liked among the Dakota, but not all of them trusted me. However, and more importantly, I had Little Crow's trust. Despite this fact, I was a U.S. Interpreter. My duty belonged to Major Cullen and the U.S. Government. I was caught between both perspectives but belonged to neither. I wanted the best outcome for each side.

This was a tense time along the frontier. Customarily the annuities were paid to the Dakota in late June. In order to receive payment, the Dakota flocked to the Upper and Lower agencies in the thousands. The Indians came prepared to receive their money and also to celebrate. I cannot blame them for their discontent when the superintendent informed them that they would not be paid. Major Cullen had already been to the Upper Agency where they firmly declined to go after Inkpaduta. The Massacre, which had occurred in early March, created a tense situation along the frontier causing many whites to flee the area. Since that time the fears of the region have calmed, but the need to capture the culprits of the massacre has caused renewed tensions between the government and the Dakota. That is why we now stand in council.

Major Cullen returned within the hour looking agitated and in need of rest. It had been a long few days for him. He was alone and without Agent Flandrau who had left for St. Paul to attend to his duties as a member of the Constitutional Convention of the territory. "It is time for your response," Major Cullen called out.

The Indians gave no acknowledgement.

"I must have your response," again shouted the superintendent.

As Major Cullen opened his mouth to speak again Little Crow appeared before us.

"We believe it unfit to punish our band for the wrong of another band," Little Crow began. He spoke in his usual stoic demeanor. "Now you say we must shed our blood to find your criminal. We give you our land and you vow to supply us with goods. Now you say no. We cannot survive without the goods you promise. We do not think it is right, but you have given us no other way. We must feed our children and provide for our women. We will go after Inkpaduta. You will see we are good. Then the Great Father will give us his favor."

Little Crow's words were followed by loud and sporadic shouts by the Indian warriors who squawked like birds toward the sun.

"Before we go, you must know we are poor," continued Little Crow. "We have no guns, we have no bread. We will die if we have no supplies."

"I understand," was Major Cullen's quick response. "I will furnish you with the necessary provisions and I will make a requisition on Major Sherman for transportation. Surely we can supply you with a wagon and mules."

Major Cullen paused for a reply but Little Crow only nodded. Major Cullen nodded in return as if acknowledging and thanking Little Crow for his obvious service in quieting the disturbance and expelling the malcontents.

The men dispersed in all directions seemingly undisturbed. But the magnitude of what just occurred felt heavy on me. Whether by force or manipulation the Dakota now had to chase and capture one of their own. Not for peace or justice or even revenge. They were made to go out of necessity; necessity for their own lives and the well-being of their families. And it was not just this moment, but years and years of an unbalanced treaty system that led to this moment. Leverage was gained by the government and now that leverage was being utilized to force the Dakota to do the will of the white man. Pursuit and capture was indeed necessary and in fact dutiful, but to see it contrived through such manipulative means made my heart heavy.

Saturday, March 21
Fort Dodge, Iowa

Dear Eliza,

I have never been one to journal. I have always wanted to, but for some reason it does not maintain my interest. But now, I would like to take a different approach. I will write to you. I am not certain whether you will ever see these words. That is not important. Rather, writing to you somehow motivates me to write. And as I enter this perilous and unknown stage, I believe it vital that a record be kept. These are my letters to you; this is my record of our attempt at rescue.

What happy times were so recently passed with your family at Okoboji. When I came to survey the new settlement I never anticipated I would meet such a fine and diligent family such as your own. Your father treated me as his own brother and your mother's hospitality was unmatched. And the children, oh, the children that made it such a gay and happy home. What wonderful evenings we passed here on the beautiful and bounteous frontier with not so much as a care.

But how things can turn dreadful in a moment and what sorrows I carry. I never did express to you how I felt. Your youth which brings me to life. Your smile which lightens the room. Your eyes which pierce my heart. Oh how I have longed for you throughout this cold and dark winter. But now I fear the worst. We have received word of an Indian massacre at Spirit and Okoboji Lakes. I know not the fate of you and your family. That is why we gather here at Fort Dodge. We gather to form an expedition to rescue those who have been attacked and to pursue and capture those who incited the attack. My heart aches with uncertainty, but remembering that you had departed with Dr. Strong for Springfield last fall I find a glimmer of hope that you are still safe. There are so many things I left unsaid and I now fear that I may never get the chance to. Together with other brave and intrepid men, we will make our way to you, through all toil and trouble.

Lovingly yours,
William

A Fatal Mistake

July 13-21, 1857 - - The following days were spent in selecting the men who would undertake the expedition to capture Inkpaduta. This work was done mostly between Major Cullen and Little Crow who labored night and day in organizing the party. Immediately word was sent to the Upper Agency to inform those Indians on the decision to form an expedition. In this resolve they were joined by the Sissetons and then the Wahpetons. Each chief of the four eastern tribes; Mdewakanton, Wahpekute, Sisseton, and Wahpeton, were in fact required to provide a quota of warriors. Ultimately, one hundred six warriors were selected as a part of the expedition. Little Crow was placed in command; there were no objections. As Major Cullen's interpreter I was also selected to go, along with six other half-breeds which included my brothers John and Baptiste. Being as ready as possible, we departed in pursuit of Inkpaduta from the Yellow Medicine.

I did not have much fear or apprehension concerning the expedition. I was not a warrior and it was doubtful I would encounter a life-threatening situation. I merely wished for justice in the same way all others did.

This was not my first expedition of the summer. Just several weeks prior I was part of an expedition sent to capture or kill any of those from Inkpaduta's band who were rumored to be at Yellow Medicine; Yellow Medicine being the Upper Agency because it lay forty miles upriver from the Redwood or Lower Agency. This expedition was organized by Agent Charles Flandrau. Agent Flandrau was a young lawyer from

New York. He was intelligent, social, and highly charismatic. He was also energetic and strong with a wiry physique and legs like an antelope. He was appointed as an agent to the Dakota in August of 1856. Immediately he proved himself to be honest and capable and he worked in close contact with the Dakota Indians. Agent Flandrau was industrious and ambitious and he spared nothing of himself in that summer of 1857.

In late June, Agent Flandrau had received word from Sam Brown that Inkpaduta and his band were in the vicinity of the Yellow Medicine. This startling information came from a reliable source as Mr. Brown was a trader at the Yellow Medicine and a brother to the respected Indian Agent Joseph R. Brown. At once Agent Flandrau consulted Colonel Alexander at Fort Ridgely in order to consider the best course of action. Colonel Alexander agreed that an effort should be made to pursue and punish any of Inkpaduta's men at Yellow Medicine. The Colonel gave Agent Flandrau a lieutenant and fifteen men for the duty. In addition to these soldiers, Agent Flandrau selected several well-known and useful men. This included my two brothers, John and Hippolyte, and me. Also, there was Mr. Morse, a graduate of West Point and son of Samuel Morse, the famous telegraph inventor. Then there was Mr. Charles Jenny, a most interesting character. Mr. Jenny was a great traveler, having seen most of the world, but having traveled by sea, he had never learned to ride a horse. James Magner was a young Irishman who was a great horseman and a splendid fellow. I was impressed by his physique.

As soon as we were ready we set out from the Redwood Agency toward the Yellow Medicine, a distance of about forty miles. We traveled on along the Minnesota River, I on horseback along with the other men chosen by Agent Flandrau while Mr. Jenny and the soldiers traveled in several mule-drawn wagons. We each had a shotgun and a revolver. We traveled steadily upon the level prairie. It was a beautiful country with great green timber along the river and long rich prairie grass stretching beyond as far as the eye could see. If one stopped and listened, all that could be heard was the sound of the grass blowing and swaying in the wind.

Halfway between the Redwood and Yellow Medicine Agencies was a curious butte or elevation. It was a well-traveled butte since the Indians from time immemorial had traversed its path. Indians sought high routes since they were always on the lookout for the enemy.

When we reached this butte the Indian Anpetutokeha or John Other Day was there to meet us. He was sent as a guide by Agent Joe Brown. Other Day was a cut-hair, an Indian who had converted to Christianity, wore white-man's clothes, and took up farming. Despite his calico shirt, brown pantaloons, and short hair, through his presence alone he appeared remarkably like a Dakota Indian. He was seated Indian fashion with one leg curled over the other at the summit of the hill with a long stone pipe in his mouth. His skin was dark and his face was stern as if in deep contemplation. As he sat he did not show the slightest sign of recognition or interest, but waited until spoken to.

"John Other Day," Agent Flandrau finally said. "John Other Day," he said again in a raised tone.

The passive Indian gave a look and a nod.

"I am Agent Charles Flandrau of the Lower Agency," explained our expedition leader in a formal manner. "I have received word that certain members of Inkpaduta's band are currently residing in or near the Yellow Medicine Agency. I have come, along with my small expedition of capable men, in search of these renegade Indians. I have been told that you might guide us in locating them."

John Other Day inhaled on his pipe once more as if he were disinterested. "They are here," he finally said with smoke escaping his mouth.

"Where? How many?" Agent Flandrau asked hastily.

"I did not count them. I do not know," replied Other Day, who was still seated casually. "The lodges that belong to the band of Inkpaduta are at Yellow Medicine."

"Can you take us there?" urged Agent Flandrau.

"The camp is not hard to find," said Other Day, who seemed disengaged. "It lay upriver. It is about half a day's walk past the white man's buildings. But it is separate from all other camps and is easy to see. I count several lodges, but not all belong to Inkpaduta."

Agent Flandrau paused and Other Day took another breath from his pipe. "How do you suppose we can distinguish the men of Inkpaduta from the innocent Sisseton of the Upper Agency?" asked Agent Flandrau after a few moments.

"Charge the camp," replied Other Day with little hesitation. "The guilty men will run or show fight. The innocent men will remain passive."

Agent Flandrau did not answer but instead looked toward me. I could not argue with Other Day's logic so I nodded in agreement.

"Very well," replied Agent Flandrau. "We will make a charge on the camp and the guilty parties will make themselves known."

We left for Yellow Medicine with Other Day as our guide. We traveled through the night. It was rather impressive to watch our guide. He was sleek and silent with an innate sense of direction. He reminded me of a wolf whose ears are constantly pricked for sound, and who seems to sleep with one eye open.

We arrived at the Yellow Medicine River just as the sun was beginning to rise. On a high plateau just across the river and in plain view sat the camp which we sought. We were still about a mile off and at this point we began to move with stealth in earnest. It was near incomprehensible the way John Other Day could move noiselessly and snake-like through the trees. I knew much about Indian life, but I had never before been on the war-path with them. No panther ever stole upon its prey with more deadly silence and certainty than we did on this occasion, under the conduct of this native Indian.

There were six lodges scattered about the open prairie. As we gathered along the north bank of an adjacent stream I felt fear for the first time. Until then the idea of conflict was only an idea. Now it lay just in front of me. It was not an overwhelming fear, but I could feel it inside me. It felt like a band wrapped tight around my chest that constricted my breathing.

The banks of the stream were covered with dense chaparral which provided excellent cover. This allowed us time to plan our attack without fear of being discovered. The plan was fairly simple. Lieutenant Murray was to take the soldiers on the double quick straight up the river bank and directly toward the camp in order to cut off any retreat for the river. The mounted men were to round the camp on either side so as to surround the camp. As a mounted man I took to the left end. Not knowing what to expect, my heart was racing.

"Forward!" commanded Agent Flandrau in a hushed but commanding tone.

Suddenly we were off racing toward the camp. We did not yell or scream, but our speed created a dull roar over the prairie. It was not long before our presence became known to the inhabitants of the camp. As we rapidly approached the camp we could see an Indian holding a woman by the hand who then furiously took off for the river. "That's our man!" I shouted. Without hesitation the men turned and their rifles began to crack as they fired toward the fleeing Indian. One shot after another struck the earth around the feet of the fleeing Indian. We could not tell if he was hit, but he made the river successfully. He lay low and returned fire, forcing us to keep our distance. His first shot struck the cartridge of one of the soldiers destroying his ammo and sending it flying in every direction. He fired three more shots all of which were errant. The flash of his rifle allowed us to locate our target and we riddled the spot with bullets. Our efforts were met with silence. No more shots were returned and eventually a soldier crawled up and dispatched the Indian with his sabre bayonet.

"Take the Dakota woman into custody," commanded Agent Flandrau as if by routine.

"What of the remaining Indians?" I asked as I looked toward the huddled and frightened men and women of the small camp.

"They have no use for us," returned Agent Fladrau. "The woman is all we need to identify the departed."

We did as Agent Flandrau ordered, but the apprehension of the woman proved to be an error in judgment. As we returned down river and toward the Upper Agency the Dakota woman kept up a terrible howling of distress in such a way that only an Indian woman could. The commotion created by the woman brought the attention of thousands of Upper Agency Dakota men. Each man had a gun in his hand and appeared quite displeased with our small entourage of white soldiers. It appeared we were at their mercy. However, we reached safety in one of the log buildings at the agency. But, even in the relative safety of the building, we felt fear of attack at any moment. We remained there under tense circumstances for two whole days before we were relieved by Major Sherman, who had been ordered up from Fort Snelling to attend the payment. This vanquished our present anxiety.

As we finally learned from the apprehended woman, the Indian killed was the one called Roaring Cloud, the eldest son of Inkpaduta and said to be a ruthless Indian. He came to Yellow Medicine to visit his sweetheart. This became his fatal mistake. He was the only one from Inkpaduta's band that was present that day. Such was our first attempt at pursuit and capture.

Sunday, March 22
Fort Dodge, Iowa

Dear Eliza,

I know now with certainty that you were not present the day the Indians attacked Okoboji. Though I grieve and brood most heavily my heart is overjoyed and relieved that you, my dear Eliza, have escaped tragedy. Where just shortly my heart was constricted and torn, I now have new hope; a new chance to confess what I ought have confessed long ago. I only fear now that danger is still lurking; that tragedy will stalk you. Therefore I shall come for you. No hardship will be too great. For nothing can be ill if you be well.

There was a town meeting in the schoolhouse today. Every able bodied man in town was there. This is how I confirmed that you escaped the immediate tragedy. The speculators Orlando Howe, Cyrus Snyder, and Robert Wheelock were present at this town meeting. They were among the first to discover that the lakes region suffered a much unexpected Indian attack. They came to Fort Dodge as quickly as was possible and told their tale to the very last detail. Many listeners shuddered in horror and fear, but it was necessary that all men knew the urgency of the situation. Still, it was hard to believe and thusly Major Williams required them to sign a sworn affidavit.

Upon their march to Fort Dodge, the messengers learned that they were not the first to discover the tragedy at the lakes. It seems that prior to their own discoveries, a trapper named Morris Markham had happened upon the deathly scene. Unfortunate though it may be, Mr. Markham came first to your home – the Gardner home. I record this detail because Mr. Markham reported your sister Abbie was not among those slain. It is believed, rather, that she has been taken captive by the ruthless Indians. Captivity is an unenviable result for poor Abbie, but at least she is still alive. And it gives us all the more reason to move quickly and diligently in order to find and punish the guilty party. Unfortunately, we fear the Indians may strike again. Perhaps at Springfield. I shudder at this thought.

By the end of the town meeting it was resolved that at least two companies of volunteers should be called for and sent to the lakes. Our mission then will be to rescue the living, bury the dead, and, if possible, overtake and punish the perpetrators of this massacre. Despite the risk of life and limb, nearly eighty men have come forth to volunteer for the expedition. All of them are brave and willing, just as I am.

At the closing of the meeting it was determined to send Mr. White as messenger to the nearby townships of Homer, Border Plains, and Webster City. We must assemble quickly, for no time can be spared, but we must also not leave in haste. We need every good man the frontier has to offer.

I cannot express my fear nor my courage. I must find you and I must find you well, at any cost to myself.

I remain, most humbly yours,
William

Chasing Inkpaduta

July 22, 1857 - - It was here that we halted, along the endless prairie, on a sun-splashed July afternoon. We had traveled about ten miles from the Yellow Medicine Agency and everyone was in need of a respite. I will admit that the group was an attractive one. One hundred and six full-blooded Dakota warriors mounted and in search of prey. They appeared almost glamorous under the bright sun, their skin glistening, their war paint intimidating, and their headdresses enchanting and prodigious. It was indeed a remarkable sight. What attracted me most was their unique military savvy. These offspring of the wilderness represented a lethal cavalcade prepared for any and all military engagements. They moved in unison across the prairie without need of orders or direction. They were trained and tested through years of self-discipline, countless conflicts, and deep personal ambition. Indians were taught to withstand all sorts of privations in order to prepare themselves to become adult warriors. They were forced to go without food or water or they would spend a night without rest. I recall when the uncle of my young friend challenged his nephew to fast with him all day simply as an exercise in self-discipline. And through all of this the boys were allowed to show no sign of weakness or cowardice. Indeed, bravery in battle was the highest honor for the Dakota man. It can be said that a young Indian warrior sought to be a brave man as much as any young white boy sought to be a great lawyer or even President of the United States.

In battle it was considered a great and courageous feat to touch a living enemy. This was called counting coup and any warrior who achieved this was bestowed with a single eagle feather to be placed upright at the back of the head. The Indians had many traditions such as this that might escape the eye of a white man but were distinct to the Indian warriors. These battle charms greatly added to the allure of the Indian outfit I was now traveling among. Each man had his own personal headdress which represented his unique accomplishments in battle. Some carried whips on their right wrist to signify that they had stolen a horse and others wore a bear paw on their right foot to show they had taken a scalp. Men who had been wounded in battle wore a fox skin around their neck. Even the Indian horses were personally designed and painted and encouraged for bravery. Those horses who had been wounded in battle had eagle feathers tied around their tails or manes and a red cloth hung round their necks. The entire group then was an elegant mixture of colors, costumes, decoration, and trinkets. But it all had purpose and meaning. And when added to the athletic physique and the intense military discipline of the Indian warrior, it made for a fearful yet majestic sight.

"Joseph," called the Major with a slightly raised voice. "Where do you stand in all of this?"

"What do you mean, Major?" I replied with an honest tone of confusion.

"In this," the Major replied with his hands held out wide as if it were obvious. "You are a mixed breed, but you have a white wife, you work for the traders and you are an interpreter for the government. Do you yet sympathize with the Dakota?"

"I hadn't much thought of it," I said candidly.

"You must wish to protect your young family," stated Major Cullen as if trying to convince me of something.

"That goes unsaid, Major."

"Very well," answered the Major.

"To what are you referring?" I asked.

"You have quite an important role in our work out here. Do you support the commissioner's decision to withhold payment and send the Dakota people after their hostile kin?"

"I am bound by duty, Sir," I answered quickly.

The Major turned his head away and sighed. "An abiding answer, but not what I was looking for."

"I don't understand."

"Whose side are you on?" the Major stated succinctly.

I paused in some sense of disillusionment. I often avoided confrontation and I never took sides. I believed too willingly in the goodness of people; in their better intentions. To find fault, to choose one side over another bred anxiety within me. I knew the answer the Major wanted from me, but I also couldn't reject the notion that both sides meant well.

"To thine own self be true," I answered.

"This above all," replied the Major with a smile and a laugh. "Very well Mr. Campbell. The time has come to impress upon these Indians the importance of their mission. Will you kindly gather them?"

"Of course," I said and swiftly turned toward the reposed Indians.

Once gathered, the Indian warriors stood at attention. It was nothing like the earlier conference at the agency. It was as if a switch were changed in their heads causing them to no longer act like disgruntled children but more like disciplined servants. They appeared ready and willing.

The superintendent, Major Cullen, finally approached the group. He stood erect and looked handsome in a wry sort of way. He dressed elegantly in his long brass-buttoned blue frock coat, a red sash, tall black leather boots, leather gloves, and a rather garish feather cap.

"Gentlemen," cried out the Major in an almost nasal tone. "Set before you is a vital mission. Criminals, nay, murderers from your nation now roam free on our frontier. These men—some of them your brothers, all of them your compatriots—have committed heinous crimes against the people of the United States and they must be punished for it."

The Major threw up both hands to emphasize his voice, but his gestures appeared awkward. Remarkably, the Indians stood stone faced throughout showing no signs of approval or otherwise.

"It has been pressed upon you," continued the Major after a brief pause, "to capture this band of hostiles. Because they are your people, because they are your brothers, because you know this land so well, you must now go sparing no zeal or courage to bring in the hostiles. If you do not," the Major stated with a sudden change of tone, "if you fail, your people will suffer. Your annuities will not be paid and many of your wives and children will not survive the long winter."

Audible grunts of dissatisfaction came forth from many of the warriors but they made no real sign of protest. The Major sneered at the grunts but then continued.

"If you fail to capture Inkpaduta, the people of the United States will suffer as well. Already a great terror has swept over the frontier. Fewer settlers are coming in and those who have settled are now fleeing. This will continue as long as Inkpaduta is free." The Major paused his garrulous speech and looked out over the Indians. I do not believe this pause had its intended effect, as Major Cullen realized his previous statement may have just encouraged apathy on the part of the Dakota.

"For these reasons it is your duty to find and capture or kill Inkpaduta. Again, if you do not, your annuities will not be paid. Furthermore, because of the actions of your nation and your failure to atone for those actions, your Great Father will have just cause to make war upon your people. To avoid this harsh future, to win the favor of your Great Father, to amend for the sins of your people, your solemn duty is to capture or exterminate the hostile band of Inkpaduta."

The Major completed his speech in a loud voice with his head held high as if he expected to be exalted. The Indians gave no immediate reaction almost like they were waiting for Major Cullen to continue speaking. But then Little Crow came forward, unmistakable in his fabulously adorned headdress.

"I shall not return until the band of Inkpaduta is exterminated," pledged Little Crow in his native Dakota tongue.

Little Crow was followed by Iron Elk who made the same pledge. Then Good Road came forward followed by Red Owl, and then Black Dog, and suddenly there was a long line of warriors all waiting to pledge their loyalty to Major Cullen and the expedition at hand. It was an admirable sign of Indian faithfulness toward their Great Father and his white children.

We marched on from our resting place in the direction of Skunk Lake where it was presumed that Inkpaduta and his band were located. Superintendent Major Cullen did not continue with us. For as long as Agent Flandrau was absent, Major Cullen was needed at the agency, especially during this time of unrest. As we moved along that day I could not shake an uneasy feeling that wrest inside me. I thought more and more on the provocation of Major Cullen. *Whose side was I on?* I shut the world out around me as I meditated on that thought, but I could not even bring myself to understand the question.

After what seemed like many hours of mental gridlock I recognized the old Indian Apahota, or Grey Leaf, riding in front of me. When I saw Grey Leaf I had an epiphany of sorts. Until that time I only knew what I had heard. I only knew what had been passed along from mouth to mouth as mere gossip; each mouth with its own personal convictions. But I knew nothing more. I knew not exactly why or how or who. I must, I decided then, I *must* make a conscientious effort to discover these details. In particular, I wanted to know about the Wahpekute Indians who incited the massacre. I cannot choose a conviction or pick a side based on hearsay and rumor. It was with this newfound notion that I approached Grey Leaf.

Grey Leaf was a prime target for my inquiry. He was an old man, probably too old for an expedition of this kind. He suffered from rheumatism and he was constantly in search of opodeldoc and British oil to sooth his restless bones. But he was energetic. He was also kind and affable and made for a good neighbor. He was often telling stories that ran on and on, but this was a small sacrifice to endure. Grey Leaf was never known to beg or borrow. His physical appearance was quite unique. He was tall and slender, a full six feet in height. He had a long, thin face with an odd-looking aquiline nose. His mouth was small and his eyes were large and expressive. His whole appearance seemed to indicate a higher intellect than the ordinary man.

But it was not for these reasons that I sought his council. For he was a Wahpekute. A Shooter Among the Leaves. He was of the same band of those who incited the recent trouble. It is likely, I thought, that he was well acquainted with many of those involved; those we now sought to punish. He, perhaps, could enlighten me.

"Ho!" I called out sprightly. "Apahota, I should think they would leave an old man like you at home."

"Joseph," he answered with a smile, "there is a use for this old man yet. Though my body is slow as the tortoise, my mind is sly as the fox."

"Ah," I said with a raised brow, "you are a spirited elder. No doubt you will be of valuable service. Do your joints still cause you pain?"

"Only if I use them," he replied with a laugh and a spark in his eye.

I laughed but my reaction was inauthentic.

"Are you troubled?" Grey Leaf asked somehow noticing my insincerity.

"It is true I am bothered by something," I answered somberly. "May I seek your advice?"

"Ho," Grey Leaf nodded routinely.

"Before his departure," I began, "Major Cullen asked me whose side I was on. I suppose he wanted me to choose either the side of the whites or the side of the Dakota. But I did not know which side to choose."

Grey Leaf appeared glaringly inattentive as he stared off in the distance. Nevertheless, he answered me promptly.

"You are right to be skeptical, son. When we tame the bear, the bear does not unreservedly join our clan. We must coax the bear and give him what he wants. Then he will follow us." Grey Leaf spoke easily like water down a swift-moving stream. "Do not be deceived, Joseph," Grey Leaf continued. "There are no sides in this matter. You cannot love your brother but hate his children. You cannot admire the mountain but despise the rock. The wasichu seek dominion over all things. They pit father against son, man against earth, white against Indian. They conquer and destroy and see it as good. They are overseers of life and of destiny. They see the world as those who are weak and those who are strong and they wish them to be in constant struggle."

I listened intently as Grey Leaf spoke in the most natural tone. He seemed calm and at rest without pausing to think. He kept his eyes forward and his posture straight.

"The Great Mystery teaches us to be in unison. We do not control the fish of the stream or the deer of the forest. We do not claim the land or the water. The deer are our brothers and the streams are our blood. We care for them as we care for our own children. We survive only because the animals taught us how. Even the trees, like people, have their own individual characters; some are willing to give up their life-blood, some are more reluctant. But if the tree is reluctant, we do not cut it down. We wait, and return when the tree is ready."

Grey Leaf finally turned his head and looked at me.

"The eagle flies high and sees all other beings living beneath him. But the eagle claims no dominion. It soars happily above the clouds and takes only what it needs. There are no sides, young Joseph. Examine the life around you. Seek its wisdom but do not challenge its virtue."

Grey Leaf lowered his head and turned forward again, appearing much more like the old man that he was. I was silent, not in thought or in reverence, just at ease. Grey Leaf's words were wise, but I was not convinced. I had more questions.

"But what about Inkpaduta's band?" I asked, breaking the silence. "You are a Wahpekute, are you not? Do they belong to your nation? Why did they commence violence?"

"Do not be anxious," Grey Leaf replied as he lifted his hand toward me. "You are right to ask such questions. For it is said, 'Do not judge your neighbor until you walk two moons in his moccasins.' But you are anxious and proud. You must first let your heart wander and then you will find knowledge."

I was enlightened by Grey Leaf's words, but I could not grasp his mindset. I spoke again, this time in a more composed manner.

"Forgive my impatience, elder. I am grateful for your wisdom. But I still wish to know something more about the Inkpaduta band. What do you know of this band and what can you share?"

"You are a stubborn young man," Grey Leaf said with a smile and a lighthearted tone. "I will share those things that I know." Grey Leaf took a breath and repositioned himself with a groan. I waited patiently as the old man collected himself like a bird about to fly for the first time. "To understand Inkpaduta," he finally began, "you must first understand that for the Dakota, all war is defensive. We take up the bow and arrow to protect our land and the land of our ancestors, or we take the war path to avenge the deaths of our kin. We will not attack wantonly or unprovoked. This you must remember."

I nodded in agreement.

"Our people are separated into many tribes. Our tradition holds that there are seven major tribes known to us as the Oceti-Sakowin or Seven Council Fires. We form many bands and spread out among the land from the great river here in the east to the great mountains in the west. We carry with us the same tradition and knowledge and we gather for council each year when the earth is new again."

Grey Leaf spoke plainly; much more plainly than I can ever remember him speaking. I listened attentively.

"The Wahpekutes are among the eastern most of the Dakota people. We once lived and hunted in the land surrounding the Mississippi and also south among the headwaters of the Des Moines." Grey Leaf paused briefly as if in need of rest. "We lived this way for many seasons. But not long ago, when I was tenderfooted, like the fawn, things began to change. The Sac and Fox, who dwelled in the east, were forced west. They came upon our land and hunted our game. Then the wasichu came and made their homes here. The buffalo became scarce and we had no food to survive the moon of difficulty."

"The moon of difficulty?" I interrupted.

"The time you call winter," replied Grey Leaf without much hesitation.

"It was at this time," continued Grey Leaf willingly, "when our people were going hungry and dying of disease, that Wamdisapa split from the larger band and led his own band. Wamdisapa, along with his son, Inkpaduta, became a small nomadic clan of Wahpekutes who clung to our traditional way of life. But things had changed and life would never return to the way of our fathers and grandfathers. Soon the great white chiefs came to us and promised to protect us. They promised to give us food and money in exchange for land. We did not understand this proposal, but we did not know what to do. We signed this agreement. Inkpaduta and his band stayed on the prairie. They were reluctant to give up their land and their way of living. But Inkpaduta's reluctance was barren. After the Dakota agreed to sell our lands the wasichu came more numerous than ever before. For every Indian there were ten white men. They forced themselves upon our native land as quickly as my eye blinks. For Inkpaduta and his band this created much conflict. As life became harsher Inkpaduta came for the money promised by the white chiefs. But he always returned to our ancestral home and lived off the roots where there was no game."

Again Grey Leaf paused as if he may be finished. I waited and could see that he was in thought.

"Inkpaduta is a good man," he continued suddenly. "He is quiet and soft-spoken; he never drinks of the fire-water. He is a courageous warrior; zealous, and capable of enduring hardship. But when pushed he is known to have a temper and to act severely."

Grey Leaf sighed and I could see that he was afflicted. His youthful energy and gaiety was replaced by a more somber mood. "Every Dakota carries sorrow in his heart," continued Grey Leaf. "It is a sorrow, I believe, that cannot be repaired. That is all I have to say."

"Thank you," I said softly. I felt apprehensive as if I should say more. But the sun was setting and we were nearing camp. We rode in silently.

Monday, March 23
Fort Dodge

Dear Eliza,

It is quite late now, but sleep has become irrelevant. I cannot imagine what these days are like for you; I can only hope you are alive and well. Forgive my insensitivity, but I am left to wonder if you think of me during these unfortunate times as I now think of you.

The men of Webster City arrived tonight to a rousing ovation, a full twenty-eight in number. These men traveled twenty miles in just eight hours over nearly impassable roads. It is a true testament to their spirit of determination that these untrained and undersupplied men made such a hazardous trek so rapidly.

The day was spent gathering supplies for the expedition. In this endeavor the town showed a remarkable outpouring of assistance and support. There was not scarcely a man or a woman in this little hamlet that did not offer up something: guns, ammunition, food, gloves, wearing apparel, blankets, or other articles that might prove useful. Many of the contributions came from older men who were barred from joining the expedition due to the inclemency of the weather and the nature of the mission. But they still generously contributed whatever possible to help outfit the company. Supplies varied in nature and usefulness from the worst conditioned shotgun to the finest Sharps rifle to be found on the frontier. Nevertheless, all supplies were accepted with gratitude for we consider it impossible to foresee and prepare for the trials to be faced on the expedition. In addition to these we have secured two or three ox teams and wagons to haul the food supplies, bedding, and camp equipment. We have but one wagon for each company which shall greatly limit the amount of supplies we are able to carry. The grain, for instance, must be left behind, which means the poor cattle will be forced to forage food for themselves at the various camping or stopping places along the route.

The evening was spent in selecting officers and dividing into companies. The decision was made somewhat precarious by the fact that none of the men had any military experience. Charles Richards, a well-educated man from New York, was chosen as Captain for Company A. The lawyer, John Duncombe, was chosen to head Company B. I was placed under his command in Company B. Company C is made up of Webster City men and their Captain is John Johnson. Captain Johnson seems to be well-liked and he was the obvious choice for the Webster City group. I met him only briefly, but I ascertained that he has a fine physique as well as a generous, frank disposition. I pray his leadership abilities are as keen as his manners.

Major William Williams was chosen to lead the battalion. This was clear from the outset for many reasons. Firstly, after the closing of the military garrison of Fort Dodge, Major Williams was commissioned by Governor Grimes to take such measures as might be deemed necessary to protect settlers from the Indians and to preserve the peace. He was chosen by the Governor as such because of his undoubted ability and vigor as the first postmaster, first mayor, and first citizen of Fort Dodge. He is indeed the most respected citizen in the town and surrounding areas. Furthermore he has a wealth of military experience, whereas the rest of us have none. He is in fact a very well respected man and I cannot be more proud to have him as commander of this expedition.

All things considered I believe we are reasonably well prepared for this mission. Nothing can truly prepare us for the hardships that lay ahead, but we consider it our honor and our duty to relieve the pain and struggle now faced by our fellow frontiersmen. Tomorrow we set out.

Oh how my heart has ached for you these few days.

I am yours, willfully,
William

Frontier Alarm

July 23, 1857 - - *Crack! Crack! Crack!* The sound of gunfire rang through the night. All around me I could hear a wild commotion. The loud war-like shrieks of the Indians echoed in my tent and the sound of impetuous warriors rumbled the ground beneath me. By the sudden and tumultuous uproar it appeared certain we were under attack.

"What has happened?" my brother Baptiste shouted frantically from his bedroll.

The noise continued but seemed to be traveling away from the camp rather than toward it. *Crack! Crack! Crack!* More shots were fired. War-like shrieks continued from the Indian men as I could now hear the gallop of the horses added to the confused melody. My fear, which was great inside me, began to wane as the noise carried off toward the woods. Whatever was happening, our camp was not under attack.

"I'll venture out to discover the excitement," I said to Baptiste who was noticeably startled.

I walked out slowly to see the camp was dark and appeared undisturbed. Gunfire rang again but this time it came notably from a distance. I wandered slowly in the direction of the conflict while trying not to arouse any further excitement. I could hear voices of men still in their tepees apparently unalarmed. Finally I came upon a group of warriors looking off in the direction of the woods with their rifles in hand.

"Joseph," one of them said as he turned and noticed my slow approach. In the dark of the night I could not be sure which Indian had called to me.

"There is no cause for alarm," said Lone Village in his native Dakota tongue as I finally recognized him through the blackness of the night.

"I feared the entire forest had fallen down upon us," I replied with a grin.

The warriors responded with a laugh. It was clear that we were in no danger.

"We have no more reason to fear than the buffalo calf as he learns to walk," replied Lone Village laughingly.

"What was the cause of the commotion?" I asked after the laughter had died down.

"The Yanktons," replied Lone Village candidly. "As we move further west along the Redwood we enter their country. They are unpleased and made an attempt at our horses. But we chased them off."

"We would dare them to come again," one of the other warriors added wryly.

"Return to your tent and find yourself some rest, Joseph," Lone Village said in an assuring manner, "the Yanktons will not return."

Despite Lone Village's assurance, I was quite restless the remainder of the night. That spring and summer had been one of continual alarm unlike any on the frontier before. The heart racing drama which had just passed reminded me of the frantic atmosphere of the territory. It was something I couldn't shake from my memory. For years there was relative peace between the Indians and the settlers. The only violent threat was warfare between the Dakota and the Chippewa. But for settlers coming from the far east, the fear of the unknown was always there. The majority of inhabitants only knew what they had heard from early history, where the horrid barbarities of savages in New England and the dark and bloody ground of Kentucky are recorded. But during the spring of 1857 in Minnesota, their apprehension of the unknown showed itself.

I recall when I first learned of the massacre. My wife Mary and I were sitting in our house on a Saturday evening in April when Nathaniel Myrick burst in the door saying the Indians were driving out the settlers and burning their houses. My young daughters reacted with frantic screams as they huddled together, and I tried to assure them that the news we heard was not possible. Nathaniel, however, convinced us to leave our home and gather at the stone warehouse building on the agency. We arrived to find that numerous other families had already gathered there. The women clung to their children and had swollen red eyes expecting the Indians to come at any moment to scalp their infants. I had not given in to the panic as many of the more impulsive men had, but I realized I was better safe than sorry. The employment of the evening went on with great haste and consisted of posting sentinels, cleaning and pre-firing the guns and pistols, and taking turns to stand guard. Furthermore, men were at work fortifying the building with heavy logs. Although we managed to organize a defense, it was amidst great confusion. We knew something had happened, but we knew not exactly what.

That night was a sleepless one. The women and children huddled together for warmth and comfort. Periodic sobbing could be heard softly throughout the night. The men stayed alert and ready, their eyes fixed on the bleakness of the snow-covered prairie. Occasionally a sound sparked the attention of the weary and worrisome guards but it never turned out to be anything more than an owl.

At daybreak I was chosen along with a handful of others to head upriver and determine if any settlers required assistance. We moved slowly and cautiously but found no cause for distress. Each home we encountered we found safe and untouched. There appeared to be no sign of mischief or violence anywhere along the river.

Upon returning to the fortified storehouse the majority agreed that although we had seen no danger, it was best that we took refuge at Mankato, at least until we could be certain there was no chance of Indian warfare. Again I knew better than to believe such rumors, but it was a minor sacrifice to ensure the safety of my family.

We arrived in Mankato to an indescribable panic. The town was filled with refugees who insisted that St. Peter had been captured and burnt by nine hundred Yankton and Sisseton Dakota, and that this savage horde were sweeping down the Minnesota Valley with fire and tomahawk. The streets were a jumbled parade of frenzied and terror-stricken people who rushed back and forth to collect clothes, food and weapons. Some were just discombobulated with fear and went down the streets yelling. Into the town they rushed all day long, coming from all surrounding counties. Some came alone, but many came in teams of horses and oxen all hooked to sleds and wagons filled with all manner of household effects. Some even came with the family pet or geese, turkeys, pigs and chickens. Those with some sense remaining were laid up in any of the several fortified stone buildings. Mary and I took refuge in the principal hotel called the Mankato House which was nearly filled to the brim. In that three-story building there were as many men, women, and children as could lie on the floor. The house was so jammed full it became hard work to get anything to eat. As the day waned, fewer and fewer refugees came in, but when they did it was quite a sight to witness the interest and respect garnered by the newcomers' reports or opinions.

While hunched together in our place of refuge, I learned that Mankato had formed a volunteer militia the day prior. This, as I discovered later, was not an aberration. Towns all over the territory, even as far as St. Paul, had succumbed to the wild, sudden and superfluous panic. Many townships, just as in Mankato, had formed their own militias. In Faribault they formed a sixty-man militia under General James Shields. In St. Peter they formed a militia of forty volunteers under Captain William Dodd. From the Traverse des Sioux there was a thirty-man militia led by Captain George McLeod. That was not the full extent of it either. The townships of Judson and Nicollet and the town of Red Wing, along with the small settlement of Welsh and German settlers on the Little Cottonwood, had all formed sudden and extemporaneous militias. On top of all that, Colonel Smith from Fort Snelling sent Captain Frank Gardner and one hundred sixty armed men down to Mankato in order to secure the safety of the frontier.

I was astounded at the analogous reaction of the entire citizenry of the territory to what appeared not to be a threat. Men and women, young and old alike acted merely on rumors. Even so, matters intensified. It was not enough to form defensive militias. Several armed units decided to go on the attack. The first was Captain William Lewis and the thirty-eight volunteers from Mankato. On the very same day I arrived in Mankato, these men, unprovoked, attacked Red Iron and his band of Sissetons who were in Watonwan County trapping and fishing and making sugar from maple trees. The Sissetons ran from the assault while the Mankato militia retreated to the cabin of Isaac Slocum for refuge. Later, Red Iron and his band were met by Captain George McLeod and his militia from the Traverse des Sioux. Once again the militia opened fire and the Sissetons were forced to scatter. While camped peaceably at Swan Lake, Sleepy Eye's band was also attacked. This resulted in the death of six Indians. These innocent bands of Dakota were in no way affiliated with the earlier attacks on Spirit Lake and Springfield.

It grieved me to learn about the attacks on my Dakota brothers. None of them had done anything to provoke violence, but they were victims of mass hysteria created by an isolated incident. Many of the Dakota were either forced to flee or simply told to leave. Those that fled had to take refuge at Fort Ridgely, where they requested the protection of the army.

The only apparent benefit of these many volunteer militias was that they greatly assisted in restoring confidence to the settlers. Unfortunately, the hysteria of the moment was exaggerated and heightened by the local press reports. From all over the territory, embellished or completely erroneous reports inundated the newspapers. Each report seemed more outlandish than the previous. As with the rumors, I knew better than to give heed to such flamboyant exaggerations, but many of the naive and suggestible easterners took the reports straight to heart. The Henderson Democrat, for instance, reported that five hundred Missouri Sioux had slaughtered over fifty white persons while adding that they took their victim's scalps and mutilated their bodies. Likewise, the St. Paul Daily Times reported that the Dakota Indians had been murdering the whites at Blue Earth, pillaging and burning the dwellings, and were moving down upon Mankato determined to destroy the lives of all the whites. For two weeks, reports like these showed up in the papers every day. The reports were far too numerous and widespread to ignore. It is no wonder that the people of the territory were sent into such an unbridled panic.

Thankfully the panic was unfounded and could not last. Although it was became clear that something had happened on the Minnesota and Iowa frontiers, it had proved to be an isolated incident. Within a week the militias began to return. I could see that they were a motley crew of poorly equipped men with little military experience. It was obvious that they did not lack bravery, but their earlier enthusiasm effectuated few results as the militias found no evidence to support the claims and rumors. Homes were untouched and the settlements were quiet. The friendly Indians remained friendly and those that were forced to flee showed no signs of retaliatory violence. A week after the initial rumors spread, people slowly began to return to their homes and the panic started to abate. Within two weeks, life in the territory had returned to its customary pace, yet there remained a general wariness that lingered the entire summer. No matter what was true or untrue, the Minnesota frontier was characterized by impulsive hysteria and plagued by fear.

Wednesday, March 25
On the Prairie

Dear Eliza,

As I write to you now I am a changed man. We are all changed men. We began with vigor, ambition, and an unchecked desire for justice, honor, and revenge. But we were raw, inexperienced soldiers who could not foresee nor imagine the hardships we would encounter. And this is merely the beginning. Presently we are a few miles from Dakota City. We are taking a midday rest in the relatively pleasant sun. Though the sun warms my back and the trickling water is soothing to my ear, I know it shall not last. The snow goes off slow and the winter remains harsh. Spring is sleeping in the arms of winter.

We departed Fort Dodge about noon yesterday. We might have departed sooner save the trouble in securing transportation. We were ninety-one officers and enlisted men, all of us lacking nothing in spirit. The first day's march covered merely six or seven miles. Though the miles were few, they were hard-earned indeed. The difficulties are endless. There are no roadways or worn paths. There is truly no way to estimate the depth of the snow. Parts of the windswept prairie have less than a foot of snow while sloughs and knolls create areas where the snow is four or five feet deep. Then there exists the massive snow drifts where the oxen have floundered vainly in fifteen to twenty feet of snow. But worse even than the travel was our first night on the prairie. What brittle and desolate cold the night brings. We were without tents or shelter or much of anything to shield us from the howling depths of the frigid winter air. Each man had but one blanket and nowhere to rest his head but the nearest snow bank. Still the men did their best. With alacrity and cheerfulness they settled into camp and built for themselves three large fires. The men huddled around these fires and adapted themselves nicely to their changed environment. We are without a cook, so each man was impelled to fry up his own slapjacks and take on those tasks usually left to the homemaker. The night left us hardened. It was our first night on the prairie and I presume it will be the longest. The misery of that cold and sleepless night is something that will not soon pass from my memory.

We were up early today in hopes we might cover more ground. Major Williams proposed a new strategy this morning which seemed adroit at the time. He recommended we travel along and on top of the Des Moines River thereby utilizing it as a roadway. The ice appeared thick, the snow had been blown to a thin sheet, and there were no obstacles to encumber travel. But this proved futile. The moving water of the river created many soft spots which were not strong enough to support our weight. Continually we were forced to remove ourselves from the ice and travel along the bank. This was especially difficult because the snows were deep and the banks were sloped. Moreover, the considerable warmth of this day has created a heavy and wet slush which feels much like we are traveling through mud. Finally, many of the men are suffering from snow blindness from the intense glare of the sun shining off of the snow. Nothing thus far has proven easy. We only hope to reach Dakota City tonight where we may find shelter and regroup.

We consider these hardships but little compared to the tragedy faced by our friends and family on the frontier. I will find a way to you. I will ease your suffering and I will punish the instigators. I am moved forward by these words: "If misfortune comes she brings along the bravest virtues."

Most assuredly I am yours,
William

INDIAN GAMES

July 24, 1857 - - It was a new day and the commotion by which I was startled the night before seemed a lifetime ago. In contrast, the next day was warm and comforting. We rode easily over the ups and downs of the rolling prairie with an endless and broken blue sky above us. The summer sun was inviting in its warmth and acted quickly to melt the dew from the tall grass.

"Don't get caught daydreaming," called my brother Baptiste as if sensing my casual mood.

But I found it near impossible not to. The repetitive and methodical saunter of the horse added with the continuous and unending prairie had a way of lulling a man to sleep. It was easy to forget time and place and wander off into some distant realm of the imagination. And the pace set by the group around me showed no inclination to rush or hurry themselves and thereby break the relaxing monotony. The sun continued to shine and only the growing heat might have changed the relaxed tone of the day.

"Do you ever miss Father?" I asked Baptiste suddenly.

"Of course I do," replied Baptiste. "I miss him every day."

"Yeah," I muttered.

"We had good old fun with Pa out hunting deer or fox or weasel," Baptiste said wistfully.

"Or out on the canoe," I added.

"Yeah, I don't think it ever mattered to him much if we caught anything," Baptiste said with a snicker. "If only the fire water hadn't gotten his claws in him," he added with a sullen tone.

"Do you ever wonder why?" I asked.

"Why?"

"Why he drank. Why he drank more and more until it paralyzed his life."

"I never did figure much about it," Baptiste replied. "It just made me angry that he wouldn't quit."

"I know," I replied in agreement. "But now, looking back, I can see the way things changed."

Baptiste didn't reply, he just stared back at me and waited for me to continue. I could see that he didn't realize what I meant.

"He was never like that when we were young," I said. "Life was never like this. The only whites that were here were the French traders or the military. Things were quieter, simpler."

"You think that caused Pa to drink?" interrupted Baptiste.

"No," I said starkly. "It was more than just the influx of people; it was worse than that. It started to change when the Indians signed the treaty. It started to change when Major Taliaferro left."

"What are you supposing?" Baptiste asked with a quizzical look across his face.

"Father was the best man we knew. He was well-known, well-respected, and a diligent man. But after the treaty . . . after the treaty everything changed. Squatters came in, the traders took over, and the agents tried to control everything. Nothing seemed the same after that."

"I reckon so, but you fail to make your point," noted Baptiste.

"I think it was the greed," I said with a hint of apprehension. "I think it was the corruption. I think it was the money. After the treaty, selfish men filled with greed moved in. They took everything and left the Indians with insurmountable debt. Even those that meant well still helped to induct a system that failed in every manner to curb the avarice and greed of money and power-hungry men. That's what led father to drink. He was caught in a system of exploit and there was nothing he could do."

I paused from my now excited soliloquy.

"It pains me to say so, but it has everything to do with why we are here today," I said after a breath.

"Perhaps things will get better," said Baptiste in an effort to boost my antagonized state.

"Perhaps," I said, "but that won't bring Father back."

We stopped early that day near Brown's trading post at the head of the Redwood River. The river at that point was nothing more than a quaint brook meandering in between the rocks and around the small yet curious slopes of the Coteau des Prairies. The shores were lush with vegetation; a brilliantly green forest dominated the spectrum of vision. The sound of the trickling water was soothing to the ear and the breeze along the valley was refreshing indeed. It was a perfect setting for rest and recuperation of the mind and body.

We settled for a meal amidst a large opening in the trees. The meal wasn't much more than cornmeal and some dry bread, but it was enough to satisfy a weary traveler.

Sometime prior to the meal and without my knowledge, the warriors had elected Bright Shining Cloud as the conductor of the expedition. Shining Cloud was a Wahpeton with whom I was unfamiliar. He was not an old man, but old enough that the youth in his face had shortly disappeared. He stood confidently before the men, ready to make a speech on this calm and comfortable summer afternoon.

"Beware the white man," Bright Shining Cloud said ardently with his hand and arm sweeping across his body like a Shaman casting a spell. "The white man makes distinctions among us. He says you go here and you go there. He takes the land and breaks it. He causes us to fight and quarrel and war against our own brothers while the white chief laughs and watches us destroy each other."

Bright Shining Cloud was an excellent orator and I was captivated by his impromptu speech, as was every other man present.

"Even now," he continued, "he sends us out like the fall hunt to capture our own brothers. They say we must go or we will be punished. They say we must go or they will make war upon us. Brother," he called out dearly, "our people have no undo friction with the whites. We have caused no trouble. We did not raise the tomahawk. Yet the white chief says we made trouble upon his nation. How can this be his nation? Did not the Great Spirit create the trees? Did not the Great Spirit create the rivers and the air and the earth? Did not the Great Spirit make them all for the use of his children?"

A wave of agreement swept over the Indian warriors as they began to shout with imperceptible calls of affirmation.

"I am angry, brothers!" shouted Bright Shining Cloud before his men had a chance to calm down.

The shouts grew and what started as a peaceful afternoon began to look exceedingly different.

"But!" said Bright Shining Cloud as he raised both arms and paused for the men to settle themselves. "But I did not stand here today to invoke your anger," he continued softly. "I wish only to remind you that we are not at war among ourselves. Though the white man has divided us and placed us where he sees fit, we are all children of the Great Spirit. Life cannot be defined. It cannot be bought or sold or borrowed or traded. We are in unison with our brother. Though I am angry, I remind you this also."

Bright Shining Cloud paused and looked affectionately over the small crowd of faithful warriors.

"Though the white man be unjust. Though he be the source of our trouble. We rely on his generosity. We rely on his generosity and we must do as he now bids."

There was little response among the crowd. Only a few somber calls of agreement while many seemed just to hang their heads.

"Let us be free today, men," said Bright Shining Cloud with a more lively tone. "Let us join in game and races. Let us forget our hardships and take pleasure in the afternoon."

The men responded with jubilation and laughter. "Ho! Ho!" they shouted again and again. The men threw aside all weapons, headdresses, and clothes until they were nearly naked other than their breech cloths. The horses were sent to be watered and then allowed to graze for an hour or so. The Indian men gathered around, excited as boys to begin an afternoon of races. Each man wisely chose his opponent as they sized each other up. Wild, fifty yard dashes, one after another, were run. Each one was highly contested as the warriors showed off their deer-like quickness. They ran vigorously and were extremely fleet of foot causing a rush of air following their passing. The cheering was loud and electrifying as they hailed the competing racers. The winners were acclaimed in a unison of *hoorays* as the losers turned away in a lonesome fit of fury. Finally it was down to two men. The young, robust sprinters took their marks both now dripping in sweat. The crowd of onlookers waited in silence as they edged closer and closer to the now well-worn path. The signal was given and the men took off with a powerful burst of speed. The crowd immediately erupted in an indecipherable clamor for their favorite competitor. Neck and neck, the speedy racers showed no sign of fatigue and no hint of surrender. As they neared the line, the cheering lulled in anticipation. Into the final steps one man reached his neck forward just a moment too soon, allowing the second man to make one final thrust forward and capture victory.

The crowd erupted in cheers and furiously moved to surround and congratulate the victor. Soon they hoisted him upon their shoulders and made joyful cries as if victorious in battle. The loser went away, fully dejected by his defeat. The Indian warrior took no pride in second place.

Shortly thereafter the sun came low to the horizon and the men, now fully exhausted, settled into camp. The day waned and our task still lay ahead. It was a pleasant day and a diverting evening. All would rest well on this calm summer night.

Friday, March 27
McKnight's Point

Dear Eliza,

I remember with fondness the fall days spent at your quaint log home. Even before the logs were set or the roof was in place it was truly a home more so than any I had visited before. Oh, how I long for those days now as I know you must as well. Such sweet days with nothing but the future that seemed to shine so bright. That hope seems like only a glimmer now.

This is our fourth night out from Fort Dodge and our first with any degree of comfort. We are camped at a small settlement called McKnight's Point where we arrived about noon today. We have remained here the bulk of the day because the majority of the men are too exhausted to continue and are in dire need of rest and resuscitation. I myself am quite fortunate to be doing better than most. I am thoroughly inspired by our leader, Major Williams. A full sixty years of age, yet our peerless leader has endured with us every hardship and suffered the same privation. Still his manner is as steadfast and courageous as any man I have seen.

The two-and-a-half days since I wrote you last have been ones of remarkably tedious and repeated toil. The deep snows continue to present us with our greatest burden. We have traveled on the low, flat prairie which is manageable at times but filled with various and unpredictably deep drifts. The drifts are so deep they seem fathomless. Indeed the oxen are not even able to trod through them. For this reason it has been necessary to send the men ahead in double files to break a road for the ox teams and wagons which follow. All day, each day like this, the men have marched and counter marched in this manner until we have beaten a path sufficient enough for the wagons to pass over. In order to circumvent this trouble, Major Williams thought it prudent to send scouts in advance of the company to steer the group in the least inconvenient direction. For this task Major Williams selected Captain Duncombe, Lieutenant Maxwell, and R.U. Wheelock. These men traveled two to three miles in advance of the company and relayed signals from high points on the prairie directing us which way to travel. It came to my attention that Captain Duncombe, while a member of this advanced group, nearly perished the night before. He suffered from extreme exhaustion and fatigue, but through the courageous and self-sacrificing spirit of Lieutenant Maxwell and Mr. Wheelock he was brought safely to the cabin of the pioneer Jeremiah Evans. This saved his life.

Despite these efforts to direct the company, travel has remained nearly impossible. The snow is somewhat frozen at the top and is just solid enough for a man of light weight to pass over it easily. But for a heavier man the snow breaks and his foot falls through until his leg is practically imprisoned by the hard crust of the snow. This has made travel exceedingly difficult. What has been far worse are the ravines or stream heads we have encountered. Here the soft snow, warmed by the sun, has been formed into a bottomless slush that the men must wade through. Then, in order to bring the oxen and wagons through, ropes must be attached and the men, by sheer force and numbers, must pull the wagons and oxen through the drift. It is quite a sight to witness an ox on its side being dragged by a handful of men. The constant repetition of these tasks is truly exhausting.

Last night was another bitter night on the prairie. At about sundown Major Williams put it to a vote whether or not to camp or to continue on to the point. Most voted to stop and camp while the remainder acquiesced to the will of the majority. For supper we had only crackers and uncooked ham. There were no fires to keep us warm because there was no timber nearby. Men had merely to wring out their socks and wet clothes and then put them right back on. The wagon covers were taken off and stretched around the wagons in an attempt to block the cold night wind. Men laid their oil skin coats on the ground to serve as bedding and used their wet boots as pillows. Then we huddled together; so close that when one man turned the entire company was forced to do likewise. Even among all those comrades, the dark night of the prairie and the bitter cold of an interminable winter created a depressing loneliness and an uncommon fear.

The reprieve today will serve us well. But we know, and I know, that we must bear our burdens with courage. You are still out there, and others like you. We will be together again and in that I find new hope daily.

My utmost, now and always, yours,
William

RESCUE OF MRS. MARBLE

July 24, 1857 - - We continued our slow yet determined march west into the country of the Yankton Dakota. This was a new world to me. One without boundaries or rules or comforts. It was a world beyond civilization. All my life I had learned and loved the way of the Dakota, but it was in such a way that I consider diluted. I lived on the edge where tradition was constantly mixed and intertwined with the contemporary. New people, new ideas, new religion, new ways of life. In its own way it was a quintessential arrangement of both equal and opposite forces working to create a brave new world where the foreign became familiar and the two became one. It was this edge, this clash of culture where I took up life. Beyond this edge, beyond the frontier, life was unknown to me though it preceded me and my known world for centuries prior.

As we moved west from beyond the boundaries of civilization, or, at least, civilization as it was known to me, I imbibed my beautiful and somehow enchanted new scenery. No longer were the fields plowed or the rivers controlled or the land marked. The certain tameness that seemed to characterize the place I grew up was here missing. The land stretched from one horizon to the next, unaltered and free. Not belonging to anyone or separated by surveyors. It was pure and natural and gave off an aura of tranquility. The land spoke of centuries gone by, unclaimed and unworn by the tools of civilization. The land appeared selfless in the way it gave life over and over again. For the buffalo that grazed there, for the fauna that grew there, for the tribes that nomadically traveled through there, this land was the lifeblood of all things. The air passed serenely over the sloping meadows, carrying with it the seeds of new life. The creeks moved along slowly, meandering every crevice as if searching for something ahead. The steady and unyielding horizon, always approaching yet never reaching; so vast as if without beginning or end. Here, on the trackless prairie, the Great Mystery appears and the land is made sacred.

As we traveled I began to recall more of the springtime dramatics that foreshadowed this expedition. Following the tremendous commotion and panic of early April, it was discovered throughout the territory that the hostile Indians had with them four captive women. These women, as it became known, were Abbie Gardner, Margaret Ann Marble, Elizabeth Thatcher, and Lydia Noble. All of them were young women in the threshold of their lives. The knowledge of their captivity incited a whole new kind of panic. The people of the territory, being the good neighbors that they were, clamored immediately for the rescue of the captive women. In reality, many called for an all-out assault on the western frontier in order to find and punish the culprits of the massacre. But, out of fear for the safety of the captives, the authorities, Major Flandrau in particular, knew better. It was reasoned that if soldiers were sent after Inkpaduta and his band, the Indians might kill the captives before they themselves were captured. For this reason the authorities made the prudent decision to first rescue the captives before making any attempt at pursuing the Indians.

This attempt at rescuing the captives began in late April when the territorial legislature called an extra session to discuss the matter, at which I was not present. Whatever was exactly discussed in that session I cannot say, but it resulted in the passage of an act, approved May 15. This act, which was proposed by Joseph R. Brown, appropriated ten thousand dollars for the release of the captives through means of purchase, stratagem, or otherwise. However, before this plan could be put into action, two Wahpeton Dakota by the names of Grey Foot and Sounding Heavens had safely purchased the captive Mrs. Marble and escorted her to the missionaries at Yellow Medicine. At this time I was called to meet with these Indians and fulfill my duty as interpreter.

"Ho," I said welcoming Grey Foot and Sounding Heavens. "I am Joseph Campbell, interpreter for the Upper and Lower Agencies."

The two men sat in silence, just staring forward.

"I presume you are Makpeyakahoton and Sehahota," I said, using their Dakota names.

Again the men gave no verbal response, but nodded slightly. They were young men. Brothers. They appeared kind and willing and showed no signs of hostility. They seemed, for whatever reason, nervous.

"There is no need to be anxious," I said, trying to calm their nerves. "I just have a few simple questions regarding your rescue of the young white woman."

Again they merely nodded, this time in unison.

"How did you happen upon Inkpaduta?" I began, though not sure if they would understand.

The two men looked at each other and then gestured to one another the way only brothers might. "We are hunters," one of them stated, though I could not be sure which because they appeared so similar. "We were camped at the north end of the Big Sioux River."

The speaker, whom I believed to be Sounding Heavens, paused here.

"And?" I asked, urging him along.

"We learned from some Indians who came to us that we were not far from Red End's camp. We heard he had white captives with him and we thought we should visit them and obtain the prisoners."

"This is what you did?" I asked.

"Yes, on our own accord," answered Sounding Heavens, now appearing less nervous, but still wary. "Against the advice of our brethren who told us it was too dangerous, we went to Red End's camp." He stressed this fact, clearly wishing for me to know that he and his brother took a great risk.

"Where did you find Red End?" Red End is the one known as Inkpaduta to the whites.

"One day toward the setting sun," explained Sounding Heavens. "At Chanptayatanka. When we reached the camp we were met by four armed men with revolvers who demanded our business. Once satisfied that we were not spies and had no evil intentions, we were taken to Red End's lodge."

"And how were you welcomed?" I asked, waiting for Sounding Heavens to continue.

"We spent the whole of the night listening to Red End and his warriors recite the tales of their massacres. It was not until morning that we ventured to ask for the white women. But this was not easy. Much time was spent in negotiating. We told Red End of the enormity of his crimes but he appeared unimpressed. It was not until the middle of the afternoon that Red End wavered. He agreed to give us one captive."

"Why only one?"

"The price was high. To continue our barter would be useless," Sounding Heavens explained with his hands held out.

"What then did you pay?" I asked.

"We gave one gun, a lot of blankets, a keg of powder, and a small supply of trinkets. It was *all* we had." Sounding Heavens raised his voice to stress this last fact.

"And how did you choose which woman to take?" I asked with great curiosity.

"It was an easy decision at first," he said, which surprised me. "The woman I chose appeared so unhappy that I was moved by her. But when I beckoned her she became angry and refused to comply. Little thought was given toward the youngest captive as she appeared healthy and unharmed." This I knew could have only been Miss Abbie Gardner. "My brother," Sounding Heavens continued as he gestured toward Greyfoot, "beckoned the third woman, who agreed willingly to come."

"This was Mrs. Marble?"

"This is the one we purchased. This is the one we brought in."

"There was not a fourth?" I asked out of fear that one of the captives had perished.

"Three," answered Sounding Heavens plainly. This, regrettably, meant that one of the captive women had already died.

I asked little else of Greyfoot and Sounding Heavens. They returned Mrs. Marble in good health and only wished to remind me of the perilous business which they underwent. They claimed for themselves five hundred dollars each and wanted it not in horses or supplies, but in cash. I was in no place to provide their reward, but I thanked them for their service and assured them that I would pass along their wishes.

Agent Flandrau was quick to acquiesce to this request. Unaware of the recent legislation passed, Agent Flandrau paid the first five hundred out of pocket while the remaining five hundred he paid through territorial bond. This bond was drawn on the hope and charity of the territory and issued without authority. It was made payable three months from the date.

As for Mrs. Marble, it was laid upon me to ascertain her present condition. Being the interpreter bore with it many responsibilities, including this one. I could not imagine what she had been through having recently lost her home and her husband and having been taken captive by the hostile Indians. Although I was curious, it was not the time nor the place to bombard Mrs. Marble with questions regarding her unthinkable experience. It is likely that everyone in the territory of Minnesota wished to know, but I could not allow myself to prod at the sensitivities of poor Mrs. Marble.

From a glance, Mrs. Marble appeared in relatively fit condition. Her skin was darkened brown from the sun and her feet slightly bruised from the burned prairie but she seemed otherwise well. She was robust and very attractive looking while in full Indian garb. She was presented to the missionaries Stephen Riggs and Thomas Williamson by the parents of the two Indian rescuers I had previously mentioned. She was dressed neatly in a jaunty woman-like attire, ear-bobs, a fringed buckskin dress, trim ankles, and splendid moccasins.

"Welcome," I said, not knowing where to start.

"Hello," she replied calmly but clearly.

"I have been sent to ascertain your present condition," I explained. "Are you fit to speak?"

"Yes," she nodded, "I am well."

"Good," I replied curtly. "I sympathize with you over the tragedy you have endured, but I must know, how have you been treated by your rescuers?"

Mrs. Marble looked away and swallowed before giving her response. She appeared stunned, but not so delicate as I expected. "I have been treated quite well," she finally stated.

"What of your treatment?" I asked, urging her to elaborate.

"They treated me as one of their own," she continued freely. "It seems that the parents of the two Indians who had rescued me had shortly before lost a daughter. I believe their intentions were to adopt me in her place."

This took me by surprise.

"Every kindness possible was shown me," Mrs. Marble explained. "I soon found myself in the position of an Indian princess. A snug apartment was fitted for my use. A couch of fine robes was prepared, and real pillows of softest feathers. The room was curtained off from the main tent by print curtains. My food was cooked and the bones even taken from the meat before passed into my apartment. I remained here about two weeks, and was made to know by their actions it was their desire to keep me as their daughter."

"Fascinating," I blurted.

"Most Dakota are devoted and affectionate people," she said in an apologetic manner. "They treated me with the utmost care."

"Very good, Mrs. Marble. May I ask one more question of you?"

"Please," she said politely.

"I was told by your rescuers that at the time of your rescue there were only three captive women in camp. Do you know what happened to the fourth?"

"Yes," she responded softly, but without hesitation. "This was Mrs. Thatcher. She perished in the river."

"How so?" I asked curiously. "Why?"

"Mrs. Thatcher was weak from the outset," replied Mrs. Marble in a strangely prosaic manner. "She had recently given birth and had not yet recovered. Because of this she was greatly mistreated and forced to work beyond her capabilities. Eventually our captors decided to push her in the river and shot her."

"Well," I said in acknowledgment. "That is unfortunate."

Mrs. Marble did not reply.

"Thank you, Mrs. Marble. That is all that I need from you. You are now free among your people."

I was greatly pleased with Mrs. Marble's treatment since her rescue. Following the interview I left her in the hands of the capable missionaries. In the days following, Agent Flandrau arrived and accompanied Mrs. Marble to St. Paul where she received a celebrity's welcome. In addition to the sympathies and kindness showered upon Mrs. Marble by the people of the territory, the Governor presented Mrs. Marble with one thousand dollars which was raised for her benefit. She remained in St. Paul for a short time, after which her whereabouts are unknown to me.

ABBIE'S CEREMONY

After the return of Mrs. Marble we knew definitely that two captives remained living. We also learned the precise location of Inkpaduta and his band. With this knowledge, Agent Flandrau wasted no time in seeking out volunteers to rescue the remaining captives. Because of the ransom paid to the previous rescuers, volunteers were not wanting. Agent Flandrau chose three Wahpetons from Reverend Stephen Riggs's Hazelwood Republic. The volunteers chosen were John Other Day, Paul Mazakutamani, and Chetanmaza or Iron Hawk. Paul Mazakutamani himself was the president of the Hazelwood Republic, which was a respectable community of young Dakota men who had cut their hair and adopted white men's clothes. The Republic was a unique attempt at self-government and was recognized as a separate band of the Dakota. After selecting these men, Agent Flandrau outfitted them with a large variety of goods with which, as he stated, to tempt the savage and affect the purchase of the captives. The goods and materials included horses, blankets, cloth, tobacco, powder, corn, flour, coffee, sugar, ribbon, shirts, calico, one sack of shot, and a wagon and double harness. With instructions to give as much as was necessary, the three rescuers departed from Yellow Medicine on the twenty-third day of May. As the rescuers traveled west we could receive no word from them, so Agent Flandrau utilized this time to prepare the military expedition that would follow.

Several weeks passed without any knowledge of the rescue attempt. Some began to worry as the days turned to weeks and May became June. Meanwhile, at the agency, there began a fledgling consternation among the Dakota because their annuities had not yet been paid.

Thankfully the stress was broken when, after three weeks absence, the three rescuers, along with two Yankton warriors, returned to Yellow Medicine with the captive Abbie Gardner. Sadly they were without the other remaining captive, Mrs. Noble, whom they had found bludgeoned to death sometime prior to their arrival at Inkpaduta's camp.

Abbie was a young lady still in her adolescent years. She appeared in good health, although she carried with her a look of deep and permanent sadness.

"Ms. Abbie Gardner?" I asked politely upon our first meeting.

"Yes, I am," she said in a soft and melancholy tone.

"I am Joseph Campbell," I explained. "I simply wish to know how you have been treated by your rescuers."

"Well," she said without even lifting her head. "I owe my rescuers a debt of gratitude."

"That is all I wish to know."

Following our brief and modest meeting Abbie was given into the hands of Dr. Thomas Williamson and his family, by whom she was treated in all manner of kindness. During her short stay, the family and all those at the agency made the most gracious efforts to alleviate the suffering of the poor young girl. Though her appearance remained forlorn, I can rightly say that the goodwill of the people around her must surely have prevented Abbie from sinking into a condition of depression and helplessness.

Abbie remained at Yellow Medicine for only the matter of time required to secure some form of transportation to St. Paul. This I acquired through a Mr. Robinson, who vowed to chauffeur us in his lumber wagon. This wagon and team did not permit rapid or comfortable travel, but it was all that I could secure. We departed on a Sunday with Abbie, her rescuers, Mr. Robinson, and me. Upon reaching the Redwood Agency, Captain Bee sent a horse and buggy with a request for young Abbie to join him and his family for the day. But the Dakota rescuers were suspicious of an attempt to deprive them their reward and so the invitation had to be denied. However, we did take dinner at the Fort on Monday. Here Abbie was met by all the officers and soldiers and was presented with a purse of money and a gold ring. Also, Lieutenant

Murray, as a testament to her bravery, presented Abbie with an elegant shawl and a dress pattern of the finest cloth. Abbie did her best to respond with gratitude and affection but remained expressionless. The poor girl was broken-hearted at the loss of her family. Though she had been saved, her life had been altered forever. And for some strange and insensitive reason, I began to feel curious. I wanted to know just what Abbie had been through, but I did not dare ask Abbie to relive her experience.

We continued our cumbersome travel until we reached the Traverse des Sioux. Here we boarded a steamer bound for St. Paul. Although travel became more comfortable, things remained quiet among the occupants. The three Indian rescuers seemed to be constantly looking over their shoulders for signs of treachery and Miss Gardner kept secluded, if not in body, then in mind. Mr. Robinson maintained a somewhat lively attitude, but I was in no mood to respond to his playful anecdotes. And so we steadily and quietly passed the beautiful summer scenery of the Upper Minnesota River.

"Thank you for escorting me to St. Paul," Abbie said by surprise finally breaking the silence that had become familiar.

"It is my job," I said, "and I am pleased to assist you by any manner possible. You have my sympathies."

"Appreciated," she replied, still quiet and somber. "But not necessary."

"Regardless, I am here to help. You may ask anything you need."

Abbie nodded in acknowledgment, but nothing more was said.

Again I felt curious. Not just about what Abbie had been through, but about who Abbie was. She exhibited almost an enslaved submissiveness, an indifference to fate. Yet at the same time she was capable of deep gratitude and showed strength of character. And despite her somber mood, her eyes shown bright without shame or sorrow. There was something different about Abbie Gardner. Something good.

On the twenty-second day of June we arrived in Shakopee to a large and affectionate crowd. They gathered near the dock and cheered emphatically as the boat approached. The crowd then showered Miss Gardner with sympathy and kindness. They also presented her with a purse of thirty dollars which was raised spontaneously. We stayed not long in Shakopee and I almost had to pry young Abbie from the zealous crowd. We then continued on to St. Paul.

The scene was much the same in the capital city of St. Paul. Residents had become aware of Abbie's arrival, so they came in droves to welcome her. As the boat made dock the thunderous shouts of the crowd were almost deafening. Not even President Buchannan himself could have aroused such excitement in a crowd that day. Thankfully, there was a carriage waiting for us just off the dock. The crowd, though well meaning, was too much and therefore needed to be avoided. The carriage took us immediately to the Fuller House, a large, elegant, and exquisite hotel located at the northeast corner of Jackson and Seventh Streets in downtown St. Paul. Once we arrived at the Fuller House Miss Gardner was given into the hands of the landlady, Mrs. Long. Mrs. Long was instructed to carefully provide Miss Gardner with her every want. And, for the purpose of the next day's ceremony, she was to outfit Miss Gardner in the most becoming and effective widow's weeds obtainable in the market.

The following day Abbie Gardner was formally delivered over to the governor, the honorable Samuel Medary from Ohio. At 10:00 a.m., Abbie was brought to the large public receiving room where a large crowd of distinguished guests awaited her. This included myself, Agent Flandrau, the Indian rescuers, Superintendent of Indian Affairs William Cullen, Colonel L.P. Lee, the governor, and a variety of respectable citizens. All were finely dressed for the occasion; the women in elegant dresses thin at the bodice, wide at the skirt, and decorated with lace, fringe, ribbons and false flowers; the men with long, black frock coats, rectangular neckties, and tall top hats. The room, too, was as glamorous as its audience. A brilliant crystal chandelier hung low from the ceiling and sparkled as light passed through it from one corner of the room to another. The walls were decorated with large oil paintings depicting events in United States history and separated by fine and polished silver candlesticks. In addition the walls were colored a distinctive and opulent shade of green often used to symbolize wealth or power. And then there was Abbie. Her auburn hair parted in the center and pulled down over her ears and then back up into a bun held together by a rose-colored ribbon. Her dress was black to show mourning but was lovely all the same. The neckline was low but around her neck was a lace shawl to cover her shoulders and arms. The skirt was thin and long as it flowed across her legs and dragged on the ground behind her feet. Though fashionably dressed and in the company of those who came to celebrate her, Abbie maintained the same dull and lifeless expression. She appeared almost daguerreotyped. I knew only time could alter her bereft and isolated heart.

The reception was introduced by Agent Flandrau and included much speech-making. The speeches began with Mazakutamani who addressed Governor Medary directly.

"Father," he began reverently. "The American people are a great people—a strong nation—and if they wanted to they could have killed all our people, but they had better judgment, and permitted the Indians to go themselves and hunt up the poor girl who was with the bad Indians."

Paul's voice was strong and clear and carried the distinct sound of an American Indian. Everyone in the room seemed mesmerized and listened quietly as Paul spoke.

"We believed when we left our kindred and friends that we would be killed ourselves; but notwithstanding this we desired to show our love for the white people. Our father could have sent troops after Inkpaduta's band, but that would have created trouble, and many innocent people would have been killed. That was the reason we desired to go ourselves."

Paul paused, but did not take his eyes away from the governor. It was as if he spoke to him alone, perhaps knowing he was a representative to his so-called Great Father.

"We want to become as industrious and as able to do something for ourselves as the whites are. We have a church, and I attend it every Sunday and hear good advice. We want good counsel. There were bad Indians, but we desired to behave well. We want this known and considered by our Great Father in Washington. The whites told us to stop making war and lay down the tomahawk. The advice was good and we have followed it, and now our women can plant in peace."

Again he paused. It was clear he was prepared to conclude his remarks.

"Our father, the agent, desired us to go out and hunt this poor girl. The Great Spirit had pity on her and we succeeded in finding her. You see the girl here in the power of the white people. We have acted according to the will of the agent. We now give her up to you, but desire to shake hands with her before leaving."

As Paul finished his speech he was met with awkward silence, the room not knowing the appropriate response. Some thought to applaud while at the same time waiting for Governor Medary to give his acknowledgment. The silence was finally broken by Agent Flandrau, who took a step toward the center of the room where he could be heard and seen.

"It is well what you have done," he began, speaking to the Indian guests. Like Paul Mazakutamani, Agent Flandrau was adept at speaking and garnered the attention of each person present. "There was much excitement throughout the state following the massacre. There existed great fear that such a tragedy could befall others throughout the region. It was for this reason, to quell these fears, that the rescue was laid upon the doors of the Dakota Indians. The Wahpeton," he said with his hand directed toward the Indian men, "are loyal and brave and so they were chosen to go in search of the unfortunate captive, and thereby establish the fact they were friendly to the whites, by rendering important services. I always knew the expedition would succeed."

The silence was interrupted by *oohs* and *aahs* as the people gave their subtle acknowledgement of the Indian's service. But Agent Flandrau did not wait long before continuing and regaining the attention of the guests.

"You have gone out and done your duty well and nobly," he continued in his deliberate manner. "You are entitled to the gratitude of the white people. I am glad you came down here because it gave you an opportunity to see the Father of all the whites in the territory, and to assure him of your love for the whites. For the services you have rendered you will be rewarded to your entire satisfaction."

Finally this aroused a tenuous applause from the dignified audience. The Indians stood tall, unmoved by the show of gratitude.

Meanwhile, Governor Medary stood in the back of the room with his hands clutching the breast of his coat. He was a large, stately looking man with a long, gray beard that showed sprinkles of white. He stepped forward with a grunt and the guests parted as if making way for some royal dignitary. Medary, who was the third territorial Governor, spoke in a fatherly tone and was clearly practiced as an orator. He spoke in a manner that was completely inoffensive and almost enticing to listen to. He began by addressing the Indians.

"My Red Children," he said in a strong and unbroken tone which was directed toward the Indians. He thanked them numerous times as he spoke in just such a way that flawlessly intertwined his content and meaning. He stated his hope that this mission would bring about the renewal of friendship between the whites and the Dakotas and he warned against the occasion of any communication with Inkpaduta or his band of renegade Indians. His speech was long, but well-put. He concluded with a pledge of loyalty and gratitude. "We thank you for restoring the white women to us; and, if ever the red men, women, or children should be placed in such an unfortunate position, we hope to be able to treat them with equal humanity and kindness. In the name of humanity, of Christianity, and of that church you say you attend, and those precepts and counsels you heed, I again return you our thanks. We will take her, and see that you are liberally rewarded for all the trouble and danger you have subjected yourselves to in serving us."

Again there was a faint acknowledgement by the guests of the ceremony. All this was received with gravity and decorum by the Dakota men. They stood quietly by, polite as any Indian dressed in white man's clothes. Their typical "Ho" was the only expression they gave throughout the ceremony.

Once Governor Medary concluded his remarks, Agent Flandrau came forward with a brilliant looking war-cap to be presented to Miss Gardner. This war-cap was a gift of the Yankton chief Matowaken. Chief Matowaken owned Abbie at the time of her rescue. Abbie was seated on a stool in the center of the room and the cap was placed gently upon her head.

The room immediately lit up with lavish applause in response to the generous gift. It was indeed a beautiful and elegant cap made of soft and light buckskin. Around the crest were numerous and large eagle feathers. The quills were set just right to make a perfect circle upon which the feathers extended like a funnel above her head. Also around the crest was white weasel fur with the tails hanging down as pendants all around the cap save the front. The feathers were painted black with a stripe of pink, giving the cap quite an attractive appeal. It was a gift like none other I had seen before and must have carried great value, both fiduciary and sentimental. Once placed upon Abbie's head, and once the applause died down, Agent Flandrau told Abbie that the cap was given out of respect for her fortitude and bravery. She was also told that as long as she retained the cap she would be under the protection of all the Dakotas. It was a joyful moment and an auspicious scene, but still young Abbie remained without a smile.

That same afternoon I met with Agent Flandrau, Governor Medary, a Mr. Samuel B. Garvie and the three Indian rescuers. Here we paid each for his services four hundred dollars in cash. I interpreted the voucher for the Dakota men and signed my name as a witness. The following day we boarded a steamer headed south for our return to Yellow Medicine. Abbie Gardner, I was told, headed south for Iowa while accompanied by Governor Medary. She traveled in search of her sister Eliza, the only family she had remaining. It was a beautiful ceremony, but a sad occasion. I departed St. Paul feeling somehow unsatisfied. I lacked closure.

Sunday, March 29
Irish Colony

Dear Eliza,

Two days have passed since I last wrote you and we now find ourselves at the small Irish colony somewhere along the dragoon trail. Here reside about twelve or fifteen families who moved here from Illinois during the fall of last year. They are hearty frontiersmen who came here for the same reasons as any frontier family: to find prosperity in the promised land of the west; to chase the setting sun; to pursue the adventurous life. Their homes are nothing more than rudely-constructed cabin shelters and dugouts. But they are meant to be temporary, only to withstand the winter until they establish a more permanent settlement in the spring. Nonetheless it is a comfortable little place hidden among the groves and shielded from the cold winter air. Here also we are able to pick up some much-needed provisions, exchange our tired, worn-out oxen for fresh ones, and enlist about twenty or so new recruits. For these men we are grateful. Though they have seen our tired condition, they have bravely volunteered to join in our quest and help save even one.

Some of the men have become rather discouraged and are beginning to view our mission as futile. This was made most evident on Saturday morning before leaving McKnight's Point. One of the men (his name I do not know) who claimed to be a veteran of the Mexican War, assertively stated that he believed that to continue would be suicide. He said that to go any further would result in the destruction of the entire company. This, you can imagine, caused a tremendous ruckus among the men. But the dauntless Major Williams quickly stamped out the sudden consternation when he addressed the men. Major Williams admitted and acknowledged that this was no holiday campaign, and he declared that he would bravely go forward along with anyone willing to join him. He also declared that any man in the battalion who felt that he had gone far enough was at liberty to return. To this, the men replied with fortitude and courage. Each man, with the exception of but few, proclaimed his allegiance to the mission and said that only death could discharge them from their solemn duty.

We continued on from McKnight's Point with two new men. These were the pioneers William Church and Jeremiah Evans who had graciously taken in Captain Duncombe when he was severely ailing. In addition, on our march north we encountered four more men that were willing to join. These men had learned of the massacre and were frantically headed south to Fort Dodge to seek help. They were a welcome addition to the company.

The snow seems to grow deeper and deeper the further north we move. To us who are tired and exhausted, the drifts appear impassable as if they were mountains, while the low places seem as deep as canyons. Progress remains slow, but we are doing all we can. I fix my eyes on Major Williams. Through witness of his enduring spirit and stalwart nature, I am able to press on.

I am on my way to you, Eliza. I have seen you in my dreams and that tells me you are still living. The obstacles are great, but none shall be too great to keep me from you.

Most Truly,
William

ABBIE'S RESUCE AND INDIAN HUMOR

July 25, 1857 - - As we continued our methodical travel, and as I reminisced on the presentation ceremony for Abbie Gardner, I realized that I never much spoke to the Indian rescuers about their expedition. For some reason, the return trip south from St. Paul was as silent as the trip north had been. As we marched, it was becoming late in the afternoon, but there was still time to seek out and speak with one of the three men who had rescued Abbie Gardner. Although Chetanmaza had spoken of the rescue at the ceremony, I was curious to know more. Thusly, I slowly meandered through the separate cliques of Indian warriors. I went in search of Paul Mazakutamani. Little Paul, as he was also known, was rather unique among the Dakota of Minnesota. He was once a great and noted warrior among the Dakota, but had many, many years ago been converted to the religion of Christ. He was, in a way, the ideal Indian as far as the United States government was concerned. He became a Christian, learned the English language, adopted civilized clothing, built a permanent home and tilled the soil. Without doubt he had proven himself as loyal to the whites and had over the years done much good on their behalf.

After a few minutes of searching I finally located Paul secluded and away from the majority of the group. He was actually easy to spot being one of the few Indians in white man's attire. He wore a white calico shirt with a black handkerchief as a necktie. His pants were tan and dirtied from our long travel. Finally he wore a thin blanket strewn over his shoulder and hung over his body as a sash. His hair was dark and wavy with no signs of gray despite his age; it hung down to about the middle of his neck. From even a short distance he appeared like a white man in almost every regard other than his skin tone. Even his facial structure had a certain European characteristic, being more rounded and narrower than the typical Indian.

"Ho, Little Paul," I exclaimed as I approached him. "What offensive thing has sent you to the outskirts of our group?"

"Ho, Campbell," he returned. "Among all the talkers there must be at least one keen eye."

"Quite true," I said with a laugh. "Treachery will find those who are not on the lookout."

"What begs my attention, young Campbell?" Little Paul asked as if agitated by my presence.

"I don't intend to cause annoyance; I simply wish to speak with you."

"You must forgive me," replied Little Paul, "a long mission can grow tedious and exacerbate my nerves." Paul finally turned his head to show he was ready to engage my inquiry. "What do you wish to speak of?"

"Well," I said casually, "I'd like to hear more about your expedition to rescue the Gardner girl."

"What have I to tell?" replied Paul skeptically. "You were with us, you know the outcome."

"Certainly," I stated, "but I'd like to hear your story. I'd like to know more details."

"You have a newfound curiosity?" returned Paul with some emphasis in his voice.

"As a matter of fact I do."

"Very well," said Paul, "then I shall quench your inquisitive nature."

I blushed at his comment.

"Where shall I start?" Paul Mazakutamani asked himself. "When I first learned of the incident I was heartbroken and grieved along with the whites. But I was also heartbroken by the response of the white men to categorize all Indians as bad Indians. I determined to demonstrate that not all Indians were bad Indians just as I had done many times before."

Paul spoke naturally and was a native orator. His abilities with the English language far surpassed any other full-blooded Dakota I had met. He was calm and soothing and had a reverent demeanor about him. He was easy to listen to.

"This opportunity arose," continued Little Paul, "when the agent at Redwood, Mr. Flandrau, sought volunteers to rescue the captive women. Thinking not of the money, I volunteered myself post haste. It would be dangerous business, but it was a chance to redeem the tarnished image of the Dakota people."

I nodded to show I was listening.

"Being in good standing with the whites, I was chosen by the agent along with my Dakota brothers Hotonwashte and Chetanmaza. We met with Agent Flandrau at the Yellow Medicine where he supplied us with goods sufficient enough to barter for the remaining captives."

"Were you apprehensive?" I asked.

"Ho," replied Paul with a nod of the head. "The Dakota to the west are a warrior people. They might have seen us as a threat. Or the hostile band guilty of this horrible conduct might have sought war with us. We carried few weapons and knew we would be at their mercy."

Paul turned his head forward and paused. I knew not whether to wait or to ask for him to continue.

Finally Little Paul continued in his dignified but somewhat monotone manner. "There is little to tell about our journey west," he said. "We moved slower than we might have otherwise, being weighted down from so many materials. Also we could not be sure where to find Inkpaduta's camp. We only knew that he would have been wise to move farther west after the rescue of the first captive. So we moved west toward the horizon until after several days we discovered the body of a young white woman who was recently killed."

"Mrs. Noble," I interjected.

"Yes," Paul replied, "Mrs. Noble. She appeared to have been bludgeoned to death. We said a prayer over the body, wrapped it in a blanket, and buried her in the ground. We knew then there was only one remaining captive and that she was close. So we continued west along Inkpaduta's trail. The following day we crossed the James River and located a vast Yankton camp near the mouth of Snake Creek. The camp consisted of one hundred ninety lodges."

"I have not seen such a large camp," I said with astonishment.

"The Yankton are a strong band untouched by civilization and still fed by the wild buffalo which are limitless as the grass," answered Paul. He looked to see if I might make another inquiry, and once satisfied, he continued. "We approached the camp slowly that we might not startle the Yankton. As we neared we could see that there was a minor commotion among the camp dwellers. The commotion did not signify violence and gave us no need to worry. Rather, it appeared that the excitement was caused by the young captive girl. Many of the Yankton had not before seen a person of white flesh and were mesmerized by her. This fascination was then transferred onto us."

"What fascination did they have with you?" I promptly asked.

"Our clothes," replied Mazakutamani with equal quickness. "These Indians had likely never seen a red man in white man's clothing. They found it strange and had many questions for us. To them we appeared about as customary as an eagle who swims or a bear who speaks. Although they could not come to comprehend our appearance, they welcomed us into their camp."

As Paul continued to tell his story it occurred to me that we had never much spoken before. Somehow I began to feel the goodness that swelled inside of him. There was something different about this man, I thought. It had nothing to do with his so-called whiteness or his Dakota heritage. It was unique to his own personality and character. I could see nothing but a kind and patient sentiment about him.

"It did not take long for the Yankton to discover that we were there for the white girl," Paul said as I refocused my listening. "They led us to a large tepee in the center of the camp. Within this tepee sat the young white captive along with several Yankton warriors. She appeared unharmed."

"Was Inkpaduta present?" I asked.

"He was not," answered Paul. "It seems Inkpaduta was eager to unload the captive, so the young girl had been sold to Wamaduskaihanki or End of Snake. End of Snake desired to take the girl west to the

Missouri where she might be sold at the white fort. We negotiated with End of Snake and many others from within the tepee. After several hours we adjourned to the open prairie where we continued to negotiate throughout the night and well into the next day. We gathered in a large circle and passed the peace pipe amongst each other."

Little Paul paused to take in the summer air. He seemed to drift in and out of the present moment.

"Finally the Yankton agreed to our price," Paul said as he suddenly continued. "We succeeded in buying the young girl for two horses, seven blankets, two kegs of powder, one box of tobacco, and some other small articles. That night a celebratory feast was held in honor of the young girl. It was a dog feast which, in the Dakota tradition, is considered the greatest compliment a stranger can be given. It seemed as though the Yankton chief revered the captive girl for the heartache she had been through. This of course was made more obvious by the elegant war bonnet he presented to the girl. Though the feast was made in her honor," Paul said with a sigh while showing his first change of expression, "the girl did an unhandsome thing to remain in her tent the entire night. However, I might understand her condition and her prejudice to dog soup."

"And what of the return trip?" I asked. "Did you encounter any trouble?"

"None much to speak of," Paul continued in his prosaic manner. "We had with us an escort and safeguard of two Yankton warriors. It was feared that those of Inkpaduta's band might attempt to recapture the girl, but the Yankton are a well-respected warrior tribe and we knew their presence would stave off any molestation. Thus we made our return to Yellow Medicine and so ended our rescue." Paul then paused and looked off toward the falling sun. "Are you enlightened?" he asked, as if rejoining the present.

"Indeed," I said. "You have done a great thing. You have demonstrated sagacity and compassion."

"But has nothing changed?" replied Paul. "Does the Great Father acknowledge only our bad deeds?"

"Be that as it may," I returned, "you have given that poor girl a new life."

Paul merely smiled.

We encamped that night at Lean Bear's village which was nothing more than ten or twelve lodges. Lean Bear was a Sisseton chief and he welcomed our company with companionability. Though in the presence of allies, Little Crow ordered that sentries be posted one hundred yards out on each side of the camp. In addition, a small scouting party of three Indians and one half-breed was sent ahead to seek out any indication of Inkpaduta's band. For the remainder of us it was an enjoyable evening. The night air was warm and the breeze felt agreeable. Men relaxed, ate meat, gathered together, and told stories. It was a picturesque scene of amiability and merriment among the Dakota warriors. Not a sore heart could be found among them. The scene was made most memorable by the laughter. I cannot truly describe the affable and warm feelings created by such boisterous and exuberant laughter. Never have I heard such hearty laughter as I have heard among the Dakota.

That night I sat inside a large tepee alongside thirty or forty others. We were cramped arm to arm and leg to leg, but it gave us no discomfort thanks to the lightheartedness of the setting. The chiefs and warriors sat in a circle passing a long stone pipe while leaving just enough room in the center of the tepee for a speaker and the fire pit. Crowded and crouched behind were all others: men, women, children and any who wished to regale in the evening's festivities. In the center stood Yellow Bear, a wise elder from Lean Bear's village. From what I could tell he was a natural speaker and enjoyed the limelight of center stage. He appeared particularly dazzling covered in the full skin of a grizzly bear. He began with a story of his brother-in-law. It was customary for the Dakota to tell jokes about their brothers-in-law and sisters-in-law, even those that were rather personal. No one ever resented these jokes; for to do so would be an unpardonable breech of etiquette.

"Tamedokah!" Yellow Bear called out with his arm directed straight for his brother-in-law. "I have heard you tried to catch a dear by the tail!"

The crowd chuckled derisively and waited expectantly for a response.

"It was a singular mishap," announced Tamedokah.

"A singular mishap?" Yellow Bear replied in a mocking tone. "That is an odd way to place such a whimsical occurrence. Why, not since the pale-face brought us the mysterious iron or the pulverized coal that makes bullets fly has a man tried to catch a deer with his bare hands."

The crowd was engrossed and lively. They grunted and moaned and chided poor Tamedokah.

Tamedokah paused for a moment while all of the attention was directed toward him. "Yes," replied Tamedokah with a smile, "I thought I might outdo the tale of the young man who rode atop an elk while screaming like a woman."

A repeating laughter broke out to Tamedokah's witty response.

"Ahh," replied Yellow Bear with a laugh. "But that was mere legend. This is a point of fact, for I have seen it with my own eyes. I admit you have a strong grip, my brother, to hold the tail of a deer until it came off in your hands. Honestly speaking, I could not tell who was more frightened, you or the deer. For you both had your eyes bulging from your sockets. Indeed it will go down among the traditions of our fathers."

By this time the lodge was completely overcrowded as newcomers continued to pour in. The tent was warm and well lit by the burning embers. Shadows flickered here and there against the buckskin wall as smoke percolated through the open flap at the center. Women stood holding young ones tight to their breasts while men sat, knees to chest, and held tight as if creating for themselves a rocking chair.

"Share with us the story," cried one of the newcomers. "I wish to hear the whole matter."

Yellow Bear enjoyed a puff of the pipe and then passed it with a smile to his brother-in-law.

"It is a comical matter," began Yellow Bear in a wry sort of way. It was clear that the old man enjoyed being the center of attention. "I narrowly believe what my own eyes beheld."

The crowd seemed to urge Yellow Bear forward with their anticipation alone. The speaker fed off of their desire for more.

"This is what I saw," continued Yellow Bear with his hand outstretched and his eyes wide open. "I was tracking a buck and a doe through the woods when suddenly I heard a loud and mysterious boom. I looked all around and saw nothing. But then, like the sky when it flashes, came a deer with its pursuer attached to its tail by both hands while his knife was securely held by the bite of his teeth. 'Tamedokah,' I shouted, 'Haven't you got the wrong animal?' But in a moment they both disappeared within the tall trees."

The crowd giggled and grunted to show their approval and enjoyment. Yellow Bear was animated and lively as he recounted the story. Like a true showman, every word was followed by a gesture or facial expression. Over the years I have learned that Indian humor relies heavily on gestures and inflections of the voice and is really untranslatable.

"I began running toward the place I last saw them," said Yellow Bear as he continued his tale. "But from the other side of the clearing the deer came leaping. I started laughing hysterically and could not help myself. I held my side and tried to stop laughing, but the sight was too humorous. It almost killed me. Tamedokah held the tail tight, the knife now fallen, and he kept his feet under him. His backside was high in the air as he leapt forward while he tried to keep pace with the deer which was frightened out of its wits."

The entire lodge was in an uproar which filled the inside of the tepee with laughter. Men and women alike had to hold themselves steady to keep from pitching over. Meanwhile Yellow Bear continued to prod and excite his audience through his embellished gestures of the scene.

"By the third appearance of the deer and his stalker," Yellow Bear continued, "it seemed as if the prairie itself were moving. Tamedokah had lost his feet from under him, but his grip remained tight as a clamp. He began to skid and bounce along the prairie from behind the frantic and frightened animal. Once they moved among the trees I could hear his hair whip against the tree bark as the deer maneuvered between the trunks. Back on the prairie, Tamedokah skipped across the grass like a smooth pebble thrown against the water or like a grasshopper learning to hop. I fell down with laughter."

Again there was a pause as the audience released an even greater uproar than before. Side by side, men embraced each other as they tried to withstand their convulsive laughter. Some men were in such hysterics that tears began to roll down their cheeks. Even Tamedokah himself could not help but laugh at the whimsical tale.

"And how did the matter conclude?" cried one of the guests.

"I do not know," replied Yellow Bear while in the midst of laughter. "I lay on the grass. When I woke Tamedokah was pouring water on my face. When I saw him I burst out laughing again."

Once again there was an uproar as everyone was intoxicated with laughter.

"I knew nothing," Yellow Bear shouted over the noise but could barely collect himself enough to spit it out. "I knew nothing until the sun passed midsky!"

"Ho! Ho! Ho!" the audience called with approval as they continued their boisterous parade of hysterics. "Tamedokah has been made famous among our annals. Henceforth this story will be told from generation to generation," shouted Yellow Bear.

As the crowd of happy Indians began to catch their collective breaths, there was heard a rustling from outside the lodge. It was the sound of men moving swiftly through the grass. The tent became silent as we listened for a more definite sound. Then came a man's voice. "Little Crow," he called in a hushed tone. "Little Crow!" he called again.

"In here," responded Little Crow in his native Dakota from inside the lodge.

The man entered and I drew a sigh of relief when I discovered that it was merely one of the men from the advanced guard.

"I bring news from the advanced guard," he stated, somewhat out of breath. "Shall we speak alone?"

"No," said Little Crow. "What is told to me may be told to all."

"We discovered a lodge," said the warrior confidently. He appeared unnerved by the situation as only an Indian would be. "About half a day's walk to the west. The half-breed crawled on his belly to discover a lodge with two men, one woman, and five children. This may be those of the band we seek."

"Ah, it may," replied Little Crow to show his acknowledgement. "Do you suppose they are of any immediate threat?"

"It seems doubtful," replied the warrior.

"And our half-breed," inquired Little Crow. "Does he remain within eyesight of the lodge?"

"He does," replied the warrior quickly.

"Keep him posted near the lodge. Have him keep watch like an owl who sees through the night. We will visit this lodge after the sun rises on the morrow," advised Little Crow.

"Ho," responded the warrior as he turned and departed into the night.

"I have enjoyed enough festivities for one evening," announced Little Crow. "Let us take rest and ready ourselves for the hazards ahead."

With this the evening ended in abrupt fashion. But what a joyous evening it was, and how wonderful it felt to be among my Dakota kin. It seemed natural. As a half-breed, I rarely have these moments. More often than not I feel oddly out of place. But in moments like these; moments when I am fully immersed in a part of my culture; this is when I feel most at home and most comfortable. I feel most happy.

Wednesday, April 1
Granger's Point

My lovely Eliza,

Oh what great joy I now feel! To see you once more, to know you are safe. From such dark, abominable depths my heart has been rescued. No more imprisoned and shackled but now flying and free. No longer am I acquainted with pain, no further am I familiar with anguish, no more am I spiritless nor woebegone. For now I am familiar only with hope, and what an abundant hope it is! I am new again and my heart beats for you.

Eliza, you must forgive my candid and unrestrained jubilation. For once I thought and feared that you had perished. And in that thought I too perished. But I have seen you and I have life again. Yes, my heart aches for your loss, for your grief is my own. Though not all is lost. We can go on. We can go on together. When this is over, when our duty is complete, I will return for you. Oh, that you would be rejuvenated and that you would know the hope and joy that I now feel!

It is of great fortune that we came upon you and the seventeen others from Springfield. Though painful to imagine, it is indeed possible and in fact probable that you and the other refugees might have died on the frozen prairie if our advanced guard had not discovered you. The fortune which preceded this discovery began the day prior, on Monday. That morning we had left from the Irish colony feeling much refreshed and with new recruits. We owed most of our newfound strength to the meat we ate after butchering a cow. It was not prime rib, but it was well beyond anything we had eaten on the expedition thus far. As we marched that day, we recognized evidence of an Indian presence. The further we marched, the more evidence we discovered. We saw moccasin tracks as well as dead cattle which were killed in such a manner that only an Indian might have done. When we reached the Big Island Grove, we discovered a lookout in the treetops from where the Indians could spot their enemies. On the lake we observed fresh fishing holes. We knew we were getting closer to the lakes and the scene of the massacre, and the evidence of Indians created quite a stir among the men. Some feared the Indians were headed south bent on a war of extermination, however unlikely. Because of these discoveries, Major Williams decided to form an advanced guard of ten men to go ahead of the main column and scout the area for hostile Indians. I was not among the ten selected. William Church was chosen as the commander of the party since he knew the territory so well, having traveled it many times between here and Springfield. The advanced guard did not leave that evening, but waited until sunrise the following morning. And what a beautiful morning I can say it was. The ten men of the advanced guard moved out much quicker than the company could follow. We, of course, were still burdened with the tasks of shoveling and beating down the snow to create a passable roadway, a task which was unforgiving and never ending. We were trudging along, much like we had each day. Then it happened, the most exciting news of this long and forbidding march. Frank Mason and Roderick Smith came running, a full eight miles from the front. Frantically and well out of breath they announced that they had encountered refugees along the prairie: refugees from Springfield! At this my heart leapt as I knew you were likely among them. A meeting of the officers was held and it was determined by Major Williams to send forward Mason, Richards, Duncombe, and Dr. Bissell as rapidly as possible to the aid of the refugees. It was reported that several of them were badly injured and in need of medical attention, so we knew there was no time to spare. The four men pushed ahead and the main company pressed on. I longed to go with them, but my duty was with the company. As we pressed on, we did so with a renewed courage at the knowledge that we might finally affect some good for all our efforts. I was clinging to hope and filled with anxiety that you were found and found to be well, or at least well enough.

It was not until midnight that we arrived and then rains came pouring down. A cold and dismal spring-like downpour only added to the already wretched conditions. What mixed emotions we all must have shared that night. To see the refugees tattered and worn was hard to endure. The women with their worn-out shoes, their torn dresses fringed at the ankle, and the children crying with hunger and cold.

And there were those in need of surgical aid such as Mr. Thomas, who had been shot in the wrist, and Miss Swanger, who had been hit in the shoulder. Despite the cold and the rain and the conditions, I was proud of the way the men set out through strenuous efforts to provide some sort of comfort. Dr. Bissell dressed the wounds while some of the men stitched together blankets to act as a tent. Major Williams ordered men out to guard the camp from any possible attack. Few, I believe, slept that night. Then there was you, Eliza. I went about my duties, but longed to go by your side. I did not know what I would say. I did not know how you felt or what you were going through. Just before I was called away to stand guard our eyes met and in that moment you smiled the most subtle and gentle smile. It filled my heart with warmth and it let me know that you were okay. I am sorry that I did not go to you. But I was so nervous that I was more likely to approach a grizzly bear than the object of my affection. Love makes us irrational, does it not?

As I write to you now, it is a day later since I saw you, and you were sent south this morning. I am exceedingly tired. We have reached Granger's Point, but everything has changed. Tonight we were visited by a messenger sent from Captain Bee of Fort Ridgely. The messenger has brought with him the information that Captain Bee and his men have already arrived at Spirit and Okoboji Lakes. Unfortunately, as the messenger stated, after being repulsed at Springfield, the hostile Indians hastily fled to the north and west and are probably a hundred miles distant by now. This was disappointing to the extreme. Every man in the company hoped that if we did not reach the scene of the action in time to provide relief to the settlers, we might at least be able to chase and capture the dreaded culprits and dole out justice for their unspeakable actions. It comes as a surprise to me that Captain Bee and his men did not pursue the Indians when they were seemingly so close. This is quite unaccountable. Even so, we are filled with pride that if nothing more, our efforts resulted in the salvation of eighteen perishing refugees from almost certain death by exposure and starvation. This has adequately repaid all our hardships and trouble; myself most of all.

The chase has been abandoned and tomorrow the majority of the men will return south to Fort Dodge. As for me and a handful of others, we have been assigned to burial detail. We will proceed to the lakes and provide a proper burial for those fallen. We will do our best to provide some level of dignity to their earthly bodies in their final resting place.

I have great joy knowing you are safe. I will find you upon my return. I will share with you everything.

I remain, yours,
William

Unknown Lodge

Be it a curse or a blessing, I often wondered to myself. A mixed-blood, a half-breed, they called me. It rolled off the tongue as naturally as the cry of a newborn babe. It became every part of the natural order of things and yet could ever and only be unnatural. Still, it was unquestioned, it was undisputed, it was an afterthought. If an Indian was a savage, if an Indian was subhuman, if an Indian was without rights, than a half-breed was an abomination. He was a creation of ill-fate. He was never meant to be. The half-breed is a whole new kind of being. Though useful in bridging and navigating the gap between languages, cultures, and religions, we are shunned and deplored. It goes without saying that we are somehow different and so we live as an outcast of fraternity. It is not as if we are pointed out and cast aside, rather there exists an unsaid stigma against those of mixed blood. It has crept into the hearts and minds and context of these times so thoroughly, so adequately, that it emanates in every manner of feeling and doing and being. This prejudice, if you will, has been branded into society and is so overwhelmingly accepted and practiced that even those with the aforesaid stigma do not argue its definition but rather take shame in their distinction. I and my family have fought hard with this distinction of owning the blood of both Indian and white, but it is something with which we have yet come to terms. Yes, we make our living and we get along, but not without the inescapable notion that we are somehow unwholesome, unwanted, and disregarded. My very own wife, Mary, has kept hidden her identity as a Cherokee mixed-blood. She would rather live a life of disguise than to face the negative intercourse that comes with being known as both

Indian and white. My sisters too, have sought to hide or change or manipulate who they are. Both Madeline and Harriet have married and both have transformed their names so they sound more white: Madeline's from Rassicot to Roscoe and Harriet's from D'Yonne to Young. And I am no less guilty than my sisters or my wife. I can recall as a boy my grandmother saying, "Remember always, you are an Indian." How she might shudder and cry to know what has become of my identity. It is not that I am shut off from my native heritage. It is not that I do not find pride, respect, and curiosity in my background. Indeed, I share familial ties with the great Chief Little Crow. Rather, the white way is the only acceptable way. The way of the wasichu seems the only way to live and succeed and thrive. The native tradition is looked down upon and thrust aside in the name of progress and so-called destiny. And so I live in the manner of the whites. Not with pure intention, but in a somber conciliation of what must and can only be.

My reminder of this disparaging reality visited me last night while among the fun and folly of that effervescent Indian lodge. What a gift I can say it was to so be so freely associated with my native kin in such an atmosphere of amusement. Here, with the Dakota, I feel unencumbered by what ought to be and what not ought to be. There are no expectations to live up to, no manner of dress or speak that is unacceptable, and no standards on how to live. There is instead a circle of living and a certain unspoken respect and dignity for everything in that circle. Thus I find a feeling of being unshackled whence I never realized I was imprisoned. With my Indian brethren I am made full of life, cheerfulness, and sociability. Not the less, the struggle continues in my innermost being not knowing how or if to embrace my Indian blood.

July 26, 1857 - - We made our way cautiously that morning in search of the forewarned lodge. It is not as if one hundred mounted warriors with an ox team and a load of materials could move soundlessly over the prairie, but there was an unspoken understanding that inconspicuousness was necessary. Even the elements seemed an ally in our mission. The air was brisk and calm, almost autumn-like. And the cloud cover was thick and grey allowing little light to pass through. The birds too cooperated and were less numerous that morning. The entire scene felt strangely ominous.

We came within striking distance of the lodge just before mid-day. "I need six men to make a charge on the lodge," announced Little Crow. A brief meeting was held between Little Crow and the other chiefs or band leaders. They conferred for several minutes in what appeared to be a passionate discussion. But before long they agreed upon the six men to advance upon the lodge. The six included three of Little Crow's advanced guard while the others were young men of varying loyalties.

The lodge was within a small grove that grew alongside a creek bed. The plan was to surround the lodge and leave no place from which to escape while the six men crept upon the camp in an act of surprise. And so we moved silently and spread ourselves along the edges of the grove. From my vantage point I could only catch a glimpse of the lodge and could detect no real movement. The six chosen warriors also spread themselves out so that they might come from all directions. Like snakes they slithered along the ground without so much as breaking a twig. We simply waited as the stealthy warriors went to work. We were instructed to wait upon the war cry at which time we would descend like locusts upon the lodge of unknown Indians. The time passed slowly as I waited to hear the war cry. There was not much to feel nervous about, for we greatly outnumbered our potential opponents and we had the advantage of surprise. Still I could not avoid a feeling of apprehension. I would not describe it as fear, only as uncertainty.

"Heee!" came the loud shriek of the war cry as it echoed like a ball bouncing off the trees. In a snap the warriors pushed ahead holding their rifles high in one hand and screaming in such a manner to strike fear in the heart of any man. In and out and through the long shadows we descended quickly upon the lodge. Little Crow, being the first to enter the open area, came to a sudden halt, and like a chain reaction, so too did all who followed. There we were, a tight knit circle of over one hundred warriors primed for conflict while leaving no means for escape. But the scene, as I came to realize, was anything but threatening. The six Dakota warriors who went in advance had the unknown Indians surrounded and huddled helplessly together. These men, women, and children appeared frightened and rather harmless. One of the warriors began asking questions. "Who are you? Are you associated with Red End? Why are you alone from your band?" But there came no answer. The small huddled group was too startled to reply and all that could be heard were the cries of the young children.

"Lower your tomahawks," said Little Crow.

The tension was broken and the warriors backed away. Everyone became relaxed like a tight string suddenly being released. Little Crow approached the frightened group as they began to console each other as any family might.

"From what band do you belong?" Little Crow asked bluntly.

"We are Sisseton," cowered one of the men, still huddled next to his family.

"What brings you to this region of the Yankton?" Little Crow continued his questioning.

"The trade," answered the man quickly. "We have traded goods with the Yankton and we are returning to the homeland."

"Pardon the intrusion," said Little Crow with a change of tone. "We seek another."

Little Crow turned away with a sigh in his expression. It was somewhat of a disappointment to make such an extraneous discovery. We had been traveling many days and we were anxious for results, though we knew it was too soon. But it was also a relief, at least for me, to know that we avoided a potential conflict. In reality, I do not think anyone as a part of this expedition sought a great battle which might risk or claim lives. We had a duty to fulfill and it went little further than that. For the Dakota it was a matter of survival; something that must be endured in order to provide for themselves and their families. We had to hide our disappointment, apprehension, and frustration. We had to press on.

Soldier's Expedition from Fort Ridgely

That afternoon we continued west with the same degree of caution we had that morning. The farther along we trotted, the more prudent caution came to be. We knew not exactly who or where our enemy was. The weather had turned from gloomy to downright treacherous. The clouds had gathered strength and began to pour down rain with sustained alacrity. There was nothing to be done but to trudge through the muck and mire while trying to remain sanguine enough to maintain alertness. At times the mud became so utterly oppressive that the ox were unable to pull the wagon forward, forcing us to dismount and physically push the wagon ahead. But as burdensome as the conditions may have been, I knew it was like nothing in contrast to the military expedition from Fort Ridgely that was sent out in March. Though I was oblivious to the misfortunes and perils of that expedition at the time, I learned about it soon afterward as it was specified by Agent Flandrau and recorded through military reports. The attack on Spirit Lake occurred sometime in early March. While the rest of the region carried on with its mundane and everyday troubles, this is what happened to those who discovered and sought to alleviate the Spirit Lake Massacre.

The horrible scene was first discovered by a trapper named Morris Markham. Mr. Markham intended to settle in the Okoboji region, but was away trapping at the time of the incident. Upon his return, he was shocked and mortified to find all of the inhabitants either killed or missing. After visiting each cabin in the settlement and finding no one alive, Mr. Markham proceeded to the home of George Granger, approximately eighteen miles distant. All this he did under deplorable conditions and under below-freezing temperatures. Resting only briefly at the Granger cabin, Mr. Markham and Mr. Granger made their way north to the small settlement of Springfield to warn the settlers of another possible Indian outrage. Their warning was properly heeded and the people of Springfield made ready for an attack. In addition to preparing a defense, the Springfield residents deliberated whether or not to send a relief party to the lakes. In the end, they rightly determined to send messengers to Fort Ridgely, which lay seventy miles to the northeast, and was the nearest military garrison. The two young men chosen for this task were Joseph Cheffins and Henry Tretts. The two messengers left immediately from Spingfield with a written statement of the facts which had been signed by the Springfield residents. But despite the haste of the messengers and the urgency of the matter, conditions made travel nearly impossible and therefore the trip took almost a week. It was not until March 18 that Agent Flandrau received the message and became aware of the situation.

You must understand the difficulty in travel faced by the two messengers. The previous winter was extremely harsh and prolonged, lasting well into April. Because of the deep snows, the two men had to take a rather indirect route, which extended their travel from seventy to more than one hundred miles. Additionally, they could barely see due to snow blindness. That they arrived at all is a testament to their will and courage.

Upon receiving the message, Agent Flandrau acted swiftly and went immediately to interview with Colonel E.B. Alexander of the tenth infantry, who was at that time in charge of the post at Fort Ridgely. Between these two men it was decided to send a relief expedition at once to Springfield and if necessary, Spirit Lake. Captain Bernard E. Bee was selected to command the expedition with his Lieutenant Alexander Murray. The two guides selected were Joseph La Framboise, a young half-breed who was reputed to know the country well, and Joseph Coursolle, also known as Gaboo, another half-breed who was well known throughout the surrounding country and acted as a trapper, trader, and intermediary between the whites and the Indians. As his interpreter, Agent Flandrau selected Philander Prescott, a trader and sutler and a man who had lived among the Dakota for many years.

By noon the following day, March 19, the expedition of forty-eight soldiers departed for Springfield. The men immediately encountered the same obstacles faced by Cheffins and Tretts. The snow was deep and nearly impassable. It was also thick, wet, heavy snow which made it rather difficult to walk through. In order to circumvent the trouble of traveling by foot, the expedition began with sleds drawn by mules. The intention was to move in a direct route in order to reach the afflicted peoples as soon as possible. This proved impractical and the caravan instead had to take a circuitous route as far as South Bend. Captain Bee reported that travel was completely unsuitable for military operations. With each step the men sank deep into the snow and were made wet from morning 'til night. They were forced to cut through the snow with the spade and shovel while often extricating the mules and sleighs from sloughs or dragging them over steep hills. Agent Flandrau called the first day's march appalling. And not only were the conditions appalling, but the troops were ill-equipped to contend with them. As Agent Flandrau described it, the poor troops were about as fit for such a march as an elephant is for a ballroom. The first day's march was so discouraging that Agent Flandrau thought it hopeless. He considered the time that had elapsed since the murders and the additional time that would elapse in traveling to the region, and he told Captain Bee that if he wished to return at once to the Fort he could do so. But, being the true soldier that he was, Captain Bee declared that despite the obstacles faced and the likelihood of accomplishing much good, his orders were to proceed to Spirit Lake and so he would do so until it was physically impossible to go further.

It was at this point that Agent Flandrau and Mr. Prescott returned to the fort, for it behooved them to do so. The military, however, pressed on. After reaching South Bend they continued in a southwesterly direction until they had reached the farm of Isaac Slocum. Slocum's was the western most settlement of that region beyond which laid an unbroken waste of snow. From here they set out across the prairie. On

March 26 they received a tip that some thirty lodges of Indians were encamped at a grove some eight miles above the Springfield settlement. With this knowledge, Captain Bee and his men struck across the land with as much haste as possible. But the journey was indeed arduous. Captain Bee reported that his men had to march in columns of four in order to break a road in front of them. Every twenty minutes the men rotated in order to alternate the tired men at the front.

After three days of rigorous marching, the company found themselves near the grove where it was believed the Indians had been encamped. The men loaded their rifles and were instructed to be ready to throw off their knapsacks and make a run for the camp. Upon Captain Bee's command the men threw aside their scarves and gloves and moved quickly on the grove. But the nest was found empty. The camp was indeed located, but by the looks of it, it had been abandoned several days earlier. The trusted Indian guide Gaboo, however, was confident that the Indians could be found at Heron Lake, approximately fifteen miles further west. At this point Captain Bee was faced with a decision: either pursue and overtake the hostile band of Wahpekute or hasten to the scene of the massacre. Having been told only dead were to be found at the scene of the massacre, Captain Bee determined to call upon volunteers for pursuit. With no less than twenty volunteers, it became unanimous among the men to pursue the Indians.

Early the next morning, the entire command set out toward Heron Lake. The path of the Indians was easily discovered by the guides, and thus the route of the soldiers followed directly the route of the Indians they pursued. By approximately 1:00 p.m., the company reached Heron Lake and prepared once again for battle. Quickly they surrounded the lake and instructions were given that a single shot fired by La Framboise would act as a signal for the rapid ingathering of the troops. With the camp located, the shot was fired and the men fell upon the camp, only to find it abandoned just like the camp before. Within the deserted camp lay every bit of evidence of the destruction of the settlements. This included all sorts of plunder and rapine such as books, scissors, articles of feminine apparel, furs, and traps. The guides reported that the camp was three or four days old, making any further pursuit futile. However,

I later learned through the testimony of Mrs. Marble that the troops came so near that the Indians could see them. The Indians made ready an ambush and were prepared to kill the captives if the soldiers attacked. I suppose it is just as well that the Indians were not discovered, thus sparing the lives of the captives, but I am left to wonder if treachery was involved on the part of the guides who falsely reported the oldness of the deserted camp. Perhaps I shall never know.

By this time supplies were quite nearly exhausted and there was little left for the expedition to accomplish. From Heron Lake, Captain Bee and his command marched to Springfield. Here they located just two men who happened to be recent amputees and were unable to flee with their companions following the Indian attack. They were found on a Saturday evening, while the Indian attack on Springfield occurred Thursday evening. Unfortunately, the military expedition was two days too late to prevent bloodshed. Henderson and Smith, the two crippled men, related the story of the attack and informed Captain Bee that the people of Springfield had fled south toward Granger's Point. At once Captain Bee sent a man out to overtake the refugees and tell them it was safe to return. This man was unable to locate the party, though he did locate the expedition sent north from Fort Dodge. Meanwhile Lieutenant Murray, along with twenty men, went as a burial detail to Spirit Lake. This detail went only as far as the Marble cabin where they found and buried Mr. Marble's body and then returned to Springfield. Once the expedition had done all it could, Captain Bee returned to Fort Ridgley to report matters as he had found them. At Springfield there remained a detail of twenty-eight men under the command of Lieutenant Murray. These men were to secure the region should there be any renewed Indian hostilities.

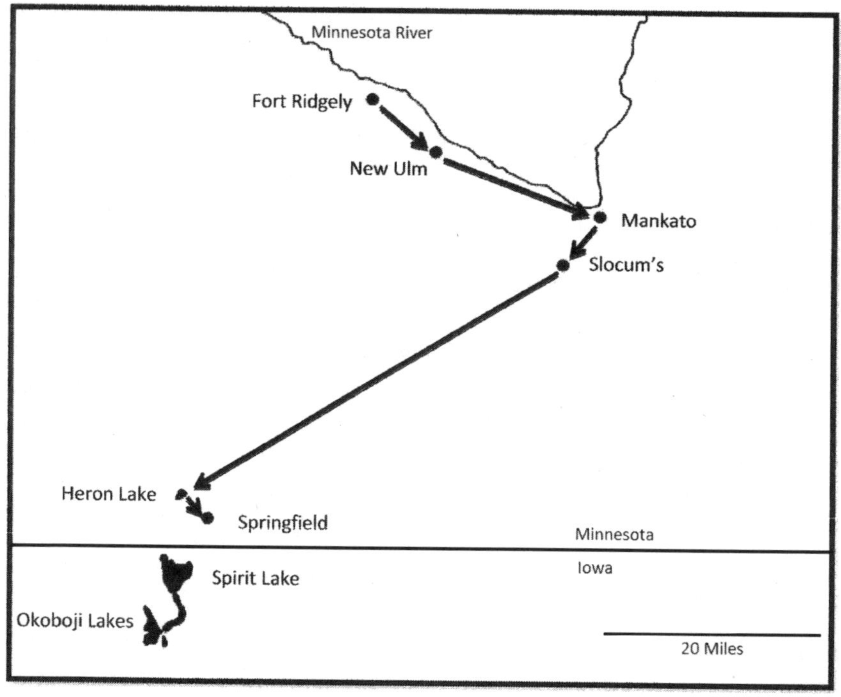

The route followed by Captain Bee and the U.S. Troops from Fort Ridgely

Although the military expedition was unable to find and capture Inkpaduta, it is indescribable the courage and fortitude shown by those soldiers. They endured the harshest winter weather over a trackless and barren prairie while being undersupplied and ill-equipped. But, as Captain Bee reported, they did it with cheerfulness and patience. As I now trek over this endless western range, I cannot fully imagine the toil and burden those men must have experienced while struggling through such deep snows and perilous weather.

My group of brave Indian warriors went as far as Hole in the Mountain that day; this being the day that began with the discovery of an unknown lodge. The weather eventually subsided and the clouds cleared, making for a brilliant western sky as the sun approached the horizon. It was calm and cool and there was a somewhat comforting feeling about the evening despite the malignant weather just hours earlier. I determined that I ought to write a dispatch to be sent to the superintendent. Certainly the events that transpired that morning were worthy of correspondence, and the superintendent would also be curious to know our progress. Thus I found solitude on the outskirts of the camp and made my reports while there remained enough daylight to do so. I informed the superintendent of our location at Hole in the Mountain and I shared the details of the unknown lodge of Sissetons. I also forecasted the future of the expedition, explaining that we would continue our search on toward the James River and as far west as the Missouri if necessary. I remembered well the enthusiasm with which the Dakota warriors had shaken hands with Major Cullen, and they seemed to have lost no strength or will since that time. I was confident to say that they were determined not to return home without apprehending the murderers.

"Do you now work?" came a voice from behind me.

"I turned to see Left Hand Bear approaching me casually. He had a large fur pelt pulled over his head, making him barely recognizable through the shadow that covered his face.

"Indeed, I do," was my assertive reply.

"Why?" he asked.

"Whatever do you mean?" I replied. "It is a part of my duty as the interpreter."

"Are you not a Dakota?" he said curiously, now standing just a few feet in front of me. "I have seen your mother, she speaks with Crow. Is he not also your blood relative? Why do white man's work? Why turn against your people?"

"A man must work," I said in a soft but defensive tone. "I mean no disrespect. My father was an interpreter and I follow in his steps."

Left Hand Bear merely grunted and turned his head. Not satisfied, he continued with his questioning. "But you are a tool of the wasichu. They seek to wipe the Red man clear from the earth. Do you believe the white man is just? Why do you help him?"

I sighed just slightly, not totally offended, but not knowing how to reply, either. "You must understand," I said. "I did not create the tension between the whites and Indians. The struggles that exists today existed long before I was born. I merely act as a mediator, a facilitator, a go-between. I assist both parties that they might be able to communicate and reach an understanding. I do not seek to uplift one side over another. I do not wish to stamp out my Indian blood and my Indian kin. Like you I am only desirous of peace."

"Ah," Left Hand Bear replied with another grunt still obviously dissatisfied. "But look at what the white man has done. When the fish swim, they do not swim against each other. Why then does the white man rub us like sand paper? They have taken the land and made it a prison. They have cleared the trees and with it, the homes of the animals. They say we must do the same. They say we must break the soil. They say we must learn their language, their history, their religion. They say we must lose the spirit that we were born with and live only as they do. And you say you are a facilitator. Why do you facilitate this?"

I was heartbroken in that moment. I listened to the words of Left Hand Bear with reverence and respect and I understood what he had to say. I held the emotion and confusion inside of me and tried to reply as objectively as possible. "I understand your vexation, confusion, and pain. The issue is a complicated one. Again I remind you that it was not I who initiated this process. It seems that the world is changing and we must change with it. The white people are growing and they seem unwilling to compromise. They do not wish to wipe you clear from the earth as you presume; they simply wish to help you become a part of this new world. Certainly the white man is not without corruption and greed, but the great many more seek peace and prosperity for your people. They do not wish for you to break the soil; they wish for you to till the soil that you might share in its abundance. They do not seek to destroy your language, they only wish to help you communicate your wants and needs and to share your perspective. The white man does not wish to swim against you, but to swim with you."

Left Hand Bear remained expressionless as he stood before me. "At one time the native Indian grew as naturally as the wild sunflower. He was a part of the earth just as the great buffalo or the soaring eagle. But now I ask, where are the Pequot or the Mohican or the Narragansett? Where are the Dakota that were once thick as the grass? As snow before the sun they have vanished. We must protect the land just as we protect our children. Life is a circle and everything in this world is of that circle. But once it is gone, it is gone forever. How then can you tell me that the white man means well?"

Once again I was struck by the words of Left Hand Bear and I had not a sufficient answer. I bowed my head in thought. "Perhaps there are no answers. I only desire to do what is right and you must believe me, there are others who would do the same."

"You are a man with a good heart," replied Left Hand Bear, "but remember that we will not be known by the tracks we follow; we will be known by the tracks we leave behind."

Thursday, April 2
Okoboji

Dear Eliza,

Of all the days spent in this unforgiving wilderness, this has been the worst. Of all the toil and trouble, of all the fear and hardship, nothing has been quite so dreadful as the realities confronted here. Until now it was only rumor and hearsay. Even with the knowledge we were given, nothing could prepare us for what we found. No words can adequately describe the horrors that must have occurred here. It is a sad tale for which my soul now aches. This once happy, hopeful, and majestic place now needlessly destroyed and torn by tragedy. I ask who would commit such an illicit act. I ask what could justify such a crime. I could search all the days of my life and I would never find an answer.

The boys and I are getting along as well as can be hoped for. We made the march from Granger's Point to the lakes without incident. Although I should mention that the crossing of the Des Moines was rather difficult. So difficult that Captain Richards and another mounted man were unable to cross and had to return to the main body. That dropped our numbers to twenty-three able men in the burial party. We arrived at the east shore of East Okoboji Lake just past midday and located Thatcher's cabin shortly thereafter. Here we found the door shut and only the cook stove and bedsteads inside. Strangely there were feathers all about the clearing which had come from the torn and emptied beds which lay outside. In the rear of the home we found poor Mr. Noble and Mr. Ryan. Both had been shot in the breast and evidently put up no fight. We buried them at the foot of a large oak tree.

From there we proceeded to the Howe house just a few rods to the south. The scene we encountered there was far more grim than the previous. We found seven bodies, all brutally murdered and thrown in a pile. There were two adults and five children. In the opening we found the mangled remains of Thatcher's infant child. What a grave and unfortunate scene for Joseph Thatcher to discover. Joseph himself had just narrowly missed the outcome of his child and neighbors. He had gone to Waterloo for supplies and upon his return he had to wait at Shippey's Point because of his exhausted cattle. This happened to save his life. The fate of his wife, poor Mrs. Thatcher, is yet unknown. We fear she has been captured and must endure the misfortunes of captivity.

By the time we finished the burials at the Howe cabin darkness had begun to fall. We retreated for the night to the Thatcher cabin. Here we rest, all twenty-three of us in this cabin of just fourteen by twenty feet. It is a place of relative comfort. I shall try and sleep, but the images of today are loathsome and I would rather pass the minutes as hours than to encounter those images again tomorrow.

Yours truly,
William

Discovering the Culprits

July 27, 1857 - - "I have not seen an Indian in such a fine coat," I remarked.

"Nor I," replied my brother John. "I should think he could have only stolen such a coat, or taken it off a corpse."

"His pantaloons, too, seem quite splendid," I added.

"They must be of the group we are searching for," said John willingly. "Where else could he find an outfit such as that? Especially all the way out here, where the traders dare not even come."

"Well that's not necessarily so," I returned. "This is Crooked River; this is a very fine stream. I suppose the traders may come out this way. And who's to say . . . maybe the articles were traded to him from another Indian who had come from the east and had himself traded with a white man."

"Now you're just being trivial," said John.

"I suppose I am. I just do not wish to jump to any conclusions. This is risky business we tred."

"What do you mean?" My brother raised his eyebrows and furled his brow.

"We cannot be too careful," I began to explain. "Everyone is a suspect. Everyone is a possible danger. While at the same time we don't want to wrongfully accuse and detain innocent men and women."

"I guess we cannot win, can we?" replied John. "But I say they are all guilty. Until we capture the culprits they must be guilty. Otherwise they might fall upon us like they did those innocent settlements."

"That may be so, John. That may be so."

For four hours our newest suspects were detained and questioned. We found them camped along the open prairie where it was impossible to surround them, but they made no attempt at flight or escape. We did as John suggested and treated them as a vile and dangerous enemy. Not because they were, but because we could not be sure that they were not. Among them were three Indian men, two women, and four children. We presumed with caution that this group may have been a part of Inkpaduta's band for which we searched. But hours of questioning proved otherwise. Though I am unaware of the details, Little Crow found no reason to detain them and therefore let them go. It may have been an unpleasant day for our guests, but by this time we needed to take every precaution.

The next day we pushed on from Crooked River in the direction of Skunk Lake. Although the capture the day before proved inconsequential, there remained a strange sense of intimacy that hung over the group. Not intimacy to each other, but intimacy to our goal. I could feel a tangible sense of proximity to the fiends we sought to apprehend. And with each mile, each quarter-mile even, the feeling grew stronger. I cannot understand why or where the feeling came from, for we had no clues or evidence to suggest we neared our target, but the feeling could not be denied. I could see it in each man as he grew more quieted, more reserved and stealth-like. No longer were there casual conversations or any non-pertinent communications. There was no wandering or resting one's eyes or stretching one's tired legs. No—now the group was firm, ready, alert, and aware. Even their posture had become animal-like as if waiting to pounce on its prey. Whatever apathy might have existed at the beginning of this expedition had now been completely lost or transformed into something that could be defined as nothing other than pugnacious. I could see and feel that in an unspoken way we were preparing for battle. In that moment I recalled the wisdom I had once read in the ancient text, *The Art of War*, by Sun Tzu: "Now the general who wins a battle makes many calculations in his temple ere the battle is fought." We had made our calculations and we were ready for war.

As we moved slowly but readily along I thought once more on our enemy. It was an enemy I knew little about and, despite my earlier conversation with Grey Leaf, I still felt muddled and confused. All of us, in fact, were torn over the duty before us, but we had little choice. Throughout the territory rumors and hearsay were bound to sprout regarding Inkpaduta and his band and they very well did. Inkpaduta was seen as a vile fiend and an inhuman monster. He was considered as the most savage of the savages from which only evil erupted. Even his appearance aroused both fear and wild exaggeration. From what was said, Inkpaduta was a tall, evil-looking figure with deep scars on his face and squinty black eyes behind which festered his dark and sinful nature. Many referred to his appearance as revolting and repulsive and they considered him an enemy to be feared and distrusted. No doubt his physical appearance contributed to his heinous reputation. But I knew all this could not necessarily be true. Especially after learning what Grey Leaf had to say. There were other rumors too, about the events leading up to the massacre and about the provocations that may have led to such an event. It was not all hearsay, wild characterizations, and flamboyant, derogatory allegations. It was known in fact that last fall Inkpaduta carried on good relations with the settlers of Northern Iowa. In the towns of Peterson, Cherokee, and Peary there were reports of peaceful and friendly interactions with Inkpaduta's band. I had been told that while at Peterson, Inkpaduta's sons, Roaring Cloud and Fire Cloud, competed with the white settlers in shooting and wrestling contests. Relations were apparently nothing but positive.

But there occurred an inexorable change. On December the first of last year there was a massive snow storm that lasted three days and left the region with near three feet of snow. Over the northwest frontier winter had set in. Food was no longer expendable. What each family had, they had to make last through the winter.

Still, relations remained positive. There was no expectation of violence and there never had been. The Wahpekutes were known to move near a settlement called Smithland where they established several lodges near the farm of Elijah Adams. At the time of their arrival, Inkapduta and his band smoked the peace pipe with the local settlers and proceeded to visit with them daily. Though the Dakota's were hungry, they remained friendly, always trading for food and never killing a live cow. But things changed.

As conditions worsened and food supplies became scarce, the citizens of Smithland began to resent the presence of the Dakotas. This created tension which led to a series of negative incidents. In one such incident, as it has been rumored to me, the Wahpekute women dug out unhusked corn left behind during the fall harvest. After realizing they had missed some of the corn during the harvest, the white settlers accused the Wahpekute women of stealing. The settlers then whipped the Dakota with switches and forcefully took the corn back. In another, more repercussive event, a settler's dog attacked the Indians while they were hunting elk. One of the Wahpekute hunters then shot and killed the dog. In retaliation, the owner of the dog attacked the Indian responsible, beating him and taking his gun. These are just some of the incidents of which I became aware.

In any case, the citizens of Smithland decided to raise a militia to drive the Indians away. Despite differing opinions, the majority of the white settlers determined that they could no longer accept the Dakota presence. A small militia was raised and in early February they set out to find Inkpaduta. Upon locating Inkpaduta and his band the militia requested that they leave the area immediately. Simple as that may have been, the militia also requested—rather, demanded—that the Indians give up all their firearms. This could only be perceived as an unreasonable request because without their guns, the Indians would be unable to hunt and would surely starve. It was a death sentence. Though Inkpaduta pleaded that his band be allowed to keep their guns, the militia was adamant in their demand and ultimately the guns were confiscated. What occurred from this point I can merely speculate. The Dakota's, now angry and hungry, proceeded northeast along the Little Sioux River trading for food, guns, and ammunition. Cast out and left for dead, the roving band of Wahpekutes would eventually retaliate with deadly force.

I could not be sure of Inkpaduta's present condition as it concerns hostility. It was now late July, a full four months since the last violent incident between the whites and Indians. The hostile band we sought no longer carried with them any captives and they were apparently well beyond the boundaries of white civilization. I consider it likely that whatever anger had provoked earlier hostilities had since passed, or, at a minimum, was not at the forefront of their minds.

"There!" I suddenly heard the voice of the warrior Mahpiya as he pointed to the west in a granite-like pose.

It was a single solitary lodge situated alongside a small grove of elm.

"Proceed with caution," added Little Crow. "Send two on each flank."

We went forward as cautiously and carefully as possible, but once again being out in the open, we were not provided much opportunity for concealment. As we grew closer, the scene did not present any immediate danger. There was no one about and all seemed quiet, but we could not be sure that those possible enemies had not spotted us first and hidden themselves upon our approach.

"Keep sight," was all Little Crow said as we got closer.

We were now within about one hundred yards of the lodge. I cannot imagine what our column of weapon-clad Indian warriors must have looked like to an impartial onlooker. Over one hundred men all mounted, painted, and ready for battle stretched out across the entire prairie. It had to be a fearful sight to anyone who crossed our path.

The lodge looked to be deserted. The fire pit was black with cold ash while white bones had been stripped clean and laid along the perimeter. There was not much else beside the lodge itself and a few articles of clothing and pelts that hung on the branch of a tree. Whoever made their home there had evidently not lived there long.

"Reveal yourselves!" called out Black Dog. The entire army was now within fifteen yards of the lodge, all with rifles pointed.

"Make yourselves known," continued Black Dog. "We wish to avoid a fight."

We waited second after second, weapons aimed and ready. Silence and a burst of wind was the only response.

"Move forward," Little Crow commanded of Black Dog and several other warriors.

The warriors, led by Black Dog, moved surreptitiously forward like a small army of ants after a morsel of food. Without making a noise they surrounded the lodge. After a brief and silent communication, Black Dog opened the flap to the lodge and the three warriors went in as quick as a gopher down a hole.

"It is deserted," announced Black Dog. "Just some bedding remains."

The warriors emptied the tent and all turned toward Little Crow as if by magnetic force and awaited instruction.

"Check the grove," said Little Crow in a rather impassive manner. "Be cautious, they may still be near."

It was another source of disappointment to find an empty lodge. Though the Dakota men sought no conflict, the expedition was wearisome. I believe they would rather find their enemy and risk conflict than continue along the indefinite trail west. For the third day in a row we had located a suspicious lodge but each had proven insignificant. In this case, at least, we had not disproven anything. The lodge may yet have been one of Inkpaduta's.

After ensuring that the lodge and its surrounding area was deserted, we continued on our way west. Despite whatever frustration existed among the warriors, they showed no signs of indiscretion, but continued with the same vigilance. It was not long before another lodge was found. Then there was another and another. Altogether we found six lodges scattered along the trail within about three miles of each other. And each time the scene repeated itself. We made a careful approach, surrounded the lodge, and discovered that it was empty. But we were getting close. Though we found no one, there seemed to be almost no doubt that these lodges belonged to none other than the band of Inkpaduta. It created for me a certain exhilaration, but also a nervous tension. Meanwhile the warriors demonstrated only a professional, war-like demeanor. They knew the task at hand and everything else they put aside.

Little Crow gave the order to scatter the men in all directions. Surely if the enemy was near we would find them. I was chosen to follow down the principle trail. In addition to Little Crow and me, this group included my brothers John and Baptiste, John Mooers, Good Road, Iron Elk, Sunkasake, Wasuhowaste, and Hehanduta. In flawless military fashion the armed warriors scattered and set out in search of the potential enemy. The region was no longer prairie, but rather a sparsely-wooded forest with thick brush and plentiful undergrowth. The thick undergrowth made it easy to follow the path of the principle trail, but the sparse woods made it difficult to move inconspicuously. Still, the full-blooded Indian warriors demonstrated a keen style and grace in their movements. They knew every turn and dip and bend of the trail before it came about. It seemed as if they had traveled along that same path hundreds of times, although I am certain none had ventured along that trail even once.

We continued down the trail with grit and determination showing no signs of fatigue or lethargy. Mile after mile, hour after hour, we kept up our awareness and maintained our unspoken bond of service to each other. Yet the forest remained quiet. The environment remained still as if it had never seen a single visitor. The day grew long as the sun passed from east to west and the shadows turned from one side to another. There was nothing but us in that forest.

"Halt!" commanded Wasuhowaste. He sat upon his steed like a hawk upon a perch, one hand stretched behind him to indicate that we hold our position while his eyes stared straight ahead through the trees. Oh, to be a painter with an easel in that moment! The powerfully bright sun set in a direct path behind Wasuhowaste turning him into a fantastic and shadowy figure while dark clouds gathered straight overhead and rain began to fall. It was a surreal image in a very real situation.

"They are there," pointed out Wasuhowaste. "I see women and children among the reeds." The entire group of ten men had now gathered in a circle. It suddenly occurred to me that we were near a small lake. The others and I peered through the trees and the orange sunlight and we could see in the distance what looked like two women wading through the water.

"Crow," continued Wasuhowaste, "you ought to call them out of the lake to speak with them; determine whether they are friend or foe."

Little Crow paused for a moment as he tried to get a better view of those in the lake. "That would not be wise," said Little Crow. "If they are the enemy they would surely recognize me as the chief of the Mdwekanton and they would kill me. I also fear they may turn and run and then might escape."

"But you are well respected and there are none among us who would be better received," argued Wasuhowaste.

"I agree with Crow," added Sunkasake unexpectedly. "It would be a great risk to send our chief."

"Who would you send?" asked Wasuhowaste in an irritated manner.

Almost involuntarily, I said, "I will go."

"We cannot send a half-breed," replied Wasuhowaste. "That would be more dangerous than sending Crow."

"I suppose it would," I agreed automatically without really evaluating the truth of the statement.

"It must be you," said Sunkasake while looking straight toward Wasuhowaste. "You are a full-blooded Dakota of Mazakutamani's portion of Iagmani's band. They have no reason to suspect you are an enemy."

Wasuhowaste paused without giving reply. He turned and looked once more toward the reeds and the lake. "The sun is low," he said. "The clouds are gathering. I have learned patience from the owl. I have learned cleverness from the crow. And I have learned courage from the jay. I will go."

With that there was nothing more to be said. Wasuhowaste turned and slipped away, making a path that was unnoticeable even to ourselves. The rest of us dismounted and crept slowly down the path. We moved with caution and stealth in order that we would not make ourselves known. Finally we came within striking distance of the unwitting people of the lake. The rain was now coming down steadily but it did not seem to bother the women and children as they waded through the reeds.

Suddenly Wasuhowaste appeared on the shore of the lake off to our front and left. "Ho!" he called out while raising both arms high above his head. The women looked with curiosity and then looked at each other. "Come to the land so I may speak with you," called Wasuhowaste. "I am a friend."

The two women in the lake began to speak softly with one another, certainly discussing whether or not to meet the unknown Indian. Just then it became clear that there were many more Indians among them as they came out from the reeds to discover the commotion. I could not count exactly, but there were nearly ten men, ten women, and a dozen children in the group we now found. At that moment I was certain we were in for a fight.

After some squabbling and an inaudible discussion, two women and one child came out from the lake to meet Wasuhowaste. The meeting appeared cordial at first as both parties shook hands. From our spot behind the trees we watched carefully, ready for anything. In the meantime the people in the lake also observed the meeting and called out, "They are friends—they are shaking hands." For a few moments all seemed well as if perhaps this was not the band we had been searching for. But then the women and children mysteriously began backing away from Wasuhowaste. The Indians in the lake now cried, "No! He is an enemy!" In an instant the men and women in the lake turned and ran in all directions. It was clear now these were the Indians of Inkpaduta's band, for why else would they run? Fearing they would escape, Wasuhowaste was the first to raise his gun and fire. "Boom!" His rifle echoed across the water while the ball fired struck a man in the back shoulder causing him to drop his gun and fall in the water. Before the rest of us could provide support Wasuhowaste fired his other barrel. "Boom!" The shot rang out once more causing the ground itself to shake. An old man was hit and before he fell he yelled out, "They have killed me!" I believe he dropped dead right then and there. Wasuhowaste dropped back to a defensive position to reload while the rest of us came forward to an exposed position and began to fire on the now-scattered crowd. After just a few moments the enemy had retreated out of the lake and behind the trees where they finally returned fire. Having lost our advantage, we fell back to a position that provided cover. The rain was now coming down heavily and the sun was nearly below the horizon, making it almost impossible to locate our enemy. Bullets whizzed rapidly overhead, sounding much like bees, while the occasional shot struck and ricocheted off the fallen logs to our front. Regardless of the danger, we kept up a healthy fire in the direction of the reeds. After a few minutes the enemy's fire began to dissipate, but it was still frequent enough to keep us behind cover. "Don't let them off yet!" urged Little Crow. I squinted and peered through the darkness, searching for any movement at all. Occasionally something caught my eye and I fired, but I doubt if it had much effect other than to remind our enemy that we still meant to defeat them.

For thirty minutes the fight was kept up with an exchange of volleys. Meanwhile, the gathering storm had worsened and the darkness had thoroughly set in. At last Little Crow called us to retreat. We slipped away not knowing how many were killed or where our enemy still lurked. It was a rather uncertain result.

RETURN TO THE AGENCY

July 29, 1857 - - The night following the attack did not provide much rest. The rain continued well into the night and was a source of great discomfort. We had no shelter from which to escape the downpour and at the same time, our nerves were still excited from the fight. I managed a few moments of sleep and a few more moments of solitude, but for the most part I was awake and alert like I might be at any point during the day.

Once morning finally arrived and the light of day provided a relative bit of safety, it was decided we would head back to the scene of the fight in search of the fallen enemy. It was assumed that the enemy that remained alive was now long gone, but we could not be certain. At the very least we wished to find and identify those who had been killed. Unfortunately this decision also brought with it a tender argument. A couple of half-breeds, not including myself, wished to scalp any bodies they found. However, Hehanduta and several others of the full-blooded Dakotas were adamantly opposed to scalping the dead because they were members of their own nation. The argument could not be settled and Hehanduta insisted that we split into groups. Little Crow agreed, so we went out that morning in small groups of two or three. Hehanduta went alone around the side of the lake.

For several hours we searched but found nothing, living or dead. All was quiet. Once satisfied that our searches had been thorough and complete, my group and I returned to camp. Upon returning we were met by the approximately eighty warriors who had split off and scattered around the region just the day before. We had learned from them that, unlike ourselves, they had discovered no enemies throughout the wooded region. It seemed that the only people to be found were those we encountered in the lake.

Of all of us, the only one to locate any bodies was Hehanduta. He first found an Indian man named Tawachineewaken, the old man, lying dead in a shallow portion of the lake. Then he found Tateiohi who was also lying dead in the reeds. Hehanduta then moved on down the trail and past the lake where he found Mahpiyapeta, also known as Fire Cloud, who was Inkpaduta's son. Fire Cloud also happened to be the twin brother of Roaring Cloud whom we had shot and killed earlier in the summer.

Three dead, then, was the total, and no more to be found. Some men may have also been wounded, but as Hehanduta stated, he no longer wished to follow the trail because he felt lonesome and unhappy. In any case, the fight was successful. We caused three casualties while taking none and at the same time, we were able to positively identify that it was in fact Inkpaduta's renegade band. Furthermore, we came away with two women and a little boy who were located by Hehanduta upon his return. They were frightened and alone and had nothing to say. Though we searched all day long we found no other Indians. Now the time came to consider what to do next. We took council.

"We have killed three of our enemy," said Little Crow from the head of the circle. "Captured three more. Taken two horses. Brought away all their baggage. The enemy now retreats toward the horizon where the sun falls and the moon rises. They move further into the territory of the Yankton, a place we are not welcome. We have seen no death, but our moccasins are worn, our horses are jaded, and our supplies are empty. Our families and kin await our return and they also grow hungry. But we must remember that we shook hands with the white chief. We vowed to capture or kill all of the culprits. We stated that we would go as far as the great Missouri to bring them in. It is not my place to decide. I lay this before you now, brothers. Shall we pursue our enemy or return to our families?"

Little Crow spoke calmly and appeared as impartial as possible for a man in his position. Around him, seated in a circle, were all of the band leaders and elders of the group. Behind them, standing and bunched closely together, were all of the warriors and half-breeds that belonged to the expedition. I was fortunate enough to be seated among the inner circle, although I might have little to add to the discussion.

While Little Crow spoke it occurred to me for the first time that we may not continue after the enemy. As Little Crow mentioned, we made a vow not to return without first capturing or killing Inkpaduta's entire band. The Indians seemed so genuine in their promise. Perhaps I was naive to take them at their word, but I knew of no other way to interpret their pledge. It was my nature. What's more, I was every bit a participant in that promise and I did not wish to renege on my own vow. That being said, we were indeed tired, weary, and low on supplies. It was quite uncertain what more we could actually accomplish. I could understand what brought us to this moment, to this council. Nonetheless I felt confounded the instant I realized what had brought us together. Until now I truly viewed our only option as pursuit.

"The question," said Iagmani in response to Little Crow's statement, "is not whether to pursue or return. The question is whether or not our annuities will be paid us if we return empty-handed. If we pursue we may starve. If we return we may be denied our annuities again. This is all I have to say."

Iagmanis' statement immediately sparked chatter among the warriors. It also seemed to spark a great deal of interest.

"I will speak of what I know," said Ukita as the chatter quickly died down. "I found in the lodges seven dollars in money. I did not wish to take the money because it belonged to people of my own nation. I do not want to pursue my own nation. But when I saw Wakeaska, who was connected by marriage to Inkpaduta's band, and the old-chief Iagnami, ready to go, I could not refuse to follow."

The chatter rose again while several warriors called out "Ho!" in agreement.

Red Owl, who was seated opposite me in the circle, then raised his hands to indicate that he desired to speak. "I do not understand the white man's promise," began Red Owl in a stoic fashion. "The white man puts a price on the land just so he can take it. He takes everything and promises to give us food and money in return. But when the time to pay comes, he does not pay. He does not follow his promise and he asks us to give him more instead."

Everyone was listening intently as Red Owl lowered his head and continued speaking.

"Now he says we must do his work. He says we must capture his enemy. Though we have done no wrong we are punished. Though we have done no wrong we are forced to prove ourselves worthy and good to the white man. I say we have done enough. I am tired. I am hungry. We have risked our lives and earned our reward. We have earned what was rightfully ours to begin with. Why should the earth have to earn the rainfall? How can we earn what is already promised us?"

"But we have," interrupted Lone Village in a way that seemed to startle everyone's ears for its suddenness.

"We have," confirmed Red Owl.

"We have done more than enough!" shouted Mahpiya, who was a true warrior. "We have done more than enough for the white man!" he continued as he stepped forth from the crowd speaking loudly and with conviction. "If we return and they do not hand over our payment, we need only to remind the Great Father what we have done. We will tell him how difficult it was to chase after our own people. We will tell him that Wasuhowaste, a Dakota warrior of the Upper Bands, was the first to fire upon those of Inkpaduta's band. We will tell the Great Father that there were others such as Matocatka, Ptewaken, and Towanhdigmani who fought the whole time. They fought against their own nation."

"Ho!" Again came the call from several of the warriors.

Mahpiya now stood directly in the middle of the circle. As he spoke he pointed his hands and waved his arms and turned in every direction as if he were telling a great story. "We have chased the enemy for many miles into the depths of the western lands. We have fought and killed them and sent them retreating even further beyond the white man's reach. There is nothing more to be done!" said Mahpiya adamantly. "And if they say to us we have not done enough—if they say we have not proven our loyalty to the white people—if they say these things, we must only remind the Great Father that the first man who went and rescued the white captive belonged to the Upper band of Dakota. He is Grey Wolf who sits among us now. If they still say we have not proven our loyalty, we will remind our Great Father that those employed and those who succeeded in bringing in the other white captive were Wahpetons and they are also of the Upper band of Dakota. They too sit among us now having bravely faced two dangerous expeditions."

Mahpiya was emphatic and his emotion spewed not only from his voice but from his eyes, his arms, and his heart. I listened in amazement and wonder at the sheer strength that erupted from his grievances. Right or wrong, he spoke as a man who was sure of himself.

"And more still," continued Mahpiya, "we will remind the Great Father who it was that killed Inkpaduta's son at Yellow Medicine. Those who gave information to the military and assisted in the expedition to kill Roaring Cloud were Wasuhowaste and Anpetutokeca, both Wahpetons and both Upper band of Dakota."

With that a general cheer came out from the small crowd of warriors. It was not loud or exuberant, but it was enough to show support and agreement for the words spoken by their fellow Dakota.

Mahpiya paused and put his hands on his hips as if exhausted. He turned his head to the right, took a breath and waited for every last sound to cease. "Have we not done enough? Have we not proven that we have no intention to harm the white man? We have lived with him many years and we have caused no trouble. Many of you have learned their tongue, and picked up their tools, and adopted their clothing. We have upheld our promise. We have fulfilled our mission. There is nothing more the white man can ask of us, nor is there anything more he can take. I beg you brothers, these things are good proof of our willingness to assist in the destruction of the murderers and our desire to carry out the wishes of our Great Father. Now, our provisions are consumed. We are much in want. We must return home to collect our annuities."

Before Mahpiya could finish his impassioned speech a cheer again rose up, this time it was much louder than the first. They grunted and shouted with approval and sounded like a thunderous cloud. The cheer was loud and sustained and showed that all seemed to agree with Mahpiya.

Little Crow, from his seated position, raised his arms in order to calm the boisterous crowd of warriors. "Men," he began in the same calm manner in which he spoke before. "It appears a decision has been reached."

The men began to cheer and shout but Little Crow quickly quieted their enthusiasm as he raised his arms high. "We have met our enemy and we have done our duty," said Little Crow as the men began to listen again. "We are now tired and have little to eat. We will return to the agency and we will ask for our annuities."

The decision was made. Once again the men smiled and cheered and showed their approval that the expedition would return home. I sat in silence among all the noise and excitement. For some reason I was disenchanted by the decision. Though I understood the grievances expressed by the warriors, I did not feel as if our mission was complete or that we had lived up to our promise. Certainly the Indians were in want and much deserved their annuities, but what of the criminals? If they slip away now, I thought, they might slip away forever. And then it may only be a matter of time before it happens again. The consequences would be unknown.

Sunday, April 5
West Okoboji

Dear Eliza,

Outside, a winter storm is raging. It is rather unbelievable that at this late a date we are still being visited by winter weather. One day it is warm and comfortable and the snows are melting and the next it is cold and icy with a frigid winter breeze. Today the conditions are blizzard-like with huge, heavy flakes of snow flying horizontally and carried by a stiff and strong winter wind. Even the thought of venturing onto the prairie causes my body to cringe. That is why I am so much in angst now. We are only seven here in this cabin. The others we fear must bear the brunt of this storm head on and exposed. They are liable to die in such unfavorable conditions. Today I am the fortunate one.

When last I wrote, we were huddled inside the Thatcher cabin, all twenty-three of us. We arose early the next morning and continued with our solemn duty. After a scanty breakfast we returned to the Howe cabin to complete the burying of the seven dead. However, we then found yet another body—that of a young boy who was apparently Mrs. Noble's brother. This discovery brought the total dead at the Howe cabin to nine, including Thatcher's infant baby. Before we continued our work, Captain Johnson decided to split us into three groups. One group, under Captain Johnson, was to stay and complete the burial at the Howe cabin. Another group, under Lieutenant Maxwell was to proceed to the Mattock cabin on West Okoboji. I was a member of this group. The third group, under the direction of Mr. Wheelock, was detailed to find, if possible, the wagon with supplies that Howe and Wheelock had abandoned on the prairie the night they had discovered the massacre on their former trip. This assignment was of crucial importance because we were at that time depleted of all provisions.

As I proceeded to the Mattock cabin with the Lieutenant and others, we discovered the headless body of Mr. Joel Howe on the ice. We took Mr. Howe's body to the shore and buried him in a bluff some distance southwest of his home. We arrived at the Mattock cabin to find it in ashes. It was by far the most sinister scene we had yet encountered. The bodies were widely scattered around the home and along the trail toward the Granger house. I am uncertain if any bodies had burned up in the flames. Here was shown the only sign of much resistance. Dr. Harriot was found with a broken rifle in his hand and may have succeeded in injuring one of the attackers. We buried eleven at the Mattock cabin.

Just as we were completing the work at the Mattock cabin, the parties of Wheelock and Johnson joined us. The men who had gone with Wheelock found the abandoned wagon without difficulty and they secured as much as they could comfortably carry. This included flour, pork, coffee, and sugar, for which we were grateful.

As an entire group once more we proceeded across the strait to the Granger cabin. Here we found the body of Carl Granger, horribly mutilated in such a manner I dare not wish to describe. At his side was his dog, apparently faithful to the last. We continued then to the last place. Your home. Oh how I dreaded that short march more than any other. It was like walking the plank at sea, only it was not I who would perish, but the happiness I had once found. We arrived to find six bodies scattered about the home and the clearing. I tell you now who they were because you have the right to know. My dear Eliza, it was there we found your father, your mother, your oldest sister, your brother, and your sister's two little ones. Although they must have faced unimaginable fear, they appear to have been killed quickly. We buried them together at the base of the oak tree just a few paces outside your once loving home. I am so very, very sorry. Words cannot begin to express the weight of my sorrow for you and your loved ones today. From the bottom of my heart, I grieve.

Your sister Abbie could not be found. We believe she was carried off by the savages and remains among them, still living. I fear that nothing can be done for her now, but surely the great people of this frontier will band together and she will be rescued.

We completed our loathsome work right around the time the sun was falling. We were tired and hungry and we decided to camp just north of your cabin. Although we had secured some provisions, we needed more sufficient nutrients. It was then that I remembered that your father had buried a box of potatoes under the stove to keep them from freezing. I quickly recovered the potatoes and we roasted them over the campfire. They filled our bellies nicely.

Saturday morning arrived foggy and misty and had all the indications of a coming storm. This resulted in quite an argument between the men over the return trip. Many of the men favored a more direct southeasterly route heading directly toward the Irish colony. Others, including me, favored the less direct more easterly route on which we had come. This argument could not be settled and Captain Johnson allowed the men to decide for themselves which route they would take. Sixteen men, including Captain Johnson and Lieutenant Maxwell, chose to take the direct route. I and six others chose the longer but safer route. We urged them to change their minds out of fear for the coming storm, but they could not be convinced, so we bade them goodbye. Following the main group's departure, the seven of us set out to locate the abandoned wagon. We quickly found the wagon and rather than proceed to Granger's Point, we decided to retreat to the Gardner cabin because of the looks of the gathering storm. When we arrived we hunkered down and made ready to defend ourselves in case of an Indian attack. First we secured some fuel, then we barricaded the door, removed some of the chinking and made portholes in the sides of the cabin. Before long the storm hit. In very little time the storm became a blinding whirlwind of snow and freezing air. We could do little else but wait. Feeling relatively safe and with reasonable provisions, we now find ourselves in some degree of comfort. We can only wonder at what perils and discomfort confront our comrades.

I hope you are well and safe. My return home will not seem nearly as long or quite as arduous with the knowledge that you are alright. I pray with both hope and joy that your family is in a better place and that through grace, young Abbie would return to us safely.

With my utmost I remain yours,
William

Special Agent Kintzing Pritchette

Two worlds. So very different, yet so very much the same. Both seeking happiness, comfort, safety, and survival. They love their families and they have pride for their nations. They hunt the same deer, they fish the same streams, they covet the same land. They work toward the future: toward a better and brighter future where their children can flourish. Two worlds and I live among them both. As I now travel with one I am working on behalf of the other. I am torn, conflicted, and heartbroken. I see these men, these natives of the Americas, and I see a passionate, generous, faithful, and beautiful culture. But as they march back tired, weary, and powerless to plead with their Great Father for their promised annuities, I see the inevitability of their cause. I see their world dominated and destroyed by the world of another and there appears no hope in sight. In my short lifetime alone, a mere thirty years, they have been reduced from an infinite space, an endless Eden, to a few acres of reserved and undesirable land. Their resources, once thought to be infinite, have been exhausted and their way of life has been extinguished. While the dominant world, the white world, continues to come. Year after year, more and more, they come, and they bring with them an unyielding sense of entitlement. They march over this endless wilderness, see what they want, and claim it as their own. Once claimed, they draw up rules and laws and treaties in a spurious way to justify what they have done. They confound and confuse the Indian and say "sign here" and "sign there." They manipulate the Indian by giving him gifts and becoming his friend, but this is only a clever ruse to enamor the Indian with the exoticism of the white world. The subterfuge of the whites has made the Indians addicted and dependent and ultimately suppressed and perhaps, eventually, extinct.

I see these warriors, these soon-to-be relics. I see their passion, their strength, their vivacity, but I no longer see hope. I grew up loving the world of the Indian. I respected and revered the teachings of my grandmother. I still do today. But I look around at a dejected people, a proud people, who now must beg for their next meal, and the future becomes a dismal sight. I see two worlds in a world where there can only be one.

Our return trip was relatively nondescript. We made our way quickly, camping at or near several of the same sites we had passed on our way out. The weather was agreeable and the path was easy to follow. Indeed we were low on rations and supplies. But thankfully the superintendent sent out new supplies which we received at Hole in the Mountain. This was a much-needed boost in order to maintain any degree of comfort for the final few days. My feet in fact were terribly blistered and I was in great want for new moccasins. Aside from this there was just one noteworthy incident to report from our return trip. On August 1, our third day from Skunk Lake, we encamped at the Redwood River. Here we were met by three or four Indians who demanded our prisoners. Of course we were unwilling to concede, because without the prisoners we had little proof that we had overtaken Inkpaduta's band. The confrontation nearly turned ugly when Mahpiya told them if they sympathized so much with the murderers they had better go and pick their dead men out of the lake and bury them. Thankfully the confrontation did not escalate into violence and the unknown Indians continued on their way. The days, though long, passed well enough and we returned to Yellow Medicine at 11 a.m. on the morning of August 3.

"Don't you understand what great perils the Dakota Indians have faced?" I argued. "They ask for nothing but what they are entitled to."

"The Dakota are entitled to nothing," quickly retorted Agent Pritchette.

"Well, if not entitled, they have very well earned it," I answered. "The Dakota have been nothing but loyal and good and they have done everything the government has asked."

"Whether or not they are good is of little concern to me," answered Agent Pritchette in his stale and emotionless manner. "It is of no difference to me how the Dakota behave themselves. My job concerns only the capture and punishment of the murderers. And as I understand, the Dakota are required to apprehend said murderers. Until they do, I will withhold their annuities. It is not a matter for debate."

The special agent sat back comfortably in his chair as he spoke, cross-legged and with a pipe angling downward from his mouth and resting softly in his palm. If his words were not enough to infuriate me, certainly his casual, indifferent demeanor was.

"Sir, I beg you, they live in a northern climate and winter approaches fast. If you do not send for their annuities now they will not come at all. And then winter will set in and the Dakota Indians will starve. Please, have a heart."

"Excuse me," Agent Pritchette replied with a heavy glare and a staunch tone. "I would be fit to rebuke you for such a comment. But being you are half Indian it is likely your brash tongue can be attributed to pure stupidity. Over which you have no control and therefore ought to be pitied."

Agent Pritchette did not laugh or even smirk after making such a ghastly and horrible comment. He just went on smoking his pipe as if his words were no less common than each breath of air he took. I had nothing to say in return. On a personal level both his ignorance and his acrimony stunned me deep, but at the same time I realized that there was no reasoning with such an animal as he. It was clear to me that he was incapable of a reasonable and effective dialogue. Kintzing Pritchette was his full name and he only just arrived to the agency three days prior, today being the fifth of August. Major Pritchette was known professionally as a Special Agent. He was an Indian Agent as assigned by the Bureau of Indian Affairs, but he was a temporary agent with a temporary assignment. In this case he was sent from Washington City to help plan for Inkpaduta's capture and punishment. He was a man of mature age, probably in his mid to late fifties. He was also a somewhat accomplished politician. He was born in Philadelphia and eventually became the Secretary of the Michigan Territory. Later in his career he served as the Secretary of the Oregon Territory and then as its Governor from June 18, 1850, to August 18, 1850. For the past few years he has served as a Special Agent for the Bureau of Indian Affairs.

This was the first I had met Agent Pritchette. As a first impression he came off as incredibly pompous and arrogant. He was, in his own way, much more difficult to consult with than was Major Cullen. He enraged me. But in a strange way I saw past his coarse and abrasive countenance. In the back of my mind I understood that he was a career politician who traveled many days with an assignment to fulfill. Though intolerable, though unreasonable, there was a sense of duty about him. He may have slandered me, but on a vocational level I believe he was adamant about his work. He was mature and experienced and he knew what he was sent to do. Therefore, or it seemed to me, his abrasiveness was used as a tool to accomplish his goals. Whether or not his manner was sincere was not important to him. He valued only the outcome. For that reason I was able to see past my anger and understand that quite possibly the Special Agent still had the best interest of the Dakota people in mind. If not, then he was nothing more than a bigot and a fiend.

"I beg your pardon Agent Pritchette," I said apologetically as I began my reply. "I meant no disrespect. I only . . ."

Just then a knock came at the door. I paused and turned. I then looked toward Major Cullen who had also been standing in the room. He nodded to indicate I could open the door.

"Mazaomani," I said as I recognized and greeted the man on the other side of the door. "Please, step in," I said in English knowing that Mazaomani could understand the white man's language.

Mazaomani was a Wahpeton chief who had been with the war party against Inkpaduta. I knew the purpose of his visit the moment I saw him. I think we all did. It had been a full two days since the war party returned and they had yet to discuss with the superintendent the results of the expedition or the terms of their reward. The Indians were eager, I knew, to receive their annuities, but I feared a discussion of the matter would be as vain as the argument I had just made.

"Welcome," said Major Cullen.

Mazaomani turned and gave a slight bow to the superintendent. "Ho," he said in the common Indian greeting. Mazaomani then gave a slight bow to Special Agent Pritchette, though he had never met him and must have been made curious by the Special Agent's presence. Agent Pritchette merely nodded in return.

"How might we assist you, Mazaomani?" asked Major Cullen.

"I speak for my brothers, the Mdewakantons, Wahpekutes, Sissetons, and Wahpetons," Mazaomani said softly. He both spoke and stood in a subservient manner like a child to his father. "We have tried to do what you wished."

"Indeed," agreed the superintendent.

"We have made a little scratch," continued Mazaomani. "We do not believe we have done enough yet. We suppose our Great Father is not afraid to travel through the country now. We hope our Great Father will send his braves on our track. The braves that went out have heard something that makes them feel bad," said Mazaomani, referring to the warriors who were on the recent expedition. "They hear their women and children have been hungry for four or five days. They do not deal foolishly with their Great Father. He has an abundance of money and other things. You are both our Fathers. Look around and find a little corn to feed the hungry Dakota. The farmer should know if there be anything, and if there be, he should show it to us when we get home."

"We have heard your pleas and the pleas of your women and children," replied Major Cullen. "But it is not my fault nor that of anyone at Yellow Medicine; we have no provision there." Major Cullen also spoke softly and calmly like a man trying to place ease in a troublesome situation. He leaned in toward Mazaomani and continued to speak as if no one else were present. "You have spoken well as to what your Great Father expects of you. I have told you often that your braves have done well, and I may want them again. I will send up a wagon loaded with flour for the wives of those that have been out on the war path. Let the two horses that were taken from Inkpaduta's people be given to the woman who is prisoner and whose husband and son were killed."

As the superintendent finished speaking he also ushered Mazaomani out of the room. Mazaomani made no reply, he simply bowed once more, turned, and walked away as the door closed behind him. As he left Mazaomani did not appear satisfied, but apparently he was not in the mood for an argument.

It was a mild, though charitable concession made by the superintendent. But it was clear that Major Cullen was avoiding the issue. He listened to Mazaomani only to give him the promise of a minor concession and then ushered him out the door. What appeared humanitarian on the surface was in fact rather shrewd.

"This is what I speak of," I said to Agent Pritchette. "The Dakota are hungry and destitute and are in no position to either make a second expedition or to cause any trouble among the settlers."

"Mr. Campbell," said Agent Pritchette in a slightly raised tone. "I appreciate the service you provide and I appreciate the risks you have taken. I have heard nothing but positive reports on your behalf. But I am telling you now to remember your position. I am telling you to stay within your boundaries. This is a political matter and there is a political process. I have my job and you have yours. Allow me to conduct mine as is fitting to my knowledge, experience, and expertise. Otherwise, you may end up ostracizing yourself, much like your father did."

The insult cut me like a blade. *How dare he bring up my father*, I thought. But I swallowed the insult as best I could and knew better than to answer in kind.

"Will there be a council?" I asked. "At the very least there ought to be a council."

"Positively," Agent Pritchette replied. "And I expect you will be on your best behavior."

There was nothing more to say. I turned, nodded to the superintendent, and escorted myself from the room. I spent the rest of the evening trying to forget the insolence of the cantankerous Kintzing Pritchette.

Payment Withheld

August 10, 1857 - - "Tell them that I am ready to hear them," Major Cullen instructed me from his position inside the storehouse.

"I will gather the Indians immediately," I replied as I made my way out from the storehouse and onto the agency.

It would not be difficult to gather the Upper Band of Dakota. They were already present and waiting upon Major Cullen and Agent Pritchette to begin the council. I merely had to tell the Indians to come, and they would gather in moments.

It had now been seven days since the expedition returned, and the Indians had yet received nothing more than a wagon of flour sent by the superintendent a few days earlier. Now, today, the Sisseton and Wahpeton of the Upper Bands gathered at Yellow Medicine to plead with the superintendent and his special agent for their promised, well-deserved, and much needed annuity payment. However, the government officials, Cullen and Pritchette, had every intention of rejecting their plea and withholding the annuity payment until every one of Inkpaduta's men had been killed, captured, or punished. It was an undesirable struggle between those who had the power and those who had a need. And like so many times before, I was caught directly in the middle, both literally and figuratively. I supported the plea of the Indians, but my job as U.S. Interpreter was only to convey the information given me. In other words, I was not to garner support toward one side or another. This, however, was made exceedingly difficult by the manner in which both sides fully expected that I embrace their outlook as if there were no other way. Regardless, the day was before us and the tension was palatable. A meeting, a discussion, a council, or whatever it might be: it was absolutely necessary.

"Gentlemen," called out Major Cullen to the hundreds of Upper Dakota now gathered in front of the three-story brick storehouse. "I am ready to hear you now. Make your case."

I translated as quickly and aptly as I could. It was humorous the way the attention turned from the major to me in an instant of flawless unison. The Indians made no immediate response to the major's words but stood quiet and disciplined. It was clear they had already chosen a speaker and they waited for that man to come forth.

It was Mazasa, also known as Red Iron, who finally came forward to speak. "I am appointed by all the soldiers here to speak for them," he began loudly and coherently in his native Dakota tongue. Though he spoke clearly, he did appear somewhat reluctant to be the one chosen to speak. "You have said something which I suppose is not forgotten. We went after Inkpaduta's band, as you desired us. You promised that if we would go you would pay the annuity money on our return, and we expect it now in three or four days. You are our father," said Red Iron, pointing directly to Major Cullen. "We do not expect you to change your words. Did you not say that if we went and did not get Inkpaduta that then you would send your own soldiers?" Red Iron paused here while he allowed me to translate, but for a moment it became unclear if he would continue. "We wish you to do this now," he finally said. "The soldiers have been walking a long time, and they now wish their money. That is all I have to say. All the soldiers asked me to say this. I have nothing to say for myself."

Red Iron did not wait for Major Cullen's response. He slowly backed away into the crowd. The rest turned their eyes forward and eagerly awaited the words of their so-called father.

Major Cullen took a step forward to show he was intent on speaking. He appeared much like he had at the council prior to the expedition, dressed in his blue frock coat and tall leather boots, though he was this time without his garish feather cap. Major Cullen was always one to dress for an occasion. "I am not here to ask you to go after Inkpaduta," he began, speaking loudly enough for all to hear despite the obvious fact that I had to translate his words and therefore the volume of his voice mattered little. "I wish you would finish the work you have begun. Your Great Father," he said referring to the President in a way the Indians had come to understand, "thinks it best for you to take these murderers, to save the killing of women and children. He would give you the opportunity of going again, and would wish you do it, because if white people go, we fear they may mistake and kill innocent persons."

This sounded like nothing more than a lie to me and I began to feel angry, but I knew it was no time to be angry.

"I do just as I promised," continued Major Cullen with his finger held out as if to add emphasis. "I understand that you refuse to do anything more. If the white soldiers have to do the work, and if any of your people suffer, it will be your own fault. I have no orders to pay any money until Inkpaduta is brought in."

Until then the Indians had given their undivided attention to the words of Major Cullen. But with this statement came an immediate and collective groan from the disgruntled Indians. Like rain spattering against the ground, they began to clamor in a loud and continuous manner.

"I feel sorry for you because you refuse," said the Major once it was quiet enough to continue. "It is for your good and not ours that he should be brought in. I suppose I understand you when you say that you will not do anything more. That is all I have to say on this subject."

Again there was an obvious groan; an audible discontent. Even I was surprised at the sheer offensiveness of the Major's statement. He made no attempt at reconciliation or compromise. If I can say so, he was rather audacious in his feeble coercion and blatant hypocrisy. How, I wondered, could he say one thing only to follow it up by saying the exact opposite? In my own mind I did not wish to judge or interpret the words of the Major, but I could not help myself.

Major Cullen waited while the Dakota warriors continued to talk and grumble amongst themselves. Finally he put his left hand out to his side and directed the attention to Major Pritchette, who was seated comfortably in a wooden chair behind him. "This gentlemen is sent by your Great Father," he finally continued, "to see what you have done."

This immediately quieted the Indians, who were eager and curious to see this new white authority.

"He has sent to your Great Father an account of all you have done. He is here, if you wish to say anything to him." Major Cullen took a step back as if to concede his pedestal and once again pointed toward Agent Pritchette. "If you wish to speak to Special Agent Pritchette, he is here."

Agent Pritchette made no attempt to move from his comfortable, cross-legged position. He did not even bother to remove himself from the shadow of the building. He sat back in an unconcerned fashion as if nothing were going on around him.

"I have listened to what was said," came the voice of Jagmani, a young but respected chief. "Our fields are spoken of; but if anybody is lazy, it is the man who is here to attend to it," Jagmani stated in a disagreeable tone. "I am going to speak of the treaty," he continued in a more subdued manner. "The Indians sold their land at Traverse des Sioux. I will say what we were told. For fifty years we were to be paid fifty thousand dollars per annum. We were also promised three hundred thousand dollars that we have not seen."

Jagmani was now animated in his speech. He was turning left and right, and waving his arms, and making strong gestures to match his strong words.

"I wish to say to my Great Father we were promised these things, but have not seen them yet. Why does not the Great Father do as he promised?" Jagmani paused. "I have something more to say; perhaps I may forget, but the others will remind me. One payment at Redwood they had no goods; five thousand dollars were kept back. Another time we did not get the surplus money for the chiefs and soldiers. These mills are theirs," he said speaking of the grist-mill and saw mill. "We were promised that when anything was done by the mill for others, that we should get paid for it. There has been a great deal of work done for others, and we have seen nothing. We were promised houses for each chief, they are not built yet. Last spring we ploughed their fields; I suppose we are to be paid for it. A great many of my men have cut logs for the mill; when sawed we only get half the lumber."

Jagmani stopped his speech abruptly. There was no reaction from the Dakota, just curious faces who probably expected Jagmani to continue. But Jagmani had nothing more to say and he looked toward Major Cullen, not Agent Pritchette, for his response.

"When I go to St. Paul," said Major Cullen casually, "I shall send up a man to repair the mill."

This was all the superintendent would reply. It was a curt response to a long monologue and it had little if anything to do with Jagmani's objections.

Next to come forward was was Wahpuja Wicasta. He was a young warrior who appeared angry and set on making a point. He dressed in his breech cloth and war paint and had a javelin in hand. He appeared as a memory of the once-great American Indian. "You told us you had come from our Great Father to be our father," he said loudly and fueled by passion. "The chiefs and soldiers have listened to all you said to them. You told us to go after Inkpaduta, and you promised that if we did anything and came back, that then we should get our money. We remember you said so. You have said one thing we do not at all like. You said we should have hard times; we do not like this," he said plainly. "The Wahpeton chiefs and soldiers on the Minnesota sit here and think they are looking on their money and goods now."

Wahpuja Wicasta made a turn away from the agents and toward his fellow warriors. Several of the warriors shouted "Ho!" and urged Wahpuja Wicasta to go on.

"It was not any of our people," he continued, still passionate but no longer with the same distinct vigor. "But some of the lower Indians who committed murder. The blame is with them, and they should be made to account for it."

Like a startled flock of birds, support rose up from behind Wahpuja Wicasta as the warriors were roused by his words.

"Some of the Wahpeton saw the captive white woman," he continued, "and brought her in. There was another woman there; they, the Wahpeton, went and got her. When you came and you asked us to go out after Inkpaduta; they did so. They suppose unless you tasted the meat you would not believe them. If they had said so, they would have brought you a piece."

With this Major Cullen would have no more. Suddenly he stepped forth from the shadow and rebuked the bold-speaking Indian. "I will not hear this man talk so," he said in a forceful tone I had not heard from him before. "If he cannot speak respectfully to me as the representative of their Great Father, I will not listen to him again." Major Cullen softened his tone, but he continued to speak. "I have heard what they have done; they have killed three and wounded another. This is already reported to their Great Father. I do not want to eat Indians," he stated matter-of-factly. "They should be ashamed to speak in such terms to me, when all they have had given to them so far has been out of my own pocket."

As much and as often as I was displeased with the superintendent, he was right to respond in the way he did. In that moment I could not sympathize with the Dakota.

"I am willing to give them all due praise for what they have already done," continued Major Cullen who was now somewhat more reticent. "But I cannot allow them to use such language with me. If they have anything to say in a friendly manner, I am ready to hear it. I do not desire to talk cross to them, but they must not speak disrespectfully to me."

Wahpuja Wicasta, who was still standing at the front of the warriors, now appeared ashamed. "I had not got through," he said defensively but not in a manner to suggest he wished to argue.

"I would as soon hear him as anyone, but he must not say I want to eat Indians," replied Major Cullen as if to politely tell Wahpuja Wicasta that it was time for him to step down.

The crowd was silent. It was as if the tension that once lingered had now been lost and squandered. Though the council was far from over. Not enough questions had been asked and nothing resembling an answer had been given.

Finally, in the midst of the silence, Paul Mazakutamani came forward. I was relieved to see this dark-looking Indian wearing white man's clothes and carrying an expression of lifelong wisdom. He, unlike many of the others, came from a place varied in perspective and replete with experience. I was curious to hear what this man of wisdom had to say.

"The soldier's lodge has appointed me to speak for them," he said as any humble man might. "The man who killed the white people did not belong to us, and we do not expect to be called to account for the people of another band." Paul spoke in a relaxed and conversational tone, in English, which left me to translate into Dakota. "We have always tried to do as our Great Father tells us. One of our young men brought in a captive woman. I went out and brought the other. The soldiers came up here, and our young men assisted to kill one of Inkpaduta's sons at this place. Then you," he said, pointing at Major Cullen, "spoke about our soldiers going after the rest. White Lodge said he would go, and the rest of us followed."

At this point all was silent but for the words of Mazakutamani and the words I echoed. I could see that the Major appeared perturbed. I think perhaps he was tired of the repeated argument. Still Mazakutamani carried on.

"The Lower Indians did not get up the war party for you; it was our Indians, the Wahpetons and Sissetons."

That was not entirely true, I thought.

"The soldiers here say that they were told by you that a thousand dollars would be paid for killing each of the murderers. The Great Father does not expect to do these things without money, and I suppose it is for that that the Special Agent has come up."

This was a poor assumption and I was surprised to hear it from Mazakutamani.

"We wish the men who went out paid for what they have done," he requested, though he did so with no real certainty in his voice. "Three men are killed as we know."

Mazakutamani paused here and stood in thought for a few brief moments. "I am not a chief among the Indians," he continued as he raised his head. I could see that he was once more speaking on his own accord where before he had been reluctant to do so. "The white people have declared me a chief, and I suppose I am able to do something. We have nothing to eat, and our families are hungry. If we go out again we must have some money before we go." Again Mazakutamani paused, lowered his head and returned to his previous tone. "This is what the soldiers have wished me to say. I myself brought in one captive woman. You said you had come from our Great Father. All of us want our money now very much. We have never seen our Great Father, but have heard a great deal from him, and have always tried to do as he told us. A man of another band has done wrong, and we are to suffer for it. Our old women and children are hungry for this. I have seen ten thousand dollars sent to pay for our going out. I wish the soldiers were paid for it. I suppose our Great Father has more money than this."

And that is where Paul Mazakutamani ended his plea. That is where the Dakota ended their petition. I knew the agents would have a cunning answer.

The rebuttal, or the retort rather, began with Major Cullen. "The money that man saw was the annuity moneys," he began while stepping forward and speaking out over the whole crowd. "I never promised a thousand dollars a head, or any other sum. I have never made an offer for the head of any man. I was willing to pay a thousand dollars out of my own pocket to the Indians if they went and did as their Great Father desired. I know what I say, and I will always do as I say. I put my words down when I go home—"

"Your Great Father has sent me to see Major Cullen," suddenly interrupted Agent Pritchette, "and to say to him he was well satisfied with his conduct, because he acted according to his instructions." Agent Pritchette said all this while still seated comfortably in the shadows of the storehouse. I was surprised to see him come to the superintendent's defense and I think all in attendance were surprised to see him finally come to life. As I pondered this the Special Agent threw me a glare and I realized I had not yet interpreted his words for the crowd.

"Your Great Father has heard that some of his white children were cruelly and brutally murdered by some of the Dakota nation," continued Agent Pritchette, who was now finally in a standing position. "The news was sent on the wings of the lightning from the extreme north to the land of eternal summer, throughout which his children dwell."

What the agent was referring to I could not be positively certain. He was attempting, I believe, to speak in a manner that might be familiar to the Indians. This was a futile endeavor as far I was concerned.

"His young white men wished to make war on the whole Dakota nation and revenge the deaths of their brethren. But your Great Father is a just father, and he wishes to treat all his children alike with justice. He wants no innocent man punished for the guilty. He punishes the guilty alone."

Agent Pritchette had moved himself to the front of the crowd and in the light for all to see. Although there was no podium or stage or raised floor, he expressed himself as if he were in the spotlight of a dignified affair. He dressed stately though in no way resembling the military regalia of Major Cullen. His buttoned shirt, neck tie, and his brown suit coat, which he clutched with both hands, were enough to make him appear aristocratic. Adding to his appearance of stateliness were his posture and manner of speech. He stood straight and tall with his belly out, his head back and his chin forward. He spoke in an unbroken, deep and confident tone as if reciting an important war-time speech. His experience as a politician and speaker were obvious. Whether or not he spoke from the heart I can only speculate, but somehow I doubt there was much credence to what he spoke. He had an agenda to fill and that is what motivated the manner in which he expressed himself.

"He expected that those missionaries who have been here teaching you the laws of the Great Spirit had taught you this. Whenever a Dakota is injured by a white man your Great Father will punish him, and he expects from the chief and warriors of the great Dakota nation that they will punish those Indians who injure the whites. He considers the Dakota as a part of his family, and as friends and brothers he expects them to do as the whites do for them."

Special Agent Pritchette paused here to let his words be understood and take effect. But it was difficult to know what the Indians understood at that moment as they stood quietly and stared blankly forward. They looked like nothing more than confused pupils in front of their teacher.

"He knows that the Dakota nation is divided into bands," continued Agent Pritchette, "but he knows, also, how they can all band together for common protection. He expects the nation to punish those murderers or to deliver them up. He expected this because he believed they were his friends. As long as these murderers remain unpunished, or not delivered up, they are not acting as friends of their Great Father."

Agent Pritchette spoke quickly now and I found it hard to keep up. He appeared more natural as he finally released his grasp from the breast of his coat and began to speak using gestures as any man might do.

"It is for this reason he has withheld the annuity. He has instructed Major Cullen so to say and so to act. He," referring to the superintendent, "will continue this unless their Great Father changes, which is not likely. It is because he does not wish the innocent to suffer with the guilty that he has kept his young men from warring against them. For the same reason he will continue to do so."

Finally there was a reaction among the Dakota Indians; a sign of life from the submissive crowd. I heard groans and moans and unintelligible muddles of confusion and dissatisfaction.

"If now, you have determined not to punish them or deliver them up," shouted Agent Pritchette in such a way to both quiet the Indians and demonstrate his perceived authority, "your Great Father will send his own warriors to do so, and he wants no assistance from you."

The Indians were quiet once more, perhaps in a state of disillusioned shock. The special agent paused but then continued in a less ferocious but still authoritative tone.

"If your father is satisfied that you will do nothing further, then the warriors of your Great Father will have his white children protected, and all who have told you that your Great Father is not able to punish those who injure them, will find themselves bitterly mistaken. Your Great Father desires to do good for all his children, and will do all in his power to accomplish it, but he is firmly resolved to punish all who do wrong."

Immediately after finishing his words, Agent Pritchette turned and walked quickly into the storehouse behind him. Major Cullen looked around for a moment but then quickly followed. I was left standing alone as the only government official in front of a crowd of confused and disgruntled Dakota warriors. They might have looked toward me for some sort of clarification of what the Agent Pritchette just expressed, but they were too caught up in their own bizarre demonstration of discontent. The Indians knew only that their annuities were not immediately forthcoming and they wished to exhibit their anger through loud cries and shouts. They began stomping their feet and kicking the dirt. They were pounding their chests and raising their fists. This once calm and complacent group of Dakota warriors now sounded like a flock of malicious birds or a stampede of frightened and frantic buffalo. Their demonstration was unrestrained in its cacophony of harsh noise and bitter discord. On and on they went accomplishing nothing but a bitter dirge and a futile suppuration from an emotional wound. Violence, I feared, would be next, but finally they turned, one after another, and made their way out from within the agency buildings, still shouting and crying with discontent. Away, back to their families, back to their tribes, with no real hope for the future—with no real hope for even their next meal.

Monday, April 6
Granger's Point

Dear Eliza,

Life is unpredictable indeed. Not more than a year ago I was alone in life having just moved from Indiana to make a new life on the frontier. I might never have expected to meet someone as resplendent as you. And then that this tragedy would fall upon the community and on your beloved family. I grieve moment by moment for what has been lost, but I cannot hide my newfound strength and capacity for life. Through all great struggles, even in the face of death, I am comforted . . . enlivened . . . emboldened . . . by the thought of you. I recall your voice and I am warm. I remember the soft, gentle curl of your amber hair and I am safe. I envision your brilliant, lustrous blue eyes and I am calm. Amidst any and all toil and hardship I am carried along by the mere essence of you. You are a miracle and you saved my life.

Love,
William

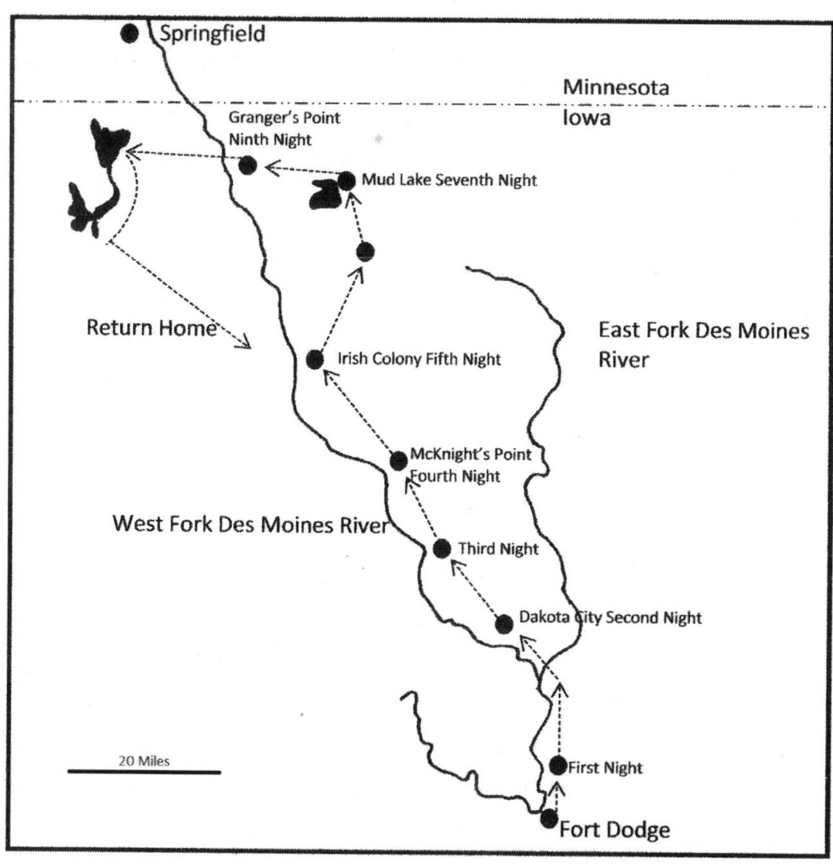

Fort Dodge Expedition led by Major William Williams

Rebuked as a Half-Breed

When I was a boy my father was often absent. He was a good provider and I know he cared for me and my siblings. But the duties of his employment kept him away and at times, overwhelmed. He was a good father. Good enough that I approach the rearing of my own children in the manner I had learned from him; in the manner in which he raised me. But as a boy I did not view things this way. I quarreled with my father. I resented him. At times I truly believed I loathed him. Through my childish and juvenile reasoning I determined that he was wrong. He had no right to deny me privileges, I reasoned. He had no right to administer responsibilities. As a boy, this was my perspective.

But maturity and hindsight have taught me many things since then. Indeed becoming a father myself has taught me many more things. And losing my father, at an age still much too young, has gone beyond teaching, gone beyond lessons, gone somewhere in the realm of hopeless perdition. It is a lesson that cannot be taught or learned. It cannot be imagined. It can only be felt. It can only be known. Because it cannot be described I can only say that it is a lesson that will find us all.

Where then, I wonder, are the Dakota in their relationship with their so-called Great Father? They speak as if the government were in fact their true father. They behave as if the Indian agents were their legitimate patriarchs. Are the Dakota no more than sullen, immature juveniles with no foresight or thoughtful comprehension? Are they like children who cannot understand what is in their best interest? Of course the Dakota know that these white men of like age are not their fathers. But the Dakota concept of family and community is much different than that of the white culture. They refer to all of their peers as brother or sister. And they refer to all of their elders as father or mother. What is remarkable to me is that this becomes something as more than just nominal. Not only do the men refer to each other as brothers, but they treat each other as brothers. The children of the tribe are cared for as if each child were their own and the elders are loved as if each one were their own mother or father. And so it is with those in authority, whether they be white or Indian. The authorities are called "father." As it is between Dakotas, the white authorities are not simply called father, but they are treated with every bit of respect and dignity as a boy would give his true father.

Here is where the line becomes blurred for me. Not only do the Dakota respect the agent as their father, but they answer in a manner fitting. That is to say, they behave in a submissive and obedient manner. I can understand and appreciate the level of respect they give in dealing with the agents, but that they also comply in a consistent and real tone of subservience is what perplexes me. Though they have no biological ties with the white authorities, their learned cultural influences seem to create an inseparable attitude between father and nominal father. They know the distinction, but they make no distinction in their behavior or even their feelings. They believe that their Great Father has their best interests in mind and they act accordingly. But like a boy before his father, they feel wronged and unjustly punished by the actions, denials, and decisions of their father. The only question then is whether or not the Great Father has kept in mind the best interests of the Dakota Indians. I fear the trusting nature and childlike obedience of the Indian will ultimately befall him.

"You cannot send them away like this," I argued with confidence despite my earlier rebuke.

"I can and I have, Mr. Campbell," replied Agent Pritchette in a definitive tone. "What have I told you about discussing matters of policy with me? Firstly, it is futile," he said with derision. "Secondly, it is not your place. You have no say in the political relationships of the United

States Government and the Dakota Indians. How could you? You are young and you are a half-breed."

"Some would argue that makes me a better fit to have an opinion on matters concerning the Indians and the government," I replied quickly.

"Not likely," he laughed. "Any who believe that are only ignorant half-breeds like yourself."

Anger swelled inside me. How could he continue to make such remarks after all I had done, after I had proven myself as loyal, hardworking, intelligent and valuable? In no way did Agent Pritchette appreciate the sacrifices I had made or the input I had to offer. But I suppressed my anger and my feelings of being undervalued. I knew it could not serve a purpose and that there were more important issues at hand.

"Let me speak," I pleaded, but not in a defeated manner. "There are important factors to be considered. There are reasons we must not send the Indians away empty handed."

"Speak if you must," was Agent Pritchette's curt and disinterested reply.

I was relieved to know I could put forth an argument, but in the same moment I realized it must be a strong and credible argument. It caused my nerves to tighten. Here before me was a man who would not listen to reason and who did not give any credence toward me. Yet it was in his power to decide the future of the Dakota.

"You must understand," I began, "that although the Dakota are one nation, they are not governed by one overarching body. They . . . they . . .," I stuttered, "they are divided without any common allegiance."

"Relax," the special agent said, "and make your point."

"Their leadership is more nominal than it is substantive," I continued, though not entirely sure where I was going with my argument. "The chiefs have no efficient control over their members. Consider the yearly payment," I pointed out. "The chiefs receive no more or less as men of superior rank to even the least respectable of their people. Because of this, because they are divided, because they lack leadership, there can be no union of action to a common end. As a consequence and furthermore, you cannot enforce a national responsibility upon the Dakota for the crime of one of its members."

I was rather satisfied with my argument to this point. Still Agent Pritchette, who had returned to his previous position in the wooden chair, sat back casually, almost aloof.

"Your argument is moot," replied the special agent. "We have already sent the Dakota after Inkpaduta. We have already withheld the annuity payment."

"But you needn't withhold it further," I fired back. "You needn't send them back out. For it is impossible to affect the surrender of Inkpaduta without chastising the entire Dakota nation. To send them out again would be superfluous and . . . and . . . hollow."

"They refuse to go," replied Agent Pritchette coolly.

"Nevertheless," I retorted.

"Are you quite finished?" asked the special agent in his wry manner.

"As yet I have not included the most vital consideration. It is something I am certain you have thought of but I will mention anyway due to the gravity of its consequences."

By this time I no longer felt a nervous tension. I had made my bed; I had put my foot forward. I overcame the frivolous notion that I was in any danger. Though I had much to lose, it mattered not in the face of right and wrong, and for some, it could mean life or death.

"If you refuse to pay annuities now, if you wait until the elusive Inkpaduta and his band are captured and punished, then the result will be serious depredations over the coming winter. If you do not pay the annuities, the Dakota will have no choice but to fight for their survival. And the loss of life," I said with conviction, "will be on your hands."

There was silence. My heart was beating rapidly, my body was warm. I was not angry. I was fueled by something but it was not anger. As I stood and waited I regained my awareness, which had been lost to passion just moments before. I noticed my finger still pointed out in front of me and I put it down. I heard and felt the gentle summer breeze as it entered through a small opening in the windowsill. I saw Major Cullen, who had been standing there the entire time, with a look of confused curiosity on his face. The room itself now seemed smaller, more confining, like the unkempt stone structure that it was.

"Is that so," Agent Pritchette finally responded, though not as a question. "I admire you, Mr. Campbell. As I mentioned before, all reports with consideration to your conduct are positive. I can see that you are an asset to the agency. You have a thorough knowledge of the language you interpret and you seem to have a good rapport with the Dakota and the whites. Furthermore, you know the region exceedingly well and you are rather versatile as an employee. It appears you are willing and able to take on any assignment. Finally, and most impressively, you are passionate about what you do with a real and veritable concern for the well-being of those involved."

Agent Pritchette sat forward in his chair as he spoke and he showed an actual interest in what he was saying. He spoke easily and truthfully and the praise rolled off his tongue effortlessly. This concerned me. It worried me to see him speaking in this manner and to know he was building toward something. He had a reason, no doubt, for speaking this way; it was not merely to sing my praises.

"I applaud your bravery. I applaud your passion. I applaud your striving to do what is right. But your perspective is limited." This is where the special agent's countenance began to change. "You believe you know what is best, but you are foolhardy and impertinent. You are presumptuous. You are careless where tactfulness is necessary. You are impetuous where discretion is required. You are mindful, but with no mind. You think you know better, Mr. Campbell, but you know nothing." The special agent's voice became stronger now. He no longer spoke in an easy and casual fashion. His indignation now came screeching forward through his words, his inflection, and the look on enmity on his face. "You, a half-breed," he said with disdain. "Born on the frontier of Minnesota territory, raised by savages and half-wits. Never leaving the region, never gaining a proper education, never seeing the world for what it is. You lack all experience! You lack all foresight! You lack all perspective!"

The special agent was fumed like a bull before a matador. He got up from his chair and paced quickly back and forth as he continued his rebuke. He became red in the face as he thought of more and more ways to tear me down. He spoke, but I no longer listened. All I could do was watch, for I sought no shouting match with him. I was instead in awe and amazement at his malicious fulmination. Was he right, what he said, this elder statesmen of high political regard? Did he speak from wisdom and experience, or did he speak from bigotry as a man filled with envy, hate, and fanaticism?

"You do not know your place!" he said loudly as he finally paused to catch his breath. "What do you think you are?" he asked, now speaking in a less demonstrative way. "Are you an Indian or are you an American? Are you even a man?" he said with a toss of his hand. "There are political objectives at stake, and you seem all too concerned with the well-being of the inhuman, savage Redskins. You poor, wretched, ignorant Métis. You need to figure out what you are and who you are. If you wish to nuzzle with the primitive, barbaric, and murderous Indian, then do not do it here, in front of me, in front of respectable white citizens. But if you wish to be respectable, if you wish to join some semblance of civilized humanity, then throw off your Indian-loving ways. Cast away all parts Indian, all parts wretched. Figure out who you support, figure out who you are, before I speak to you again: before you work as an official representative of the United States Government."

My heart sank, if it had not sunk already. Not only had I sustained severe personal insult, but now my employ was threatened; now my livelihood was at stake.

I looked toward Major Cullen, but he gave me only in return a blank and empty stare. I looked back to Agent Pritchette with my mouth half open while I searched my mind for the right words. But Agent Pritchette was already preoccupied with his next item of business, and even had I thought of the words my mouth failed to speak them. I left: broken-hearted, confused, weary.

In that moment I was beside myself. I was filled with an indescribably bad feeling. Though not quite anger, it was pain or resentment of some sort. It welled up inside me and throughout my body like a dry prairie suddenly caught fire and burning out of control. I was complete with useless energy, this pain inside. I had worked so hard. I had done so well.

Not once had I acted on a selfish motive or behaved in an unrespectable manner. My actions were not fueled by greed or avarice. My intentions were good; they were always good. How could he find fault in me? How could my conduct and my words and my efforts be seen as anything but valuable and worthy? I gave everything of myself. I risked everything. I spent months away from my family. I dedicated years of my time. I put my own life in the balance, but it meant nothing. Despite this, despite all of this, Agent Pritchette has the gall to ask who it is that I support! He has the nerve to suggest that I do not have the best interests of the United States Government in mind. He has the pomposity even to tell me that I do not know who I am!

What then am I left to do? How then am I left to act? It is true that some of the Indians perpetrated a heinous crime. Perhaps the Indians are uncivilized and at times befitting of the word "savage." The Indians are characterized as unintelligent, incapable, lazy beings who are unfit to share this vast and beautiful land. They are marginalized and outcast, strangled and destroyed. They are cut off from the world and the life that they once knew. Their past is erased and their future is extinguished. If this be the verdict, if this be the fate for the American Indian, then what be the fate for me? I am not wholly white, not even Indian. Not one or the other. Belonging to both but not truly belonging to either. For years my very own family has run from their identity. Many others too, have hidden, obscured, and concealed their true nature in favor of the dominant and superior white culture. Perhaps it was time I finally did the same. Perhaps it was time that I banish and forget my Dakota heritage and become what the world would rather I be. I had, in some ways, already done this. Maybe now I should make it complete.

As I walked away that day I did not know which way to go. I was conflicted and confused. Had I given it too much thought? Had I trivialized my own existence? I wrestled with all these things, not knowing right or wrong. Indeed, not even knowing if there was a right or wrong. I wanted to do as I was asked to do, but something about it didn't feel right. I needed answers, but I knew I could not find them within myself. Not now. Not yet. How could I settle my inner conflict? Where would I go next?

Thursday, April 9
Shippey's Point

Dear Eliza,

Grave and dreadful misfortune has visited the men upon our return home. I have been among the auspicious number who have endured relatively few encumbrances on the trip south. This I owe to the wise decision to remain at the lakes settlement to avoid what appeared to be a coming storm. But only I and few others, the remainder being more than one hundred men who had to suffer at the hands of the elements. And what extraordinary elements they were.

I and the six other men who awaited the passing of the storm departed on Monday morning. The day was clear and the sky was a magnificent plane of blue, but the temperatures were intensely cold. The mercury I can be certain was well below the zero mark. But aside from the discomfort and danger, the cold made travel discernibly easier. The Des Moines River became frozen solid, as well as the snow atop it, and it was therefore easy to walk upon. We reached Granger's Point with little trouble and were then able to procure a team and wagon and take rest for a day. We proceeded to the Irish settlement. There we encountered several of the wounded and ill from the Springfield settlement that were unable to proceed with the main command. We also found Mr. Henry Carse, who was among the burial detail but who had remained with Captain Johnson when the party was split. When we found Mr. Carse he was in a frightening condition. It seems that at one point he had removed his boots and was unable to put them back on because they had become frozen stiff. He then ripped his blanket in order to wrap his feet, but after a short time the cloth had become worn. When removing the cloth from Mr. Carse's feet, along with it came the skin on his soles. He was in no condition to walk. Furthermore, he had become delirious from exposure and exhaustion. While at the Irish settlement his mental faculties were only just returning to him.

We continued from the Irish colony now double in number. Progress was slowed by the additional numbers, but was still made easier by the frozen snow. Our next major difficulty came upon reaching Cylinder Creek, which I later learned was an even greater difficulty for those who preceded us. The creek was frozen only in spots and to affect a safe crossing required the whole of an afternoon. We continued two miles south to Shippey's Point where we now take our rest. Though rest will be difficult to achieve with the knowledge I have come by since arriving here.

The men of the main command left from here just a day prior to our arrival. Like Mr. Carse, many of the men suffered greatly and two have likely perished. I am speaking of Captain John Johnson and Mr. William Burkholder. These two men were with us on the burial detail but chose to travel in the southeasterly direction with the larger group. Apparently, as the group traveled south amidst the storm, they were separated by a large marsh and were unable to regroup as night approached. The following day Johnson and Burkholder had great difficulty in proceeding. The men with Johnson and Burkholder tried valiantly to help them continue, but the two men were simply exhausted and unable to travel. Regretfully, they had to be left behind. Later, when the party reached the main command, Major Williams sent men out to find the two fatigued men but with no success. We believe they have found their final resting place, two brave and true young men, frozen on the prairie. They volunteered knowing it was at great personal sacrifice. Ultimately, they gave their lives.

As for the main command, they encountered the harsh winter pangs without food or shelter. As the storm hit, these men were approaching Cylinder Creek which was swollen from the earlier warm temperatures. Save a few men who built a makeshift raft out of a wagon and blankets, they were unable to safely cross the creek. They could only wait on the prairie as the wind grew strong and the temperatures dipped well below zero. They built for themselves a small and temporary shelter by turning the wagons upside down and stretching the canvas along the sides. It was sufficient enough to keep the men alive, though they had to stay huddled together like animals to produce heat. For two days they remained like this and without food. I can only imagine what delirious images they must have dreamed up under such dire circumstances.

Eventually the creek became frozen enough to cross, but the men had barely enough energy to do so. They made it to Shippey's Point where they found shelter and food. From here, Major Williams ordered that the men split into smaller groups because of the great difficulty in feeding such a large number. Now I only hope their challenges are over and their obstacles passed.

I will set forth with my comrades tomorrow and should return to Fort Dodge in a few days. I cannot speak highly enough of these brave, generous, and unselfish young men. Surely there are few adversities greater than those faced on this expedition. But these proud men, knowing the hardships they would encounter, gave of themselves through toiling days and sleepless nights spent in assisting total strangers. Some gave their lives while all sacrificed their well-being and risked their future. They are to be considered most good citizens and exceptionally valuable neighbors.

Yet I know our hardships are not over. Your dear, beloved sister remains out there, somewhere. Be still and know that Providence will bring her home. A new home. A new life. One that we will start together.

From now until forever, I am yours.
William

MEETING COLONEL LEE

"There is something different about her," I said to my wife, Mary. "She is an enigma?"

"An enigma?" Mary repeated in an inquisitive tone.

"Well, yes," I began. "Abbie has been through such an unspeakable tragedy. In front of her own eyes she lost her entire family, with the exception of her sister Eliza. And then she had to endure captivity among the Indians. Yet, through her mourning . . . through her melancholy and cheerless temperament, I gleamed something else."

"What did you gleam?" asked my wife as she looked toward me in a caring and concerned manner.

"I am not sure," I said. "At the time I had met Abbie, I did not think much of it. But now, after all this, after being scorned and cast aside, now I am curious."

I had returned home after my rebuke from Agent Pritchette; after over a month away. I wasn't sure if I still had a job, but more substantially, I wasn't sure who I was. More than ever. I think I was expected to deny my Indian heritage. I think I was expected to return to my employment after a brief reprieve, ready to accept the white way as the best and the only way. But I was not ready to do that, and I knew that I never would be.

"Maybe you should go talk with her," Mary suggested.

"To Abbie?" I was surprised by this suggestion.

"Yes," returned Mary quickly but softly. "Ask her about what happened. Ask her how she got through it."

"I suppose that is not out of the question," I replied as I thought carefully about it. "I know that she has gone down to Iowa to live with her sister. It would not be impossible to find her."

"So go," encouraged Mary.

"But I have been away for so long as it is. And what could I possibly expect? I might be a hindrance on the young girl."

"You are conflicted and hurt. I know you well enough to know this," Mary said caringly. "Go. Go with no expectations. Forget the formalities and decorum. Your family will be alright. Go with an open heart and an open mind. Find out all you need to know and forget about the rest. Find out who you are; who you want to be. Don't be less, because others couldn't be more."

Mary needn't say more after that. I decided to go.

"'Tis a bright and beautiful day, is it not?" said a man who suddenly came up beside me.

"Indeed it is," I replied courteously, but without turning my head to truly acknowledge the man.

"Dare I say you look rather familiar," returned the man in a spirited fashion.

I was in my own world of self-pity and confusion and I did not wish to carry on a conversation. But the poor man's enthusiasm awoke my sensibilities and I turned my head so as to be polite.

He was a tall man, likely in his fifties. He had a full, white beard though still grey at the root. His hair was wild and disheveled and had receded to some point in the middle of his scalp. His face was stern and had large features. He was almost frightening in appearance, though it was clear that his looks did not reflect his character.

"I do not know that I recognize you," I replied truthfully.

"Ah ha!" asserted the man with a long smile on his face. "You do look familiar. You are the interpreter, are you not?"

"Why, yes," I said with hesitation. "Or, rather, I was."

"Yes, yes!" he continued with his unbridled and childlike enthusiasm. "I knew you looked familiar. It was like a bug inside me."

"I must apologize, but I do not recall our meeting," I said softly, not nearly matching the tone of my new companion.

"Oh, well," he smiled again while revealing a few yellow and cracked teeth. "Colonel Lorenzo Porter Lee," he said as he held out his hand. "Friends call me L.P."

"Pleased to make your acquaintance Colonel Lee," I replied as I grasped his open hand and shook. "Mr. Antoine Joseph Campbell. Friends call me Joe."

"A pleasure," he said politely as we released grips.

By this time I was still somewhat annoyed and confused by this man's interest with me. "If we had not formally met, how is it that you came to know me?" I inquired.

"Certainly," he said as if I had surprised him. "St. Paul," he said somehow expecting such a general hint to trigger my memory. "The presentation ceremony for the young captive girl, Miss Abbie Gardner."

"Ah," I nodded.

"I was present at the ceremony, and the banquet," he said in his pleasant and carefree manner. "I recall seeing you there, along with the Indian men who rescued her."

"My apologies," I responded. "I suppose my memory is not quite as clear."

"No need to apologize," said Colonel Lee. "I have always been one to remember faces. Likewise you were a distinct guest. I was just another well-wisher."

"My apologies nonetheless."

"What, may I ask, brings you aboard the steamer today?" politely inquired Colonel Lee.

I suddenly realized my new setting: the steamer. I was no longer chasing Indians along the western prairies, nor was I translating impassioned speeches between government agents and Dakota chiefs. I had accepted the suggestion of my wife and the prodding of my curiosity and I boarded a vessel headed south down the Mississippi for Dubuque, Iowa. This was not an expedition. I was not sent to fulfill the duties of my employment. Rather, I went upon my own accord. I went alone in search of Miss Abbie Gardner. From a natural standpoint it seemed rather imprudent to seek discernment from an adolescent girl who has just lost everything and everyone she holds dear, but I believed otherwise. Within me wrestled an unbearable conflict, while within her, despite her gravest circumstances, was a calm endurance that spilled through her subdued and pensive expression. And so, though it may be an unforgivable imposition on her fragile character, I sought her out. I wanted to know. I needed to know. Firstly, I wanted to know what happened that day at the lakes. Just how exactly did the Indians go about their fatal business? And more importantly, I wanted to know how young Abbie came through it all. How has she accepted her situation? How can she go on after such an irreplaceable loss? And how has she managed to dispel the anger, grief, and resentment that must have at once been rife inside her?

I did not know the propriety of my quest. I did not know if there were any answers. Still, I ventured in search of some understanding, some hope of reconciling the conflict within me. I hoped, somehow, to resolve my lifelong conflict and to return to my job and my family as a man ready to accept his lot in life. I hoped to return as a better father and a better husband.

"I beg your pardon?" I finally said in response to Colonel Lee.

"Why are you aboard this steamer headed for Dubuque?" he asked again.

"Oh," I said while trying to gather a natural sense of composure. "In all honesty, I am in search of Abbie Gardner. I wish to interview her."

"Delightful!" responded the Colonel with a wide grin. "She is a fine young lady, that Abbie. Poor thing did not at all deserve what had befallen her."

I made no response as I believe we both allowed the silence to speak for itself.

"And what is it that brings you aboard this steamer, Colonel Lee?" I asked, finally breaking the silence. "You speak like a man from out east."

"You are of keen mind," returned the Colonel in his jovial fashion. "New Britain, Connecticut to be exact. I am a retired business man and former Postmaster. I made my mark in manufacturing and over the years have become connected with various other institutions and business pursuits." The Colonel smiled and I could see that he enjoyed speaking of himself. "I was traveling here in the great northwest when Governor Medary invited me to join him at the presentation ceremony of young Abbie. As it were I was fortunate enough to hear Abbie's sad tale as she shared it with me."

"Ah," I responded with pleasure as I was glad to know that Abbie was willing and able to talk about what happened.

"Yes, it was on this very same trip from St. Paul to Dubuque that I had the great pleasure to commune with Abbie," explained Colonel Lee. "Now I am on my way back east to write down Abbie's harrowing tale. It is interesting," said Colonel Lee with a change of thought, "but if this had occurred in New York or any more populous eastern city, Abbie would be exalted as a national celebrity. I tell you the papers would have trebled their circulation with daily tales of the horrors and monstrosities. Social circles would for weeks talk of nothing else while the streets, saloons, barber shops, rail cars, businesses and so on would ring with discussions of the barbarous massacre. And Abbie, oh Abbie would become a heroine of the most enviable notoriety. She would not escape the crowds nor escape the throngs of people seeking even a glimpse of her angelic yet pain-stricken face."

It seemed as though the Colonel was no longer speaking to me, but to himself—or for himself. He spoke with a lyrical eloquence and I could almost imagine his words flowing from his mind, to his pen, to his paper.

"As it is," he continued, "few will come to know Abbie or her story. The easterners, with their daily hustle and bustle, care little for the people or events of the frontier. To them it is a strange world; an isolated world. Imaginary, if you will. As children we read of the exciting and bloody battles fought by the early settlers. We are told of the barbarities committed by the Indians at Saratoga or the impassioned tales and fortunes of Daniel Boone and his brave companions in Kentucky. But I swear this to you," said Colonel Lee, now becoming less eloquent and more serious, "I doubt whether there hath ever been bloodier tomahawks than those which visited Spirit Lake that day, nor hath greater fortitude ever been exhibited than that which so heroically shines in Miss Abbie Gardner."

I could not gather a clever response and decided I ought only affirm his passionate opinions. "Very well said indeed."

"That is why I must write this story," explained Colonel Lee while staring blankly forward as if he was not focused on anything but his own thoughts. "I must share her story so that people know what has happened here; so that people realize what is real and what is fiction."

Again there was silence. The mood was thick, like fog.

"You say you wish to interview Miss Gardner, is that right?" asked Colonel Lee, finally evaporating the metaphorical fog.

"I do, certainly I do," I said, now nervous for some reason.

"I reckon then you know where to find her?"

"Actually I am not all that certain," I replied truthfully. "I know her sister is living in Iowa and I would suppose that after leaving St. Paul Abbie would go to stay with the only family she has remaining. I figured to start in Fort Dodge. Someone ought to know of her whereabouts."

"Ha ha!" laughed Colonel Lee with his hands to his protruding belly. "Such fortunate irony."

"Pardon?" was all I said under a bit of confusion.

"Forgive me dear sir," said Colonel Lee as he began to calm himself. "I know where you can find Miss Gardner," he continued excitedly. "That's the irony that led us to meet here."

"You know where she stays?" I asked rather inquisitively.

"Why, yes," said the Colonel with his healthy grin. "She is living at Hampton in Franklin County, Iowa. She is living with her sister Eliza who is now married I believe."

"This is fantastic news you have shared. Undoubtedly it will save me a great deal of toil," I remarked genuinely.

"Well, you will find her there," said the Colonel who suddenly turned stoic. "And I rather hope you find whatever else you may be looking for."

"You are more perceptive than you appear," I replied with a timid expression feeling almost ashamed that my inner conflict was outwardly apparent. "You have my regards, Colonel Lee. Best wishes writing your story. Perhaps I'll read it someday."

"Perhaps," replied Colonel Lee.

I turned away.

ELIZA GARDNER

Two days by steamer, six by stage. Eight days travel before I arrived in the small rural community of Hampton, Iowa. The town, about sixty miles east-northeast from Fort Dodge, was rather plain. There was no railroad or river, just a small creek running through town on the north. It was hard to know even why it was settled, other than perhaps as a point of rest and replenishment for the traveling stage coaches. Although I imagine the farmland was rich.

It was now mid-August, August 20, to be exact, and the weather was hot and dry. The town was quiet as I arrived. It seemed abandoned as if people were hiding from the noontime sun. But I could see that it was a new and probably growing establishment. Along the main thoroughfare were several buildings that had not yet completed construction.

"Hello," I uttered as I walked into the town trading post. I was hesitant, being a stranger in a small frontier community. "Hello," I uttered once more as I cautiously stood near the front counter.

"Just a moment," came a hearty voice from another room.

I waited patiently and anxiously as I looked around the trading post. It appeared typical of any frontier post with groceries, dry goods, hardware, and ammunition. All of the necessary items a burgeoning town would need.

"Hello, stranger," said the storekeeper as he wiped his hands on a towel and made his way toward my direction. "Name's T.T. Rawson," he said with a friendly smile as he held out his right hand.

"Joseph Campbell," I said confidently as I shook his hand.

"What can I do for you, Mr. Campbell?" he asked eagerly.

"Well," I began, unsure how to place my request. "I am looking for Miss Abbie Gardner. I was told she lived here in Hampton."

"Surely," replied Mr. Rawson. "That be the poor captive girl, were she not?"

"Yes, yes," I responded with a pleasant assurance.

"If I may, what be your business with her?" he asked.

"Of course," I said. "I am an interpreter with the U.S. Bureau of Indian Affairs. I recently met Miss Gardner on her release from captivity and her travel to St. Paul. At the time she was in no condition to speak on her experience. Now, a few months removed, I hope to interview her."

"A terrible thing she and her sister endured," returned Mr. Rawson with a look of grief on his face. "But they come out here to start a new life, to put all that behind them. Besides, you kinda look like one of them Indians."

"I beg your pardon, Mr. Rawson," I said apologetically. "I mean no harm nor disrespect. I have traveled many miles at my own personal risk. I merely seek clarity. Clarity I can only find in Miss Gardner."

"I must say you do seem rather genuine," replied the storekeeper. "I am merely being protective of those girls. I wouldn't want them bothered unnecessarily."

"And I agree," I said willfully. "I mean no imposition upon them."

"Very well," said Mr. Rawson with a keen look toward me. "I will show you the way."

Mr. Rawson kindly directed me toward the farmhouse where Abbie and her sister now lived. He offered a buggy since the house was more than a mile distant, but I declined. My legs were in dire need of use after so many days' travel by carriage. I could understand Mr. Rawson's reticence with me. These were alarming times on the frontier. After what occurred over the spring there was a heightened awareness to the possibility of danger. It did not stop nor even temper the unyielding march of progress, but still the uneasiness hung in the air like smoke. All possible danger aside, I could also understand the polite nature of Mr. Rawson to respect the privacy of young Abbie. Certainly she had been through more than anyone could fear or imagine. Now it was important that she be allowed to move forward in whatever manner or means that might be possible. I knew this all along but I made the journey anyway. My self-pity was trumped only by my selfishness. I had days to ponder this. Was I in the right? Was I in the wrong? Was my poor soul even worth the enlightenment I sought? And more importantly, would I find it? Despite all these things I deliberated, I never turned around. All the while, my feet marched forward over the lonely road.

"Can I help you?" asked the man at the door.

I was quite nervous, unsure if I was even in the right place. I hadn't a single notion whom the man in front of me may have been. He was a handsome and stout man. The deep wrinkles at the corner of his eyes showed his age while his thick brown hair had evidence of grey.

"I am looking for Miss Abigail Gardner. Is this her residence?"

"Why yes," answered the man. "Who calls upon her?"

"I beg your pardon," I responded quickly. "I am Mr. Antoine Joseph Campbell, U.S. Interpreter for the Upper and Lower Bands of Dakota Indians. I met Abbie earlier this summer when I helped escort her to St. Paul." I paused to catch my breath as I was speaking nervously. "I missed my opportunity to speak much with her and I was hoping I might do so now."

The man seemed unconcerned and I could not determine if he was skeptical or just caught in a moment of emptiness. "Well, come in," he said in a somewhat disinterested tone as he ushered me into the house.

"Eliza," he shouted, "we have a guest!"

"Please show him to the sitting room," returned a female voice from the opposite room.

The home was a large, two-story, wood-frame structure. I could see that it had recently been built and I could still detect the smell of fresh cut wood. There was an abundance of supplies, tools and furniture throughout the house as if the couple were stocking up for something.

A few moments passed, but only a few, before a young lady, not more than eighteen or nineteen years of age, came swooping into the room with a pitcher on a silver tray.

"You'll have to excuse the untidiness," she said. "We are still getting settled around here."

She was a striking young lady. Curly hair of a not-so-rich but still alluring red color, a light, flowing blouse, and a perfectly attractive smile. At first glance she carried little resemblance to Abbie but was radiant to a whole other degree. This, I thought, must be Eliza, Abbie's sister.

"Your home is lovely," I managed to spurt out.

"That's mighty kind of you to say," she replied habitually as she poured water in my glass and proceeded to sit directly across from me. The man, who I could only presume was her husband, sat to my left.

"What brings you to Hampton?" she asked with a smile. "It is not exactly a travel destination."

"He is here to see Abbie," said the man to my left.

"Oh, wonderful!" she responded with the same bright smile. "My sister will be glad to have a visitor."

"You must be Eliza Gardner," I blurted impertinently.

"Eliza Wilson," she said, correcting me. "Forgive my manners. I never did introduce myself. I am Eliza and this is my husband, William. William Wilson," she said as she dropped her right hand in her husband's direction.

"Pleased to meet you," I said in the obligatory fashion. "I am Joseph Campbell, U.S. Interpreter."

"Oh, how interesting," said Eliza in a somewhat compulsory manner. "You deal then with the Indians?"

"As a matter of fact, I do," was my curt response.

"William here was a part of the expedition to capture those hostile Indians this past spring," explained Eliza. "He and the other men suffered greatly while traveling to rescue the victims and capture those Indians. He wrote me all about it; all about those hardships."

"The Fort Dodge expedition?" I asked though I already knew.

William and Eliza nodded in unison.

"I understand you and your family have been through unspeakable tragedy," I responded politely. "You have my most sincere sympathies."

"Thank you," was all she said with a soft nod of her head. "Why is it that you wish to speak to my sister?" questioned Eliza.

"Well, it is difficult to explain," I began nervously. "I was with Abbie on her way to St. Paul shortly following her captivity. There was something about her that struck me. Something about the way she carried herself. Something intangible. I noticed it before, while escorting her to St. Paul, but have now become much more curious. Also, it has occurred to me that despite all the work I have done over the previous few months in search of the hostile Indians, I still know very little of what happened at the lakes. I am ignorant both in fact and in feeling. And, to be candid, I have recently been cast away from my employment and left torn between right and wrong. Torn even over my own self-worth. I don't know wherein lie my answers."

There was a silence and I worried that I had overstepped my boundaries in the company of two strangers. I worried that I had said too much.

"My sister is not present," Eliza finally said, but with a distinct change of tone and character. "She is honeymooning in Fort Dodge. She will return shortly."

"Joyful news," I replied politely, though admittedly I was surprised by this unpredictable news that Abbie would be married so shortly following her captivity. But what plagued my constitution more was the sudden and distinguishable change of mood in the room. William sat much as he had been, but Eilza dropped her welcoming and enthusiastic tone. Rather she adopted a more stern face and humorless countenance.

"Dear William, would you excuse us," Eliza instructed her husband, who obeyed without question. William got up, nodded toward me politely, and left the room.

"Mr. Campbell, was it?" asked Eliza with a straight face.

"Yes," I replied, worried another rebuke was coming.

"I do not like to talk about the gruesome scene that so recently afflicted my friends, family, and community. I carry with me an indescribable suffering that I fear will never leave me."

As I sat across from this poor, tortured woman, I felt a rush of anxiety and sincere regret. I feared I had traveled all this way for nothing and that I had made a brash mistake. I feared my presence was of no use here—or anywhere for that matter.

"But," continued Eliza, giving my anxious heart a breath of hope, "I want my story to be told. I want *our* story to be told," she said with an emphasis on our, referring to herself and her sister Abbie. "I want people to know what happened. I want people to know the dangers of the frontier. I want people to understand the value of preparation. And I want my family to be survived by history."

There was a pause and I knew it was my turn to speak, or to at least acknowledge what had been said. "I welcome your story, difficult as it may be to hear; difficult as it may be to tell. I want to know."

"Somehow I trust you will do right by me, by my sister, and by my family," uttered Eliza in a soft, almost motherly tone.

Finally I could feel that the deep, sort of lugubrious mood had been lifted from the room. Eliza remained serious but her countenance became much more relaxed. I no longer suffocated on my anxiety, but sat eagerly and anxiously to learn the dismal reality of this spring.

Attack on Springfield

"For me it began the previous October," explained Eliza in a plain, capable manner like someone reciting the facts of life. "Dr. Strong, who I later learned to be a coward, visited my father that fall. He wished to survey the lakes area for a place to settle, but ultimately chose to settle at Springfield. His wife, being of delicate health, persuaded me to accompany them to Springfield that I might be her caretaker until her health returned. Little did I know I would not see my beloved family again."

As Eliza began her story I did not know whether to interject and give my heartfelt sympathies or to listen in strained silence. Although Eliza lowered her head briefly in a sorrowful gesture, she spoke in an emotionless tone as if she were not a part of the story she told.

"The health of Mrs. Strong returned after several months," she continued, "but, due to several heavy snow storms in quick succession of each other, I was prevented from going back to my family and the settlement at Spirit Lake. I was disappointed to remain in Springfield, but I assumed the pleasure of spring would result in a more joyful return. How narrow and vain our plans can be."

Again I felt the agonizing silence, not knowing what to say or how to say it. "Joy comes in the morning," I blurted softly in reference to the Psalms. Eliza gave no direct response as if she may not have even heard me.

"As you know, the winter was harsh and prolonged," continued Eliza in the same plain tone. "I was reasonably well taken care of, but I worried about my family who was spending their first winter along the truest of frontiers. I could do nothing but wait for the annual appearance of the spring sun to melt the snows away. But tragedy struck before that could happen. A rather unbelievable tragedy."

"How did you learn of the attack?" I interrupted, forgetting my manners in front of the woman who had experienced such tragedy.

"I cannot describe how it felt," she said, seeming to sidestep the question. "The fear. The uncertainty. Not knowing whether the reports were true or false. Not knowing whether my family was living or dead. It was the most unwholesome, undesirable feeling any human being might ever have to suffer. It is a contemptible fate, fit not even for the lowest sinner."

"I dare say," was my soft response.

"But I digress," said Eliza snapping back into her more casual, sort of unbothered form. "We learned of the attack sometime during the middle of March. We were visited by a Mr. Morris Markham and a Mr. George Granger who had traveled north from Granger's Point. Mr. Markham, who is a fine and brave man," she added, "had been returning to the lakes after picking up supplies when he discovered the massacre. After a few days, he and Mr. Granger came to Springfield to warn us in order that we might be prepared for the Indians' return. However, the story they told us was quite unbelievable."

"What did they tell you?" I asked.

"That everyone was killed," she responded, "or taken captive. Never had the Indians posed a threat before. All of us at Springfield were bewildered because we had an amiable relationship with the red men who frequented the area. It seemed so untrue that George and William Wood, the traders who founded the fine settlement, steadfastly refused that the attack had happened or that a massacre would be attempted at Springfield."

"Are you listening?" Eliza asked suddenly, like a teacher to a pupil.

"Oh . . . yes," I stuttered, as she had caught me in a blank stare. "I was just caught up in your details."

"As I was saying," she continued, "George and William Wood did not believe the Indians had or would attack. The remainder of us, about thirty in number, also found it hard to believe such a tale to be true, but we decided to err on the side of caution. First we gathered in conference to decide what we ought to do. The majority thought it was necessary to send a relief party to the lakes at once. But after some deliberation, the general concern for our own safety prevailed and it was determined to remain at Springfield and prepare a defense. Once this was determined we also decided to send messengers to Fort Ridgely. We were few in number, maybe only fifteen able-bodied men, and we knew we could not hold off a prolonged attack. For this reason a relief party from the fort would be necessary."

"Was there much panic or fear?" I asked curiously.

"I must say the frightful news was handled adequately," answered Eliza. "Of course panic and fear was the first and natural notion among many of us, but that was quickly replaced by more rational thinking. Sound minds and quick thinking were our only allies."

"Who, then, were the messengers?" I asked, though I already knew.

"Ah," she said with a nod. "The men chosen were Joseph Cheffins, a trader who had come with William Wood, and Henry Tretts, a German. Both were young, vibrant, and single men. They bravely agreed to go, though their task was an unenviable one. They were to travel seventy miles to Fort Ridgely through deep snows and below-freezing temperatures. We bade them farewell and good fortune and then prepared our defense."

In a way it was comforting to hear Eliza's retelling of the events of that past March. I had spent so much time in my own world I had forgotten to truly consider what others experienced, what others lost. Certainly I had tried to seek out truth and to find some form of understanding, but it was only just now, looking into the strong eyes of Eliza, that I was able to ignore and step outside of my perspective. Until this time, my deepest concern was always and ever on me, regardless of how I manipulated things. Somehow the declarative demeanor of Eliza, in spite of her role in the events, brought me out of my world and into hers.

"We chose the home of James Thomas as our central point of defense," explained Eliza as she continued on. "We chose the Thomas house for its strength and size. You see, it was a double log house with two sections each being about sixteen feet square and connected in the middle by a dog trot."

I nodded in acknowledgement.

"Though not all of us stayed in the Thomas cabin," continued Eliza. "There must have been about twenty of us, while a dozen or so others fortified themselves in the Wheeler cabin. In the Wheeler cabin there was included Misters Smith and Henderson who had both recently had their legs amputated. Therefore they were both unable to put up any kind of defense should the need arise. I stayed in the Thomas cabin along with Dr. and Mrs. Strong, Mr. and Mrs. Thomas, Mrs. Church, Ms. Swanger, John Bradshaw, Morris Markham, David Carver, and several young children."

"And how did all of you prepare?" I asked curiously.

"I will say that it was another undesirable situation," answered Eliza seeming to ignore my question like she had before. "Not knowing what might come over the horizon: relief or unthinkable terror. It proved too much for Mrs. Stewart. Her mental state was increasingly poor until she became overwrought with fear of a possible Indian attack. After two or three days she, Mr. Stewart, and their three children had to leave the cabin and its crowded condition for the more familiar space of their own home. As for the rest of us, we got along as best we could. We never ventured out of doors but to gather wood. While in the cabin we created port holes through the chinking from which we could look out in all cardinal directions. Beyond that we stayed relatively quiet and waited with hope and patience upon our anticipated relief."

"Such long hours they must have been," I added. "I cannot imagine."

"Indeed it was undesirable," she said agreeably.

I sat with willingness and composure as I waited for Eliza to continue. I began to think of my own family and the fear and sorrow I would encounter if something ever happened to them.

"About two weeks had passed," spoke Eliza, interrupting my extraneous train of thought, "and not much happened. Not an Indian had been sighted nor even a fox heard lurking around. Still, might the Indians have attacked, we were relatively well prepared with food, firearms, and ammunition. But we lacked firewood from time to time.

Thusly, on one Thursday morning—or so I recall—the men were out chopping wood."

I could perceive that Eliza was approaching the fretful moment of attack. Yet her voice showed no signs of distress or sadness. She spoke only with calmness and dexterity.

"It was about 2 o'clock in the afternoon. I remember because the men had postponed the midday meal until they had completed their chore. Young Willie Thomas was outside playing while the rest were inside taking part in the meal. Suddenly young Willie yelled that he had seen Henry Tretts approaching. What great relief this news brought. We rushed outside to confirm if the report was true. There, off in the distance, was a man dressed only as Henry Tretts could be. We were so convinced that David Carver exclaimed, 'Yes, it is Henry Tretts!' But before our joy was complete came our ultimate fear. Shots rang out from the direction of the timber. The supposed white man was no more than a clever ruse to draw us away from the cabin. The Indians had posted themselves in the underbrush and behind the stables just close enough to take deadly aim."

My jaw dropped as I listened intently, but again Eliza seemed unmoved as she persisted to recite the events of that day. The manner in which she could discriminate her emotions was remarkable to me.

"In a panic we scrambled back to the safety of the cabin," Eliza stated with neither excitement nor sadness. "At least a dozen shots pelted the outside of the cabin while we continued to frantically rush inside. But despite the panic, cooler heads prevailed as the men took aim and returned fire through the port holes while I and the other women barricaded the windows. One window was barricaded by standing the table upright and forcing it against the wall while the others were barricaded with the use of puncheons torn from the floor."

"Was anyone hurt?" I couldn't help but ask.

"Well, yes," answered Eliza. "But it took us some moments to realize this. The first few minutes were difficult to understand. It was a time when thought was abandoned and impulse took over. Rather than take note of the injuries, a heavy fire was kept up. It was critical to keep the Indians from rushing the cabin and no one had time or thought for much else. Mr. Markham and Mr. Bradshaw aptly fired upon any Indian who showed himself. Then, while the men reloaded, Mrs. Church took hold of a loaded gun and, thrusting it through a porthole, fired upon an Indian she had seen emerge from the brush. After the shot the Indian was nowhere to be seen and it had been concluded that he had been either badly wounded or killed. This ended the seven or eight minutes of heavy fire that occurred since the first volley. The lull allowed us to look over the damage and attend to those wounded."

Eliza paused for a moment. She turned her eyes up and moved her head to the side as if clinching to her next thought. It was her first display of even modest emotion. It was the first expression that demonstrated she was really there, rather than just an innocent witness or an all-knowing bystander.

"Willie Thomas was nowhere to be found," she finally stated after regaining her composure. "In our haste we had left him outside the door. His older brother said that he had heard groaning on the doorstep after the door had been closed. We presumed the boy had been killed and decided it would not be wise to open the door and invite further injury. We later discovered that Willie had been shot through the head and probably died in a brief time."

Again Eliza paused, this time taking a deep breath, a sigh really. I sat as still and quiet as possible. My heart was heavy and silence seemed the best response. And, as near as I could tell, Eliza did not need an audience. She was caught in her own memory, reliving the story to herself and herself alone. I acted merely as the ignition.

"There were others," she continued with unexpected suddenness. "Though none killed. Mr. Thomas took a shot to his left arm and was bleeding profusely. Mrs. Church and I did our utmost to bandage the wound, but owing to its severity and lack of attention the arm later had to be amputated. There was also Mr. Carver, who suffered greatly from a buckshot that passed through the fleshy part of his right arm and penetrated his side affecting his lung. He bore the pain bravely. Finally there was Miss Swanger who was very weak from loss of blood. She was hit in the shoulder. It was she who fell to her knees and exclaimed that though she was too weak to fight, she would pray fervently to the God of Battles until the fighting was ended."

I closed my eyes at the thought of it all. Somehow I sought to brace my tender heart.

"Do you wish me to continue?" interjected Eliza, sending a sudden and uncomfortable jolt through my body.

"Yes, please do," I replied cautiously. "I would hear more."

Eliza drew her head back and kept her eyes on me, but then continued. "After assessing the injuries and doing our best to dress the wounds, we determined there were only three able bodied men remaining who could be counted on for effective defense. These were Jareb Palmer, John Bradshaw, and Morris Markham."

"What of Dr. Strong?" I asked remembering that he had been in the Thomas cabin earlier.

"Dr. Strong?" she repeated in a high pitch as if she had, until now, forgotten him altogether. "Dr. Strong had been absent during the attack. Earlier that forenoon he had gone to the Wheeler cabin to dress the wounds of Smith and Henderson. He never did return."

"I see," was my brief acknowledgment.

"The remainder of the fight was less intense than the beginning," explained Eliza as she continued. "The fighting was much more desultory in nature. Occasionally an Indian was seen skulking through the brush or around the stable and once fired upon he would return to his place of hiding. We employed six portholes to ensure the Indians were held at a distance. If we had not, we feared they might set fire to the cabin. But as it was we kept them back until sundown when the Indians appeared to make a full retreat. This brought us great, but only temporary relief. We did not know where the Indians went or if they might return. Also, we had great concern for those wounded and in dire need of medical attention."

"Do you know," I stuttered, "or, did you know, what happened to the Stewarts?"

"Not immediately," she replied plainly. "We were confined to the cabin and could not know. However, sometime after dusk came a frightened and frantic young Johnny Stewart. He was nearly mistaken for an Indian before we recognized him as the Stewart boy. Unfortunately we learned from the poor boy that his family had been wantonly massacred by the bloodthirsty Indians. Young Johnny hid behind a log in the yard while the Indians did their evil work."

"How awful," I said sadly.

"True," said Eliza, "but at that moment we could not grieve or dwell on those lost, heartless though it may have been. We had to focus on saving those that were still living. Once we felt assured that the Indians would not reopen an attack, we began to discuss our next course of action. This was by no means a simple discussion," Eliza noted. "Some believed we ought to stay and wait for relief to arrive from Fort Ridgely. But we had no manner of knowing whether relief was coming. We knew not even if our messengers had arrived at the fort. And, if they had, it was quite possible that the soldiers would not believe the incredible tale."

Eliza spoke quickly now. She maintained her plain, emotionless tone, but she was now reciting her tale in a loose, unchecked manner as if the events had only happened yesterday.

"Furthermore, we feared that if we had stayed it would only encourage and invite another Indian attack. Thus flight appeared the more prudent option. But this option was riddled with questions and uncertainties. We did not know the actual strength in numbers of the Indians. Nor had we knowledge of their location. It might have been they were hiding in the woods and waiting to pick us off. Or they may have retreated to Heron Lake. We did not know. Another obstacle to consider was the snow. It was at least fifty miles to an adequate place of refuge and the depth of the snow made travel at even a reasonable pace almost impossible. There was no trail for which to follow over the wintry wastes and we had no horses, as they had been driven away by the Indians. Additionally, there were among us three badly wounded persons whose health would be put in great danger by the cold and exposure incidental to such a flight."

"And the children," I added. "Such long and harsh travel would for them be most troublesome."

"Indeed," agreed Eliza, "under such conditions, even for the strongest and most rugged, flight would be a hard trial of endurance."

As Eliza continued her quick-speaking description, she finally began gesticulating her story. Where she once sat stale and upright, she now began to sway back and forth with the rhythm of events. Her arms and hands began to move, slowly at first, but then wide and long and all the way over her head. She became fully immersed in the retelling of events almost as if she enjoyed it, though her true emotion was one of deep loss and sorrow. In any case, I was enamored, if not by her story, then by her manner of telling it.

"We had almost abandoned the option, this idea that we could escape, when someone recalled the Thomas oxen. We knew the oxen had not been taken, and if they had not been killed they would be safe in the stable. And so, Mr. Markham volunteered to go to the stable, and if the oxen were living he would hook up a sled and return to the cabin. This was just another example of Mr. Markham's bravery as he risked his life for the welfare of us all. While Mr. Markham was absent, we who remained in the cabin made preparations for flight. About thirty minutes passed and we feared Mr. Markham had been killed, but finally he returned with an ox and sled. He said that there were no signs of Indians anywhere in the vicinity. Still, we wasted no time. We ushered the three wounded victims into the sled. Around them we placed as much as was deemed necessary such as blankets, clothes, powder, and food. Though injured, Mr. Thomas gave one final solemn good bye to his fallen son who still lay in front of the cabin where he took his last dying breath. There was no time to remove his body."

Eliza paused to take a sip of water and I did likewise. She looked at me, but with the same emotionless eyes with which she spoke. I did not know what kind of reaction she expected so I merely turned my eyes to the floor.

"Do you believe what I tell you?" Eliza finally asked, breaking away from her story.

"I neither believe nor disbelieve," I replied without much thought. "Nor is it important what I believe."

"Then why endure such great lengths to be here?" she asked. "Why do I bother to relive this horror for you?"

"I do not have any answers, Mrs. Wilson. I do not know the reasons. I know only that our enemy is ignorance."

With that, Eliza looked away and reached for another sip of water. She gave no reply, but continued to conclude her story.

"It was near 9 o'clock in the evening when we departed. We were nineteen in number. The stars were covered by clouds and it was intensely dark. Had there been any Indians, we would not have seen them. Thus, blindfolded though we were, we marched. The pace was slow and arduous, but we had made up our minds. To the front were Markham, Bradshaw, and Palmer all with loaded rifles and all ready to protect us with their lives. To the back of the sled were the women and children while the sled itself carried the wounded and supplies. We made our way with great trouble. There was no distinct trail and we were often compelled to alter and re-alter our course. Finally, after making only five miles' progress, we halted during the darkest part of the night and decided to wait for dawn."

"Where did you sleep?" I asked.

"Few, if any, slept," Eliza answered quickly. "The men stood guard while the women lay blankets across the snow. It was the most miserable night I have ever known."

Eliza paused briefly, and then continued.

"With the light of day we departed once more, happy to be moving just to keep our bones from freezing. For less than an hour we traveled before we discovered that progress through the deep snows and high drifts was well-nigh impossible."

"Impossible," I repeated. "Then you were bound to the open prairie?"

"For a time, we were," answered Eliza. "However, after some discussion we decided to send Jareb Palmer to Granger's Point, about ten miles off, for some assistance. After many hours he returned with George Granger and a team of oxen to rescue us poor, stranded refugees. By evening we made it to the Point, and with a great sigh of relief. I can readily say it was the longest short journey I have ever made. We remained at Granger's Point for two days but could stay no longer. Provisions were waning and the wounded were still in need of medical care. But before departing we were joined by the former occupants of the Wheeler cabin, or, most of them, I should say."

"Yes, the Wheeler cabin," I said with surprise. "I had forgotten all about them. What of their fate?"

"They were unharmed," said Eliza calmly. "They told us that they had heard the firing at our cabin and knew something was amiss but that the Indians made no attempt at their own lives. The morning following the attack, Mrs. Smith discovered the body of Willie Thomas, and she feared that all inhabitants of the cabin had been killed or carried off. Thus, those in the Wheeler cabin also determined that flight was their only option. But, sadly, without the benefit of a wagon or sled they were forced to depart without the crippled Mr. Smith and Mr. Henderson who were incapable of travel. The remainder of them reached Granger's Point without further distress."

"And do you know what became of the Wood brothers?" I questioned.

"At the time, no," she replied. "But after the fact I learned that they were murdered by the Indians, and that their trading post was ransacked and burned to the ground. As a matter of fact, it was they who sold the Indians the ammunition and powder to carry out their evil deeds. Ignorance, as you might say, was indeed their enemy."

I cringed at this new knowledge. Those men had not a single notion that the Indians had a treacherous intent. Not even after they were duly warned. And so they aided, unwittingly, in their own destruction, and in the destruction of so many others.

"Such a regrettable thought," I finally replied.

Eliza merely looked at me and waited for my feeling of regret to pass as if my feelings had no point or purpose. Consequently, I quickly returned to a more emotionless demeanor.

"We departed from Granger's Point on March the 29th in the direction of Fort Dodge," Eliza continued. "We knew it was a great distance away and that it would take many days' travel to reach, but we determined it was our only hope. The next day, while making slow but sure progress, we spotted what appeared to be a small band of Indians about two miles distant. We clamored in fear as we thought these were the same Indians who had earlier attacked us. But the men were brave and willing to defend us with their lives. After a hasty consultation the guns were divided among the able-bodied men and John Bradshaw volunteered to go in advance and pick the Indians off one by one. Markham and Palmer remained with the women and children to defend us to the very end. And so with all eyes upon him, Mr. Bradshaw, with unmatched fortitude, marched bravely forward. I could only brace in wretched anticipation. But what began as unimaginable fear and loathing suddenly turned to indescribable joy. The men who approached declared themselves friends and were not Indians at all."

"Who were they?" I asked, though I knew she would eventually tell me.

"They were a party of soldiers from the Iowa relief expedition sent from Fort Dodge. They had pulled blankets and shawls over their heads to protect themselves from the fierce northern wind which made them appear like Indians, but rather, they were our long awaited salvation. It was a moment of unremitting alleviation and great happiness to be finally reunited with our friends, neighbors, and selfless allies. For the first time we believed we might actually survive. Our condition was so deplorable, I doubt whether we would have survived another night. Our shoes had worn out, the wounded were in desperate need of surgical aid, and the children were crying with hunger and cold. So thankful we were those men came to our assistance."

"You must still have had a long way to Fort Dodge," I added.

"Surely we did," answered Eliza, "and the remainder of the journey was in no way easy, but it was made tolerable by the soldiers and their help. I cannot describe the joy when we arrived among our fellow settlers at Fort Dodge. It was as if we had been saved from Hell's fire."

"I cannot express widely enough my sorrow for you and the others who experienced such fear and loss," I said solemnly.

"Mr. Campbell," she replied, "that you have taken a genuine interest is sympathy enough."

I nodded in response but feared my sympathy was not genuine at all. Was it nothing more than a self-seeking interest? I realized that Eliza had her own uniqueness, but that it did nothing to sooth my inner-conflict. I had given profound interest in Eliza's story, but it left me with only feigned compassion. Although Eliza's tale was harrowing, sorrowful, and real, it in no way filled the emptiness I sought to replace. The sympathy was real. And I can rightly say that I felt some sort of compassion. But it was a worldly compassion. It was an outward sympathy. Here today, gone tomorrow if you will. I did not blame myself for this. It was just the natural way of things. I could not force meaningful emotion upon my own character no more than I could ask myself to grow two more inches. I may have gained knowledge of the events, but it brought me no satisfaction. It brought me no comfort.

"We should move on to more cheerful matters," said Eliza with the hint of a smile as she got up to gather the tray and water. "If you speak with Abbie you will need a break from all this woebegone talk."

"Your hospitality alone is enough to woo a forlorn spirit," I returned politely.

"You are too kind," Eliza replied from the other room. "Just make yourself at home."

So ended my meeting with Eliza. I was grateful for her story and for her willingness to tell it. But somehow I felt no more enlightened today than the day I departed, crestfallen and confused, from the Lower Agency. And so I waited with hope and patience. I waited upon Abbie Gardner.

INTERVIEW WITH ABBIE

I ran as fast as I possibly could. Through puddles and around tree stumps. I swerved vigorously. My terror hurled me forward and I dared not look back at the danger closing in. Suddenly I heard the shrill sound of war-whoops behind me and arrows began to dart past my head. I ducked and dodged as if I could avoid calamity, though its origin was completely unknown to me. I began clinging and clutching to the grass as I sought to pull myself forward. My legs no longer moved on their own but had to be willed along despite the obvious and growing danger behind me. But I knew I was close. I knew I was running toward something and if I could only make it a few more steps I would be safe.

"You'll never make it!" I heard the voice of Agent Pritchette call.

"He's right," said Major Cullen who suddenly appeared to my left as I ran by. "You are nothing but a half-breed: a half-human."

"No," I answered in desperation. "I have to save them. I can fix everything."

The world began to turn dark and shrink behind me. The puddles, the trees, the war-whoops; everything had faded away. Only my fear remained as it closed in nearer and nearer. One more step . . . one more step . . . one more step, I thought with my total and complete concentration on that notion and that notion alone. But suddenly, like a ball dropping, the world was pulled away. I dropped, catapulting into the darkness.

"Joseph. Joseph. Wake up," I heard the soothing voice of Eliza say. "It seems you were having a nightmare."

"I suppose I was," I said as I sat up and began to reassess my circumstances.

"You needn't worry so much," said Eliza in a motherly tone, despite the fact that she was rather younger than I. "You know you have done nothing wrong; nothing for which to feel ashamed."

"I know," I replied, "but sometimes I think right and wrong can become blurred."

Eliza did not have a supportive response this time. She just looked away solemnly until she could think of an appropriate way to break the silence. "Abbie has returned," she said affectionately. "She is happy as a clam, too."

"That is great news," I said without any real emotion. "Will she speak with me?" I felt a sudden pit of fear that she might not.

"Yes, of course," replied Eliza immediately. "I have already told her you have come. And I have already told her why you have come."

"And?" I asked, still worried I was imposing on Abbie.

"Don't worry, Joseph," said Eliza reassuringly. "It may not be a happy subject, but Abbie understands. She wants to tell her story."

"Thank you," I said with some relief.

"Make yourself at home," Eliza said as she turned to leave the room. "I will find my sister for you. You can speak to her shortly."

I pressed my lips together in a compliant and grateful manner. I didn't know what to expect next, but I tried to put my doubt and my self-consciousness aside.

Tap, tap, came two soft knocks on the door.

"It is open," I said hesitantly.

Slowly the door opened, creaking at the hinges, and I could not right away recognize the figure in front of me, only a silhouette.

"Greetings Joseph," she said in a kind and childlike voice.

"Hello," I said as I stood to greet her. I reached out my hand, made a step forward, and in an instant she became visible to me. The auburn hair, the freckled cheeks, the tall, slender figure, the curiously radiant presence: it was Abbie Gardner.

"You must forgive me," she said respectfully and with a smile, "I know we have spoken before and I realize you were of great assistance to me, but at the time I was in a rather unpleasant condition. I suppose I barely even raised my head to you."

"There is no need to apologize," I quickly returned. "I was kept to my duty and had no expectations otherwise."

"Very well," she said while speaking softly. "Please," she offered.

We sat simultaneously, not across from one another but at a slight angle. The room was empty but for a few chairs, a cot, and a table. It was quiet too. I no longer heard stirrings from the rest of the house and I did not know where Eliza or her husband William had gone.

"Eliza says you've been married," I said all of the sudden.

"Yes," Abbie answered with a great big smile. "His name is Casville Sharp and he is a cousin to the Thatchers. I am very happy. He remains at Fort Dodge to conduct business."

"Congratulations," I said honestly. "There is no greater joy than having a family of your own."

Abbie squinted and smiled. She looked happy. Not like she had before when she was subdued and morose. She carried the same grace, that was undeniable, but now it gleamed through her joy and not her sorrow. "Do you have a family?" she asked.

"Yes," I said with a pleasant tone. "I have a wife and two wonderful daughters."

"How lovely," Abbie replied politely.

"Yes," I returned. "They are a source for joy."

"You wish to speak of the massacre," Abbie said, suddenly changing the subject.

"I do," was my immediate reply. "I have spent this summer chasing Inkpaduta. I experienced the panic and fear that gripped the state this spring. I have assisted the government and the Dakota as an interpreter throughout this whole troubled mess. I have spoken with many people with varying perspectives. Now, I'd like to know yours."

"I can tell you what I know, Joseph. I can tell you what I saw and what I experienced. I want people to know what happened. I don't want it to become lost and forgotten."

Abbie, like Eliza, spoke reverently, as if untouched by cruelty. She seemed sincere and honest and willing.

"I understand and I would be grateful to hear your story," I said submissively.

"It is quite alright," Abbie returned. "I cannot change what happened, sorrowful though it may be. Do not think that you are a hindrance to me."

I sat in silence giving only my nonverbal acknowledgement. I was greatly pleased and thoroughly relieved by Abbie's words. I don't know why, but until then it seemed impossible to let go of my apprehension.

"Were you born on the frontier, Mr. Campbell?" Abbie asked poignantly.

"Why, yes," I replied with some surprise to the question. "At St. Peter's."

"Forgive my inquiry," Abbie said noticing my surprise. "I thought I might put my story into some context for you."

"Please, go right ahead," I replied anxiously.

"I was not born here," Abbie began. "My father grew up in New Haven, Connecticut. As a young man he labored in a comb factory. But while I was still very young, my family moved to western New York State. Here my father ran a saw mill and my sisters and I lived pleasantly among the fine mountain scenery, sparkling rivulets, and the fresh country air. I often wander back with fond recollection to those delightful scenes of childhood; to the joy of those happy days."

I could see that Abbie truly meant what she said. She seemed almost lost to the present and caught in her memories. She must have longed for what was, or what might have been.

"But those days were short-lived," she continued with a change of tone. "My father was not content with his success at the saw mill. He, like many others, sought the uncertainty of the west. Not only did he seek to go west, but he sought to go furthest of all, as if to keep up the race after the setting sun. And so we left our happy home and bade good-bye to our friends and mates, promising to write, promising to remain friends, but knowing we would likely never see each other again."

I sat quietly as Abbie spoke, compelled by the nostalgia she expressed. Abbie appeared vulnerable.

"The move was not a straight one," Abbie explained, "but took its course over a matter of years. We settled first in Ohio, this being where my eldest sister Mary had resided. From there we moved to Indiana, and finally to Clear Lake, Iowa. Here, at Clear Lake, was a true frontier unlike anything I had experienced before. Pioneers, as we now were, we lived an isolated life. At Clear Lake we had but few neighbors and the nearest bit of civilization was sixty-five miles away. It was strange to be so isolated and to be so cut off from the world, but it seemed not to matter because we lived among such good and hearty people."

Abbie paused here. She spent a moment in thought, perhaps bracing for what she would express next.

"What brought you farther west?" I decided to interject. "What brought you to Spirit Lake?"

"Are you familiar with the Old Testament?" Abbie asked, breaking out of her pause.

"Yes, more or less," I replied unassumingly.

"Then you know of the Promised Land," Abbie explained. "It was a rich and abundant land promised by God to the descendants of Abraham. It was a land flowing with milk and honey."

I felt confused by Abbie's digression, but showed no bewilderment.

"For hundreds of years the land was sought after," Abbie continued to explain. "This is how the pioneers such as my father view the lakes region. It is a beautiful and prosperous land yet unsettled by white men. It is seen as our promised land."

"And so you went into the uncharted wilderness to find it," I said as if completing Abbie's thought.

"Yes," said Abbie in agreement. "My father, not yet finding the object of his wishes, sold his house and land and once again uprooted the family. We headed northwest in the direction of this so-called Promised Land beyond the reaches of white civilization. Across mile after mile of trackless, boundless prairie we made our way. By day we frequently encountered the redskins and by night we were entertained by the howling of wolves. It was a pleasant, albeit tentative, march. The oxen trudged slowly and noisily forward while pulling cumbersome wagons overflowing with household goods, agricultural implements, and various provisions. But the toil was balanced by the strange and unspoiled surroundings."

As I listened, as I imagined, I could see that Abbie was charmed by her trailblazing life. She spoke with an eloquence and honesty that demonstrated her true feelings of fascination and wonder. It seemed she was but a child at the time captivated by a life unknown to most. She spoke of these things with a fondness that poured out of her.

"The far-stretching prairie," Abbie continued pleasantly, "clothed in its mantle of green, luxuriant grass, always swaying left-to-right in unison with the ever-flowing breeze. The golden stars of the resin-weed studded the prairie here and there along with the thousands of flowering plants which painted the horizons in every direction with varying hues of blue, violet and yellow. Nor were the prairies the only attraction, but the sparkling rivers and the babbling brooks which glistened in the sunshine and spoke unhesitantly of its ever-persistent journey downstream. Finally were the shady groves of oak and elm festooned with fruit and ivy and visited frequently by graceful herds of elk and deer who sought food and shelter among its peaceful shores. Amazing too were the countless wild fowl of every variety which filled the air and spotted the ground. Every spot, it seemed, was teeming with life and beauty. Such was our long journey. Tedious though it may have been, it filled our hearts with that peaceful joy which only nature gives."

"You speak with a unique fondness," I decided to mention.

"I was fond," Abbie returned. "There is nothing quite like the wilderness of the west, uninhabited and untouched by the white man. For centuries the land sat peacefully, unknown to the turmoil's of civilization. The frontier is indeed a romantic ideal and it helped me understand my father's passion for such a risky and adventurous life."

Abbie finished with a heartfelt sigh and I began to see the Abbie I encountered those few months before; the one who was forlorn and hardly willing to speak.

"When did you first arrive at the lakes?" I asked, urging Abbie to continue.

"July 16, 1856," she stated exactly. "After a long and lonely journey of one hundred ten miles we arrived at the shores of the picturesque Okoboji Lake."

"Okoboji?" I questioned, having expected her to say Spirit Lake.

"Oh, yes," Abbie said with surprise. "The region is known in general as Spirit Lake. But it consists of three lakes. These are Spirit Lake to the north, and East and West Okoboji Lakes to the south. My father chose our settlement along the southeast edge of West Okoboji Lake."

I nodded in acknowledgement.

"I can tell you it was the most beautiful and pristine place I had ever seen," Abbie continued with a smile that came deep from within. "Its loveliness was enough to reward my father for his years of toil and uncertainty. We were the first family to settle the region. But it was not long before others came, having heard of the beautiful scenery and healthy climate. Like all those coming west they too sought adventure and the unbridled hope that comes from this life unknown. By the first of November, six families, along with several single men, had settled the region, all with log cabins, and all preparing for winter."

"How many settlers in total?" I asked. "Do you know?"

"I cannot recall exactly," Abbie responded. "But I reckon forty or so. We were ten in our small and still unfinished home."

"Ten," I repeated out of curiosity.

"Yes," Abbie replied as she was ready to explain. "My eldest sister had married Mr. Harvey Luce and they had two young children, Albert and Amanda. Then there was my father, mother, Eliza, myself, and my younger brother Rowland. Finally there was Mr. Luce's good friend Mr. Clark."

Abbie's mouth began to quiver as she turned her head to the side. She tightened her eyes as she tried to withhold her sadness.

"I am sorry," I said, not knowing what else to say.

"Such was our new and hopeful setting. Brave and hearty pioneers we were alone in the wilderness. Fort Dodge lay eighty miles to the southeast and was the nearest place that could be counted on for provisions. Let it be remembered, "Abbie stated in a defiant tone, "that there were at this time no settlements west of ours."

"Did it frighten you to live on the extreme frontier?" I asked.

"Not precisely," Abbie replied plainly. "In the spring of 1855 the Indians had generally withdrawn from the Upper Des Moines and lakes region. My father was greatly encouraged that all danger from them had passed. And having met only friendly Indians, he could not have anticipated our fate."

Again Abbie paused. She slumped over as if she cared not to expend the energy to sit upright. Her eyes now seemed empty as she stared blankly into nothingness.

"If you do not wish to continue I would understand," I said out of politeness.

"Oh, forgive me once more," she said as she turned her head and her eyes up in my direction. "I was reminiscing on our humble home. Winter came so soon we never had a chance to finish it," Abbie said with a light-hearted smile. "In fact, the floors were nothing more than leveled dirt covered with prairie hay and red carpet which we brought with us all the way from New York. But it didn't matter because we had each other. I can remember our evenings spent just some months ago," Abbie continued with the fondness I saw before. "Mary would read aloud to the family or perhaps father would be helping me solve some problem of arithmetic. Or Rowland, my wonderful little brother Rowland might be at the table trying to form letters from a copy written by Eliza while my mother sat comfortably in her rocking chair crocheting or fashioning some garment into shape. What a quiet and happy home we had."

I could think of nothing to say in return. Abbie's mood was pleasant and I didn't know whether or not to express sympathy.

"These were our circumstances, Joseph," Abbie explained as if turning the page to a new chapter. "We had a happy and hopeful life. But what I recall next I recall with inexpressible sadness. I tell it to you now so that my family might not be forgotten. I tell you now so that it might save others from a similar fate."

"I understand," I replied.

To this point Abbie told her story well. She said she wanted to build context and she had done just that. Rather than jump directly into the details of the attack she had made it more personal; more real. I now knew and could identify with her family and their lifelong journey to find prosperity and happiness. They did not come all the way from New York to Iowa to take anything. They did not seek to exploit the land and reap its spoils. It was not selfish ambition at the behest of anyone and anything that stood in their way. They were hearty pioneers, nothing more and nothing less. They did not realize nor could they know the cumulative effect of hundreds upon thousands of pioneers that did and that would force their way upon the land, further and further west. They were not a part of the past that their future, and the future of so many others, came to erase. The Dakota Indian was a part of that past; my Dakota kin; my Dakota blood. That is where conflict arose and where blood was shed . . . where the past met the future. Is either to blame?

The Spirit Lake Massacre

"It was early one Sunday in March," Abbie said soberly. "The family had risen early that morning in order to prepare for Father's trip to Fort Dodge. The winter was long and we were in need of provisions which my father sought to recover. I remember it being a beautiful morning. The bright sun was made even brighter by the glare of the deep snow. It felt warm against the skin as if spring were announcing its arrival. We gathered happily around the table for breakfast when a solitary Indian suddenly entered the house. Our Indian guest was gentle and kind and gave us no reason for alarm. Mother soon set a place for him at the table. The morning meal was pleasant much like it might have been on any other morning. But it was not long before more Indians arrived. Each one wanted something to eat and mother did not hesitate to appease them. Finally there came to be over a dozen warriors in the house," Abbie said with expression in her eyes, "along with their wives and papooses. There was by this time some discomfort and anxiety among us because we were so uncertain of their intentions. Still we did not fear that our lives were in danger. The Indians dissembled friendship and it appeared that they merely sought needed supplies."

Abbie now sat upright and seemed wholly engaged in the reciting of her experience. Her lips moved easily and her expressions mimicked each detail. She did not look so young to me now, but appeared more like an authority of some kind. I sat still and listened and tried to envision the scene, but my mind wandered. Abbie held a strange power over me that I could not shake.

"Out of hospitality for our Indian guests, we doled out our scanty store until each was satisfied. But suddenly the Indians became sullen, insolent and overbearing. They began demanding ammunition, gun-caps, and numerous other things. This was the first time I truly felt afraid. I began to tremble and I held my young niece and nephew close. Without warning one of the Indians snatched a box of gun-caps from my father's hand while another, as if by agreement, sought to snatch the powder horn hanging against the wall."

Abbie reached for the air in front of her as if grabbing at the gun herself.

"Mr. Luce thought quickly and prevented the Indian from snatching the gun. We suspected now that the Indians had the nefarious intention of gathering all available ammunition."

As Abbie continued my mind no longer wandered. Abbie told her story so well, so vividly, so naturally, that I began to sink into the depths of her detail. I could imagine it myself. I was there.

"You shall take nothing more!" shouted Mr. Luce sternly as he took hold of the powder-horn.

In an instant the half-clad Indian drew his own gun and lifted it within a few feet of Harvey's head. But, acting even quicker, Mr. Luce seized the deadly weapon from the Indian warrior who grunted in displeasure.

"Be gone with you!" said Mr. Luce bravely. "You have what you need, now leave us at peace."

The three children trembled in the corner while I covered their mouths to keep them from wailing. Meanwhile my sister Mary clung tightly to my mother. My father, Rowland, stood by silently while hoping that Mr. Luce's rebuff would result in the Indians' retreat.

After a brief and anxious pause, the most vile and fearful-looking Indian stepped forward. He was not a handsome man and I found his appearance revolting. He had strange and repulsive scars on his face and his eyes were small and squinty. He began angrily shouting a string of unintelligible commands. He waved his arms emphatically and raised his voice to a pitch that could be understood in any language. He was ferocious. The other Indians grunted with disapproval as they began to exit the home, each with a scowl on his face. The last to exit was the eldest, the most ugly and vile one of them all. Only once he exited was there a sigh of relief.

"Rowland!" came the call of a man outside. "Everything quite all right? We come wishing to send letters with you to Fort Dodge."

Peering through a crack in the open door Rowland could see that it was his neighbors, Dr. Harriott and Mr. Snyder who were now joined by the Indians.

"There'll be no trip to Fort Dodge today," returned Rowland through the crack in the door. "The Indians here seem up to no good and I believe it is serious."

"The Indians are no trouble," called Mr. Snyder. "Can you not at least open the door?"

"Please," said Rowland with a sense of worry in his voice. "I must stay to protect my family. We should warn the other settlers so they can prepare a defense. You must believe me."

"It is merely a pageant to them," replied Mr. Snyder as both of the men snickered. "They will have their fun and pass by before evening."

"I implore you, please," Rowland urged again, but to no avail. The two men had already begun interacting with Indians that were gathered alongside the house. They appeared to be engaged in trade. The men were unconcerned by the Indian's presence.

Frances, my mother, was shivering with fear as Rowland closed and latched the door behind him. "What shall we do?" she clamored.

There was a brief pause as each, not knowing what to do, waited for another to speak.

"We must notify the other settlers," Harvey declared unyieldingly.

"No," cried Mary, "you mustn't leave us."

"She is right," said Rowland quickly. "We cannot afford to weaken our numbers in defense of the home. Also, I suspect it would be near impossible to reach the other homesteads without being discovered by the Indians."

"Wait," said Frances unexpectedly. "We must do what is right. We must take risks to warn our neighbors. We cannot allow them to be shot in the back," she argued.

"I agree," added Mr. Clark who, until now, had hidden himself in the corner. "Harvey and I can go. We are young and strong and know this region as well as anyone."

"It is too dangerous," said Rowland with a shake of his head. "And we still don't know if the Indians plan to incite violence."

It was clear that as the patriarch, the decision would come down to him. His approval was necessary. Amidst the crucial dialogue there was a chaos of crying and sobbing added by the young children who had not yet recovered from the recent events. As the discussion continued, the crying continued unnoticed like a constant part of the background.

"Mr. Gardner," entreated Harvey, "the Indians are in a foul mood and I fear that every one of our friends and neighbors will be cut down if we do nothing. We must at least give them a fighting chance."

"We do not know that," appealed Rowland. "Right now my family is more important. What if the Indians were to return?"

"Mr. Clark and I can outmaneuver those Indians," contended Harvey with a calmness and confidence in his voice. "They are slowed by their wives and papooses. If they should return we can make it back before them."

"We must," added Frances. "We must do everything in our power for the lives of our neighbors."

"Very well," answered Rowland reluctantly as he sent his hand waving across the air in front of him. "Harvey and Clark head out along the south edge of the lake. But you must ensure that you are not discovered. Your lives, and the lives of everyone at this settlement hinge upon it," he finished emphatically.

"Some little time was required in preparation," I heard Abbie say as I snapped out of my imagination and remembered where I truly was.

"You must have been terror-stricken," I said, finally interrupting Abbie from her story.

"We all were," replied Abbie without breaking her persistent demeanor. "We had no one to rely on for help and could really only hope the Indians did not return with malicious intent. But somehow I think we all knew that tragedy was coming."

Abbie settled back into her story, speaking in a steady and unbroken manner. She conquered her emotions for the time being and focused instead on the details. For having lived such an experience, it seemed she had a remarkable knack to recall what she otherwise might have been too terrified to notice.

"Oh Harvey!" cried Mary as she wrapped her arms around her brave young husband. "I am afraid you will never come back to me."

"I will return," Harvey said with assurance. "We are smarter and quicker than those Indians. No harm will come."

Tears rolled down Mary's face as she hugged and kissed Harvey. Sadly, she was right. This was their last earthly meeting. Harvey and Clark departed, never to return again.

As the afternoon passed, Rowland kept a constant watch, Frances and Mary worried themselves sick, and I calmed the young children by holding them and sharing short and amusing stories. After little more than an hour following the departure of Harvey and Clark there was the soft, but undeniable sound of gunfire off in the distance.

"What happened?" cried Mary.

"It came in the direction of the Mattock cabin," answered Rowland.

"Is Harvey okay?" asked Mary frantic with fear.

"He is alright," returned Rowland. "Don't fret, he is alright."

Rowland's words were assuring, but the sounds of gunfire were not. It could mean only one thing and everyone in that small log cabin knew it. The Indians' intentions were violent, and on that day, they came with the willingness to carry it out. Now, it was only a matter of time.

A few more hours passed and the fear that felt so certain before had begun to wane. The sun was becoming low on the horizon and shed a brilliant and shadowy light over the snowy landscape. Rowland, now less afraid, but still quite anxious, decided he could no longer remain indoors.

"Stay inside and remain quiet while I go out to reconnoiter," commanded Rowland as he unlatched the door.

"Nine Indians are com'n!" shouted Rowland as he hastily bound back inside the cramped cabin while dragging wet snow along with him. "They are only a short distance from the house. We are bound to die!"

Fearful screams rang out from the women while horrifying cries began once again from the children. Only I remained in a state unmoved by fear.

"We must fight to the last," Rowland said, completely forgetting, or perhaps ignoring, that he of all people should stay composed. "While they are kill'n all of us I will kill a few of them with the two loaded guns still left in the house."

"Rowland, please," pleaded my mother. "Do not speak this way. We must have faith that kindness will spare our lives. And if we have to die, let us die innocent of shedding blood."

Rowland paused, no longer frantic, no longer thinking or speaking in such foreboding terms.

"I love you," Rowland said to his wife. It was the last moment of peace the family would ever know.

With a loud crash the door swung open. Three war-clad Indian warriors forced their way inside and began demanding flour. "Flour! Flour!" the first warrior repeated while pointing with the butt of his gun.

Rowland did not hesitate to go quickly toward the scanty store of flour that still remained. But as he turned his back one of the Indians raised his gun.

"No!" shouted Frances. But her effort was futile.

With a deafening crack the rifle went off, piercing Rowland in back and through the heart, ending his life. He fell helplessly to the floor.

Another Indian raised his gun to fire, but Mary pushed it away in a futile effort of self-defense.

The Indians, whose numbers had grown to at least six, quickly seized Mary and Frances and began beating them over the head with the butt of their guns. The two women were helpless against the powerful Indians who proceeded to drag the women out of doors and then killed them in the most cruel and shocking manner. Their screams dissipated to silence.

The children now were all that remained alive. Being the eldest of the four, I tried to be brave. While seated in a chair, frozen with fear, I clung to the little children. I held them as close as possible knowing I could not save them, but offering them any bit of comfort I could in their final moments.

The Indians began an indiscriminate destruction of everything in the house. Trunks were broken open and clothes thrown aside while the feather beds were torn and feathers scattered everywhere. The Indians overturned everything in the house with a lust for destruction. For a moment I thought they might ignore the helpless children, but this was not to be. Suddenly they seized the children, tearing them from my arms one by one. First it was Amanda, then Albert. Finally, they took my young brother Rowland. Their little arms reached for me, crying piteously for protection but I was helpless to save them. With careless regard for the children's cries the Indians took them out of the cabin and beat them with sticks of stove-wood. Like their mother's before them, the cries of the children quickly became nothing more than silence.

Now left alone, I sat tearless amidst the death and destruction.

"Please," I pleaded, "take my life too. I wish to join my family in death," I said with an honest desire to not go on living.

But the Indians were not so kind. They had other intentions and I knew it. One of the savage men took me by the arm and forced me to my feet. Like a broken doll I rose from the chair without resistance or willingness. Alone with the villainous warriors I knew I could do nothing; I knew I was being taken captive.

The Indians ransacked the entire home. They took every last object and left it overturned or broken as if they sought to wreak as much havoc as possible. I was dragged outside, though I put up no fight. My family gone and my home in near ruins, I no longer cared what happened to me. As I was carried backwards out the door I took one last look at my father, who lay lifeless on the floor, killed in an act of hospitality. Once outside my home I saw the bloody and discombobulated bodies of my family members.

The beloved children lay just outside. Still alive, they moaned for one last loving caress that I was helpless to give. My poor mother lay just beyond them, faithful to the very end, now weltering in her own blood. Finally my sister Mary, with whom I shared so many intimate parts of my life, lay dead and was left in the most horrible and mutilated condition. And then there was me. Taken alive by the wretched hands of my family's executioners while the bloody scalp of my mother still hanged from my captor's belt.

There was silence. I snapped back into reality. Abbie sat in front of me, appearing neither sad nor mournful. Just silent.

"You have my deepest sympathies," I said with sincerity. In that moment I no longer felt grief over myself and my own circumstances, but only grief for young Abbie.

"I must continue the story," Abbie said with dignity.

"It is quite alright," I replied. "I am not sure I could bear much more."

"No one life is more or less important," Abbie stated with dignity once more. "There is more to tell. I want those lives remembered too."

"Dinner!" I heard Eliza call from the opposite room.

"We should continue later," said Abbie politely.

"Yes," I replied. "I rather think I need a break."

"Tomorrow then," said Abbie.

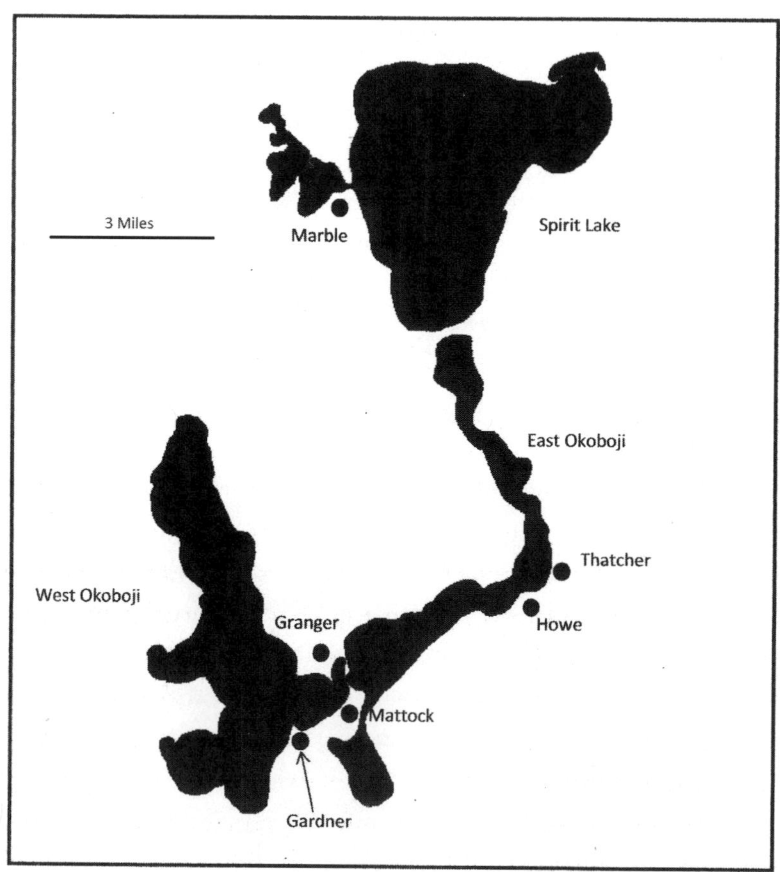

Location of the settlers on Spirit and Okoboji Lakes in March, 1857.

Final Interview with Abbie

The next twenty-four hours were a relief to me. I had, for that time, completely forgotten all of the troubles that awaited me back at the agency. I had forgotten the stubbornness of the superintendent and his special agent. I had forgotten the insults and threats slung directly at me in the cruelest manner. I had forgotten that the Dakota were starving and neglected and in dire need of their annuities. I had even forgotten my struggle within.

It was a relief to forget these things. I felt comfortable and happy and without the constant burden of duty or the relentless notion of what I ought to do or think or feel. More importantly, I no longer carried my self-doubt or the feeling I had to be someone I was not. I felt free to be myself rather than living up to the expectations of an unfledged and judgmental world. It was soothing beyond description to just be, to just exist.

My feelings were the result of Abbie and her wonderful new family. Outside of my own family, it was rare to feel such inclusion. Certainly for Abbie and Eliza it was not a life they envisioned just a short while ago, but it was a life they seemed fortunate to have. Abbie especially seemed to entertain no feelings of wrong, but only of deep thankfulness. It was refreshing and remarkable to witness gratitude among circumstances met most often with pity and remorse. There was a sense of constant joy—a sense of hopefulness. They did not dwell on the past, but looked brightly toward the future. And even more remarkable, they did not grieve over what they had lost, or what they did not have, but instead they were overwhelmingly grateful for what they did have. It was like nothing I had seen before. It was nothing I could expect. To witness and be a part of their joy, optimism, and thankfulness amidst such real loss was a blessing unlike any other.

"You have a rare and happy home," I said to Abbie as we sat down to continue our interview from the day prior. "It does me well."

"I am pleased you could be here," Abbie responded with shyness. "I am grateful for someone willing to listen."

I nodded as if to say *you're welcome.*

"Shall I continue with my tale?" Abbie asked with a change of tone.

"Please, go right ahead," I said purposely.

"Very well," Abbie said as she nudged herself forward and pushed her shoulders back as if posing for a portrait. And just like that she was ready to continue.

"I was taken by my captors to their camp which was near the Mattock cabin. I did not go reluctantly or willingly. Rather, I was in a deeply depressed state and longed for death's sweet release. What I saw at the Mattock cabin only heightened my depressed state, if that were possible. The scene I encountered, believe it or not, was even more gruesome than the one I had just departed. The cabin itself had been set aflame while two persons were still alive inside screaming with agony and fear. Scattered along the ground were several bodies whose ghastly figures were shown clearly by the light of the burning cabin. I remember this distinctly, though I wish I could forget. Among them were Dr. Harriot and Mr. Snyder, who had only just hours before refused to heed my father's warnings. Alongside the men were their rifles, which indicated to me that an attempt at resistance was made. But this effort had no effect as it appeared that no Indians were killed, though one had apparently been wounded."

I listened quietly and attentively as Abbie spoke, somewhat in shock from what I heard. I found it hard to comprehend that the person in front of me had witnessed and lived through such unbearable atrocities. This was no report or rumor. Abbie was a part of the events.

"As the Indians dragged me beyond the wretched scene toward their camp," Abbie continued with calmness, "I recognized also the body of Mr. Carl Granger. I suspected that he had been the first to be shot. He lay near his cabin with his head cut off above his mouth and ears. It was a gruesome sight."

I cringed at the thought.

"Finally, and sadly, I saw the bodies of Mr. Clark and Mr. Luce. It appeared that they had despaired of reaching the Mattock cabin and so sought to continue east to reach the Thatcher and Howe cabins, but were discovered and shot along the way. Sad as it was to see their lifeless figures, I was emotionless by this time and I met their corpses with indifference."

"I cannot imagine," I stuttered. "I cannot imagine what that was like for you."

Abbie hesitated, but when she could see that I had nothing more to say she continued, "The day's slaughter must have been near twenty lives," she said as if unaffected. "On behalf of the monsters who committed these crimes it was time to celebrate. This they did so with a war dance. Unquenched by their evil bloodshed, the Indian warriors blackened their faces and raised their fists with uncouth gestures. By the sound of the drum the warriors danced over the blood-stained snow and around the camp fire, filling the air with their wild screams and yells. For many hours they celebrated as the drum continued beating dull and slow. They celebrated long into the night until exhaustion finally compelled them to desist."

Abbie paused for a moment clearly in thought.

"Unfortunately," she said after a few seconds, "I cannot effectively describe my condition during that sleepless night, the first of my captivity. Having just lost my family and being taken by the savage culprits, only those who have shared in such circumstances can form a just conception of the terror I had been through. I can say that it was an experience that oppressed my heart and was burned into my soul."

Again I was left speechless. I had asked to hear Abbie's story but I wondered now if I had not been better off having never heard her tale. It was difficult to accept such a reality. I believed myself fortunate for not having shared in Abbie's experience, but I still felt an overwhelming sorrow for what she had been put through. Indeed I regretted Abbie's misfortune and the misfortune of her family and friends, but it was quite another experience to have it laid out before me. I suppose it is what I asked for.

"The following day brought only more carnage," Abbie said after a pause to gather her thoughts. "The Indians blackened their faces and went off from camp early to complete their evil deeds. I thought helplessly of the happy and unsuspecting families who were unwittingly set to meet their doom."

"How you must have longed to warn them," I interjected softly.

"Quite," Abbie said, but then continued her story as if determined not to tarry. "The first victim that day was Mr. Howe who was on his way to Father's apparently to borrow some flour. Without even a moment's notice the Indians shot Mr. Howe and severed his head from his body. As if this heinous act had no significance whatsoever, the Indians proceeded to the home of Mr. Howe. Here they found his wife, his son, his daughter, a young lady I did not recognize, and four young children. The Indians wasted no time and slaughtered them all, leaving only lifeless bodies behind. I need not describe how they were killed. From there the Indians proceeded to the home of Noble and Thatcher which was not even a half-mile up the shore of East Okoboji. At the Noble and Thatcher home, the Indians were met by Mr. and Mrs. Noble, Mr. Ryan, Mrs. Thatcher, and two children. Like they had before, the Indians feigned friendship and the poor occupants had no reason to suspect the Indians of treachery. I could only watch as I was held back in the woods with my mouth covered. Through their cowardly guise the Indians gained every advantage and then, in a concert of action, they shot the two men. I distinctly remember Mr. Noble crying out, "Oh, I am killed!" Next they took the children from their mothers' arms, dragged them out of doors, and killed them in the most brutal fashion. The house was ransacked and the two remaining women, Mrs. Noble and Mrs. Thatcher, were taken captive. This ended the second day's carnage."

"How many?" I asked though it may have been insensitive.

"Thirteen the second day," Abbie responded without hesitation. "I believe it was thirty-three in total."

"Your condition," I stuttered with grief. "Your condition must have been one of irreconcilable sorrow."

"Speaking now," Abbie said candidly, "I cannot truly revisit my condition. I am happy today and rather grateful for the life I have. But in those hours and days and even weeks that followed I was, as you say, irreconcilable. Frankly, I longed for death. I lacked feeling, I lacked hope, I lacked any real human qualities. I knew only indifference. The Indians recognized this and sought to challenge my indifference. They pointed guns toward my head and threaten to kill me. But each threat on my life was met with tearless acquiescence and willingness to die. This seemed to fill the Indians with wonder and admiration. They mistook my indifference for bravery, a quality they highly appreciated. Because of this they respected me and spared my life. Ironically, my desire to die was the only thing that saved me."

"A strange twist of fate," I added.

"I cannot say." Abbie responded. "I do not wish to entertain the notion of fate."

"Were there no others?" I asked. "Was not Mrs. Marble also captive among you? I have not heard you mention her."

"Unfortunately, Joseph," Abbie stated, "the massacre was not complete. For a time the Indians reveled in their achievements. They danced by night and regaled in the glory of their hideous acts by day. After a few days they struck camp and moved northwestwardly across the lake toward Marble's grove. They seemed to be ignorant of the fact that there were more whites in the region. Despite my state of apathy I was anxious they might not discover the Marble cabin. But none of us were quite so lucky. They caught the Marbles by surprise and once again feigned friendship. It was here that I witnessed their most cowardly act yet."

I furrowed my brow with surprise but said nothing.

"I was kept at a distance, but still witnessed the whole act. They asked for food, and once satisfied, they proposed a rifle trade. Mr. Marble accepted the trade and so it was proposed to shoot at a mark. A mark was set and Mr. Marble proceeded to fire several shots until his rifle was empty. As Mr. Marble moved to set the mark back in its place, he was shot through the back and he fell dead in his tracks, never suspecting a thing. Mrs. Marble, without a sound, turned to flee but was quickly overtaken and captured. For better or worse her life was spared and she became the fourth victim added to our little band of helpless captives. Mr. Marble was the last to be killed at the lakes and the only one who was actually killed at Spirit Lake."

"May I ask of Mrs. Thatcher?" I said politely, though I was filled with curiosity. "I know Mrs. Marble was rescued and I learned of the tragic death of Mrs. Noble as reported by the Indian rescuers, but what became of Mrs. Thatcher? How is it that she was killed?"

"Poor Elizabeth," Abbie said with a sorrow-filled sigh. "Of all the terrible scenes I witnessed, I believe I lament on the loss of Mrs. Thatcher most."

"Please," I said realizing Mrs. Thatcher was close to Abbie, "disregard the question."

"It is quite all right," replied Abbie assuredly. "Elizabeth and I became dear to each other and I mourn that I could not ease her affliction. But it saves me no heartache to pretend nothing occurred."

Abbie spoke with a rare maturity about the matter she now discussed. It was a quality she exhibited throughout our interview.

"Our lives as captives were harsh," continued Abbie. "Our inhuman captors were cruel and heartless and carried not even a hint of mercy among them. Day after day we were given heavy burdens and forced to plod through the deep drifts of snow without the aid of snowshoes. At times it was nearly impossible. And when we were not walking we were working. This was exceptionally difficult for us because in the Indian culture work was only fit for women. The women then are merely slaves, and we, poor captives, were slaves of the slaves."

Abbie seemed to speak with a calm indifference to her hardships, again demonstrating a unique and remarkable maturity.

"These hardships proved too much for Elizabeth," Abbie said with a sense of regret in her voice. "Elizabeth was just nineteen years of age and she only recently gave birth to a new babe. After but a few days she took a cold and then developed phlebitis fever, a combination of ills resulting in the most excruciating suffering."

"This is what killed her?" I asked, forgetting to be patient.

"Not quite," Abbie answered. "Elizabeth was resilient. With tremendous fortitude she bore her sufferings. Her limbs became swollen and black and her veins became varicose from pressure. Despite her illness she was forced to tramp through the snow, wade through the ice-cold water, drag tents, chop and carry wood, and all other sorts of drudgery. As a witness to her suffering I cannot wholly express the pain she endured or the barbarity of her heartless masters. It was amazing she did not collapse from sheer exhaustion. But she willed herself along, not for herself, but for those who loved her. That is what made her end so sad," Abbie said as her eyes moved up and caught my own. Somehow I could see the genuine humanity in the sadness she expressed. It was as if Elizabeth still lived somewhere behind Abbie's eyes.

"We were walking along one day," Abbie continued as she lowered her eyes, "when we approached a rather uncertain bridge crossing. As we reached the crossing a young Indian took the pack from Mrs. Thatcher's shoulders and ordered us forward. This was quite unusual and aroused our suspicions immediately. Before that occasion, no Indian had ever offered his assistance. Poor Elizabeth acknowledged that her time had come and she said to me, 'If you are so fortunate as to escape, tell my dear husband and parents that I desired to live and escape for their sakes.' Sadly I could only nod in agreement and could do little else. As we reached the center of the swollen stream, the same young Indian who had taken Elizabeth's pack pushed her from the bridge and into the rapidly moving stream. With what seemed like supernatural strength, Mrs. Thatcher breasted the torrent stream and struggled to shore where she clung for dear life to the tree roots. But the Indians showed no mercy on account of her resilience. They met Elizabeth at the shore and beat her off with clubs and long poles. With another desperate effort for life Elizabeth nearly managed to reach the opposite shore, but she was again beaten back and thrust into the angry stream. The pitiless Indians followed Mrs. Thatcher downstream whooping and yelling all the while. Elizabeth was barely alive when she reached the second crossing a short distance downstream when she was finally shot to death. Her lifeless body continued with the rushing water like a log down the current. I could only watch in terror while remembering her final wishes."

Abbie paused here. She peered longingly as if neither I, nor anything else now existed. She was deep in reflection.

"Of all the things I experienced," Abbie said, breaking her silence, "her death had the greatest effect on me. I was so near to Elizabeth. One moment I was literally walking in her footsteps and the next she was gone. To witness her death made me finally realize that I wanted to live. I came to see just how helpless I was to the will and power of my captors. They could at any moment decide whether I lived or died. But I also came to realize something else," she said with a new, more positive tone in her voice. "I realized what it meant to be truly selfless, though I had every reason to live with fear and self-pity."

"How did you come to realize this?" I asked not understanding what she could possible mean.

Abbie did not answer straight away. She adjusted the way she sat and seemed almost content not to say anything at all.

"Elizabeth," she finally stated like she had some sort of epiphany. "Elizabeth bore all of her bereavements and trials with meekness and courage. Despite her suffering she vowed to persevere. And this she did without even a word of complaint. She did not suffer for herself. She persevered not out of fear of the unknown, but she did it out of love for her husband and kindred. She humbly bore all her ills and sufferings for the sake of those she loved and who loved her. She did it for them. Her last words are etched into my memory."

Abbie now showed her own meekness as she reminisced on the life of Elizabeth Thatcher. She appeared pensive and sad, but also calm and accepting. She looked like the Abbie I had traveled with to St. Paul, but now without the incalculable rift between us.

"Elizabeth exemplified with beauty all the womanly and Christian graces," Abbie continued. "It is what helped me live through my unhappy experience; it is the reason I am here today to tell you about it."

All of the sudden I became curious a new way. I no longer wished to hear the details of the massacre or Abbie's captivity. That is not why I sojourned to see Abbie. Now, as Abbie reminisced on her relationship with Elizabeth, I recognized what drew me to her in the first place. I could see the effusive faith within Abbie and I wanted it for myself. I wanted, somehow, to cure my inner-conflict. "May I speak to you on something else?" I finally inquired, but without nervousness or shame.

"Of course," said Abbie willingly, "whatever you wish."

"I am not entirely sure how to articulate my thoughts," I began meekly.

"Go ahead," said Abbie as she could see me thinking.

I sat for a moment in silence, but then decided I ought to go straight to the point. "My intentions for coming here are not exclusive."

"You came to learn my story," Abbie interjected with a puzzled look on her face. "Is that not right?"

"Yes," I answered quickly. "After being a part of the expedition to capture Inkpaduta, I developed a great deal of curiosity. I wished to know more. I wished to know what happened so that I might understand it better."

"And . . . ," Abbie said, still somewhat puzzled. "What other purpose could you have?"

"I am a mixed-breed," I stated. "And, whether you can understand this or not, I have been caught between two worlds. On the one hand I am an Indian with Indian family, Indian tradition, and Indian history. On the other hand, I am a white man, working for the white man's government, and supporting the white man's way of life. Living as a mixed-breed has always left me with ambiguity, but the events of these past months have challenged my identity more than ever before. At times throughout my life I have hidden my Indian heritage. I have tried to escape it. At other times I have embraced my Indian background. But now . . . now things are different. I do not believe I can continue living in this ambiguous nature."

I was candid and calm. I did not feel ashamed; I was merely at ease as I lay out my innermost conflict. It was as if I were letting go of something—something heavy—something I had been dragging behind me.

"Before coming here I was encouraged—rather, threatened—to choose an identity. Was I Indian or was I white? And the choice was made very clear to me based on the likely consequences. I was told that I had to be white; that I had to disown my Dakota background. I was told that had I chosen otherwise, I would lose my job, my reputation, and my future. This hurt me deeply. As if by choosing a side I was rejecting my own identity and the identity of my family. I was not ready to do that. That is when I decided to come see you, Abbie. Despite all the reasons I was given to finally relinquish my Indian heritage, I was just too conflicted. I knew what I was told and I understood the reasoning and the consequences. But how could I destroy such a real and valuable portion of myself and of my family? How could I reject my Dakota grandmother who always taught me to remember who I was? How could I reject my Dakota kin, with whom I grew up along the serene banks of the Mississippi River at Kaposia? How could I hide my language? How could I hide my very nature forevermore? And how, as I watch the Dakota culture now struggling to survive, could I turn my back on my family and friends who so desperately need an ally?"

I lowered my head into my hands and took a deep breath. I was without tears, but no longer was I without emotion. My life of inner-conflict, denial, shame, and personal ambiguity came rushing to the forefront and I felt hopeless. I felt like I had let myself down.

"I understand," Abbie said sedately, sensing my condition. "But why do you suppose I could help? I am but a young, white woman, having just fifteen years and very little wisdom."

I raised my head and caught Abbie's eyes. She was startled but did not look away. "There is something different about you," I began, putting aside my deluge of emotion. "I first noticed this on the boat to St. Paul. I did not realize it at the time, but there is a peacefulness about you."

Abbie listened, unmoved, just content on comprehending my words.

"I am not sure I can explain it, and I am not sure I understand it. But you struck me. And it was more than your quiet and somber disposition. That, I could comprehend. It was something I saw behind all of that. Something I could not deny or dismiss. It was a sense of forgiveness, a sense of hope. It was a gratitude. It was a thankfulness. It was strength beyond strength that in spite of everything you had lost, in spite of everything that was taken from you, in spite of everything you experienced, you might somehow be better off. It was a willingness to accept your circumstances selflessly, without malice or hate or anger. Through your dark sadness shined a brilliant light. Not a proud or boastful light, but a humble one, available only to those who took a moment to discover it."

Again Abbie sat still, not ready to offer a reply.

"It was these qualities that drew me to you. Qualities I cannot find in myself," I admitted. "I don't know how you carry yourself with such . . ." I thought for a moment. ". . . With such wisdom, with such a forbearance to anger and hate. You seem to have a perspective vision that I just cannot fathom. And so I ask you, what is it? How do you possess this sense of acceptance and gratefulness despite what has happened to you and your family?"

Abbie sat poised and calm, just staring blankly at my now weary and desperate face. She started to crack a curious smile, revealing a childlike expression. "I believe you have given me too much credit, Mr. Campbell," Abbie finally said affably. "I am flattered."

"I could not be mistaken," I said, convinced of myself.

"I don't wish to argue the point," Abbie responded. "Perhaps there is a light about me, but I must admit to you that I am not perfect," she explained. "Though I never regarded my enemy with hatred it was quite merely out of shock, I do believe. And the condition under which you discovered me was not one of forgiveness, but could more properly be defined as an absence of feeling."

"This cannot be entirely true," I tried to argue. "Any person under similar circumstances would boil with hate and a thirst for revenge."

"Perhaps," Abbie assuaged. "Perhaps I have been too humble. You may, after all, be right on some qualities. I can truly say that I do not harbor malice. And I am indeed grateful for my life and my new future."

"Forgive my imprudence," I interrupted, "but how? How do you look beyond your pain and your loss? How do you look beyond yourself?"

"Joseph," she said with a soft tone. "What are you really asking?"

The question startled me. Abbie was right and in that one simple question she showed a wealth of wisdom and perceptiveness. I was circling the issue. All along it was not Abbie: it was me.

"What am I to do?" I asked, now realizing that I needn't avoid what I sought. "After learning about what my Dakota brethren did, I don't know how I could accept them as a part of me. Shall I hide my identity and live with a sense of shame so that I might have a better life? Is it time that I finally, once and for all, choose a side?"

Abbie smiled again, ever so slightly, making it seem like she knew something that I did not. "My father made a choice," she began plainly. "He might have amassed a fortune and had a long and happy life, in a peaceful, quiet home. The war-whoop of the Indian never would have echoed through his dwelling; the tomahawk and scalping knife never would have horrified his children; nor would his family have been brought to an untimely end. But he chose to uproot his family and chase after a life unpromised of success. He chose to follow his dreams. And though he now lay in an unknown grave on the western wilderness, I cannot regret the choice he made, not now nor then. You see, Joseph, we all have our choices to make and we all have our burdens to bear. None of us have the benefit of hindsight. And so I do not blame my father for what happened. Neither do I blame those Indians. It may not be right, what they did, but it was outside of my control. I could not make that choice for them, nor do I know or understand what led them to such a choice. And so it is with you now. As the Word says, you are worried and concerned over many things. But you need not be so concerned. This is your choice. This is not my choice or the choice of your employer, nor does the choice belong to anyone else. Make your choice, Joseph. Do not let them make the choice for you."

I sat in silence. Nothing seemed to move, nothing seemed to stir. I was contemplative.

"Joseph?" Abbie said as trying to wake me.

"You are wise beyond your years," I said, breaking out of my silence.

"I have a notion," Abbie said with a strange suddenness. "I believe you should visit the lakes. Visit my home. Grieve for the victims. But mostly, discover its beauty. Discover its everlasting wonder. See for yourself what is so cherished and charming and come to realize, just like I did, that it is something bigger than yourself. Something that cannot be taken away. See for yourself why it has been deemed the Eden of the west."

I thought for a moment. It had not occurred to me before to visit the lakes. "I might rather like that," I answered with cautious optimism.

"You have a fine heart, Joseph Campbell," Abbie said as she rose to her feet, looking more like a mature figure than ever. "Whatever you see in me, it is only because it exists within yourself. Go to Spirit Lake. I believe you will find your answer."

GRACE AT SPIRIT LAKE

At twilight the sun becomes gentle, brooding its soft apricot glow across the horizon below it and the fading sky above it. Like a yearning lover it seems to bid the world adieu, promising to return on the morrow and shed its life-giving brilliance once more. But for the night, the sun must mournfully dip away, inviting the cooler breezes, the softer sounds, and the sweeter smells of a day coming to rest. How gorgeous is its light, announcing to its beloved, "Good night! I will love you more."

Such was my first encounter with the region of Spirit and Okoboji Lakes. I arrived at sunset to a vision of beauty that can be described as nothing short of miraculous. And in one swooning moment I see and understand. Like the great Pacific long-sought by Balboa and Magellan, or Ponce de Leon's obsessive search for the Fountain of Youth, so too must this Eden of the west be prized. Before even the white admirers there were the Indian guardians who held this region sacred. Minnewaukon, or Spirit Water, it was termed by the Dakota. So translucent are its waters that the Indians regarded it with superstitious awe. They believed its waters were haunted by spirits, and that no Dakota ever ventured to cross it in his canoe. Looking out across its subtle waves I can only imagine the peace and tranquility its sparkling waters have known since the time before time.

Beginning from an outstretched promontory along its northern edge, Spirit Lake is oblong in both width and length reaching four miles in either direction. It is a huge body of water that could easily stand on its own, acting as water for the thirsty, food for the hungry, and home to countless types and forms of flora and fauna. It is a source of perpetual life and boundless beauty.

Then there is Okoboji, East and West. Known to the Indians as A Place of Rest. The quiescent waters of the East Okoboji break from the southern tip of Spirit Lake stretching down a narrow, bending channel, looking more like a wide and gentle-flowing river than a lake. For many miles it flows peacefully, not moving up nor down its channel, until, like an outstretched hand, it reaches the isthmus of the West Okoboji. Here the water is constrained no more by its narrow passageway; it opens north, south, and west, exploring every bay and inlet. Like a mirror to the sky the water settles into the West Okoboji acting as a true place of solace and rest for inhabitants and visitors alike.

But the wonder and charm of the region is not confined to its waters alone. So too can its enchantment be found in its sloping, pebbled beaches, its natural shores skirted with timber, and its rich and productive soil. From east to west the vast and lovely region is introduced by undulating, amber prairies, and withdrawn by numerous groves stretching finally into endless forests. Everything from the soil to the sun, from the waves to the wildlife, conspires to render this region a terrestrial paradise.

I did not waste any time getting to the lakes region. I departed from Abbie and Eliza shortly after finishing my interview. I gave them both my most heartfelt thanks and promised to write in the near future. But I was anxious to be on my way and to discover for myself what had so readily lured the optimistic frontiersmen. More so, I sought to discover what truth might lay there within.

It was a long but peaceful journey, one hundred twenty miles by ox cart. I was sent northwest in search of my destination over ceaseless prairie interrupted only by the occasional stream or grove. As I traveled, I tried to relax, but worry was a constant companion. I thought of everything that had happened, both to me and to all those involved. It seemed there were no victors, only losers. Whether it be the Dakota now starving and sick, the settlers now mourning and displaced, or even Inkpaduta's small band of Wapekute now alone and in hiding, everyone lost something. It was a notion that weighed on me. I also reflected on myself, knowing I had done all I could. I had stood in council doing my duty as interpreter. I had gone on expeditions and put my life in the balance. I had acted as an escort and mediator. I had sought knowledge and truth from all sides in hopes of discovering and promoting a reasonable compromise. I had done everything within my power. Still there was no solution, and perhaps I was naive. And so I listened to Abbie's wisdom and I took her advice. She, who suffered unspeakable wrong before her very eyes yet maintained a dignity and grace that few, if any, possess. I set aside my cares and worries for the world and I decided to look inward. I decided to confront myself.

I traveled south along the shore of East Okoboji. Mile after mile I trudged seeking ever so desperately to reach the ill-fated site of Abbie's former home. But the land was unending and the slow-moving water was constantly at my side. As the lake turned gently toward the west I knew I must be getting close. On and on, over and around countless trees, sloughs, and creeks I went. Finally I reached a channel. One of the lake's many outlets lay to my south while straight ahead lay the massive body of water called West Okoboji. I took a brief glance over the sparkling waters, then continued quickly to the southwest. The object of my long endeavors, I knew, was little more than a stone's throw away. With my head low I came to an opening, when all of the sudden, not fifty feet in front of me, I discovered the Gardner cabin. It was an inconspicuous little home. Though Abbie had explained its dimensions to me before, it came as a surprise to see how delicate and plain her home really was. Rectangular in frame it was a log cabin perhaps 30 feet by 20 feet in size. It had a door in the front, a window on each side and a chimney rising out of its slanted roof. Looking upon the home I could imagine what intimate family settings they must have shared. Isolated as they were, cooped up by the long, cold winter, they had no choice but to live together with peace and harmony. There was little else to call my attention. Little else but a lonely cabin among the trees and beside the lake. It was quiet now. Almost fearfully quiet.

Then, a few rods to the southeast of the house, I noticed some stones that lay in a pile. Near these stones, the sod grew thinner as if it had been misplaced. I walked slowly toward the stones realizing with a sudden shock to my body that here must lay the remains of Abbie's family. There were no headstones or epithets, just a quaint pile of stones that might just as well go unnoticed. I stood solemnly alongside the common grave looking down with sadness. It was a strange sadness, as if I owed them something, something I could not give. I thought of Abbie's father and his pursuit of a frontier life. I thought of Abbie's mother and her blessed kindness, even to the end. I thought of Mary and Harvey and the children, all of whom had their lives cut tragically short. And I thought of Abbie, who in one dreadful moment had them all taken away. I quietly shed my tears, and it felt good to cry.

Here is mixed the profound serenity of the unblemished wilderness with the utter tragedy of a conflict between cultures: between past and future. Here among this confounding setting I realized that I could not reconcile the struggles and conflicts. I have seen the needs of the Indians and longed for them to be treated fairly. I have seen the character of the pioneers and my heart breaks for them. I have learned and experienced nearly every aspect of this wretched event. And I have been asked, once and for all, whose side I would take. Not only today, but as a person forever and always, who was I to be?

I sat, deep in thought, alone in this beautiful wilderness. Like a rainstorm, memories of my life began flooding my brain. As an impetus my memories confronted me, asking me to finally decide who I was. But then, like a switch had been turned, it became clear to me. I was never meant to choose sides. I was never meant to be conflicted over one or the other. I was never meant to be ashamed. Though I was not fully Indian, though I was not fully white, I was even more. With a knowledge and perspective of both cultures, I was a link between both sides. And though I had already acted as a link, it was only now, after living between such an inextricable struggle, that I could appreciate who I was. I could not solve this struggle. But that didn't mean I could not try. I had to try. To cut myself off from one side or another would be the essence of futility and the ultimate act of surrender in the face of opposition. To choose a side would be to live in defeat.

I am a mixed-breed. I have a knowledge, an experience, and a tradition, both white and Indian. Though I cannot end the interminable conflict between whites and Indians, only as myself can I hope to understand and mediate that conflict. Only as a mixed-breed can I offer some source of strength and empathy unknown by the opposing forces. Moreover, I see now that it is not about one over another, but about one with another in a way that both can flourish.

As Abbie said, we all have our burdens to bear. I know now where her grace is found. It is found in an understanding of who she is and who she wants to be, not living in regret or anger for who she might have been. She understands her role no matter how great or small and she is selflessly willing to carry out that role. I will go forward and face the work ahead knowing all the while that I am who I was meant to be, and that I can make a difference.

March 9, 1858

Dear William,

A year now passed since tragedy and unimaginable terror visited me and my family. A year I would not relive. A year filled with constant sorrow. Forgive me if I have not been well these days. Life will never be what it was. Those joyful fall days in the Gardner cabin, they seemed so full of promise. Surrounded by the untamed wilderness and the inspired frontiersmen, the future felt limitless. It was a world all our own. We earned our joy, our hope, even our naivety. Little could we know it would all be taken away, struck from our hands as little more than a jewel box.

Then there was you. You were a stranger. You were a passerby in my unsuspecting eyes. You were nothing more than a surveyor, a woodsman, a friend to my father. I could not see you through my veil. But you were there through the darkness that had come to envelop me. You endured with me all privations and heartache. You risked your own life that I might somehow find the strength to continue my own. You were there to lift my veil.

I have not been myself and I will never again be that rosy young girl you met what seemed so long ago. Yet, how the unpropitious can change. How destruction and death can change to new life and new hope. As we welcome our first child I am filled with a profound joy. It is inexplicable and beyond my own understanding. I thought I would never know joy again or any semblance of it. But grace has found a way. Grace shall be her name.

With all of my love,
Eliza

EPILOGUE

On August 18, 1857, both Major W.J. Cullen and Special Agent Kintzing Pritchette wrote to the Commissioner of Indian Affairs, Charles E. Mix, giving their approval for annuity payments to be made to the Sioux of the Mississippi. Though the agents were not entirely satisfied with the outcome of the Indian expedition to capture and punish Inkpaduta, they determined that to withhold payment any further would "endanger the Sioux to wants incident to their condition and thereby invite temptation to depredation."[1] Put simply, if the Dakota were not given their annuity, they might respond with violence. By September 21, 1857, the annuity payment, due to them in June, was finally received by the Dakota Indians of the Upper and Lower Agencies. But this did not solve much, nor did it change the pattern of treatment by the government toward the American Indians. At the council held during the annuity payment of 1857, the chiefs and head men of the Sisseton and Wahpeton bands brought forth a number and variety of unresolved grievances. The most notable complaint was in regards to monies owed as stipulated through the treaties of 1837 and 1851. It was estimated by Agent Pritchette himself that the Dakota were owed more than $30,000. In addition to this, the Dakota had not once received their $6,000 per annum allotted for education by the treaty of the Traverse des Sioux in 1851. The corruption of the Indian System and the wrongs done to the Dakota of Minnesota is a near endless topic. But the point here is that although

1 United States, Office of Indian Affairs, *Annual Report of the Commissioner of Indian Affairs, for the year 1857,* "Northern Superintendency," 93.

payment worked to allay the affliction of the Dakota in 1857, the late payment was just one of a multitude of contributing factors that ultimately resulted in violence during the U.S. – Dakota War just five years later.

As for Inkpaduta, he was never captured or punished for his participation in the Spirit Lake Massacre. Following the Indian expedition in July, the government was still intent on the pursuit and capture of Inkpaduta. As stated by Major Cullen, "a concerted movement should be made from Forts Randall and Ridgely by mounted men, under good and trusted Indian guides, to concentrate on this band near the junction of James and Snake Rivers, where, I have no doubt, Inkpaduta and his band will be found, should the government direct the movement promptly and without delay."[2] This movement followed Major Cullen's request as early as September, 1857, when Companies G and L of the Second Artillery, as well as Little Crow, made an exhaustive search of the Coteau des Prairies and areas west of Fort Ridgely.[3] But once again Inkpaduta avoided capture. Because of Inkpaduta's already vile reputation and his allusiveness that followed, his reputation grew to epic proportions. Inkpaduta was branded as a vicious outlaw who was blamed for any wrong deed, crime, or violent act perpetrated against settlers in Iowa or Minnesota. However, following the attacks at Spirit Lake and Springfield it is likely that Inkpaduta left the region and spent the fall of 1857 mourning the deaths of his older sons while camped with the Yanktons along the James River.[4] It is doubtful that Inkpaduta ever returned to Minnesota until 1862, when he was rumored to be at Lake Benton in order to receive part of the annuity payment that year. Once it was discovered that Inkpaduta was in Minnesota, Thomas Galbraith, Indian Agent at the time, immediately requested that a military expedition from Fort Ridgely be sent to capture Inkpaduta and his soldiers. On July 28, 1862, Lieutenant Timothy Sheehan, along with fourteen soldiers, four volunteers, and one scout, went to

---

2 Ibid., 97.

3 Beck, *Inkpaduta,* 106.

4 Ibid., 108.

Lake Benton in search of Inkpaduta. But Lieutenant Sheehan found only an empty campsite and tracks that led nowhere and once again, Inkpaduta avoided capture. For the remainder of Inkpaduta's life his whereabouts would remain uncertain. He was rumored to be in the battles of Big Mound, Dead Buffalo Lake, Stoney Lake, Whitestone Hill, and Killdeer Mountain, but no one can say with certainty if he was there. It is even believed that he participated in the Battle of the Little Bighorn, although, at his advanced age, it is unlikely he did any fighting. It is certain, however, that two of Inkpaduta's sons, Sounds the Ground As He Walks and Tracking White Earth, did fight in the Battle of the Little Big Horn. Tracking White Earth was mortally wounded in the battle while Sounds the Ground As He Walks is the man credited with killing General George Armstrong Custer. A few years later, in 1879, Inkpaduta died while living free in Canada.

For twenty-two years, Inkpaduta avoided apprehension at the hands of the whites. Throughout this time he remained thought of by whites as a savage and a criminal, but to many Dakota, he became a patriotic figure to be honored and revered.[5] Ultimately, Inkpaduta's life was one of strong objection to white encroachment coupled with a stringent desire to retain the traditional life of the Wahpekutes. It is doubtful whether or not he hated the whites and uncertain if he ever committed violence outside of the Spirit Lake Massacre. What is certain is that his name has gone down in infamy as the only renegade Indian never to be captured or killed at the hands of the U.S. Government.

Interestingly, many participants and historians mark the fact that Inkpaduta was never captured as a major cause of the U.S. – Dakota War of 1862. For instance, Indian Agent Joseph Brown stated, "The failure to pursue and punish Inkpaduta and his band for the wholesale murder of our citizens at Spirit Lake has confirmed them in the belief that the government is weak and cannot punish Indian aggressions."[6] It is argued that Inkpaduta, through his resistance and his ability to elude capture, somehow inspired defiance on behalf of the younger Dakota

---

5 Ibid., 142.

6 Ibid., 99.

warriors. Upon the death of Inkpaduta, Judge Charles Flandrau asserted that Inkpaduta was "honored by his people as one of the best haters of the whites in the whole Sioux nation."[7] Proponents of this theory ultimately believe that the failure to capture Inkpaduta demonstrated the weakness of the U.S. Army while expressing to the Dakota that resistance was possible. Furthermore, it has been argued that Little Crow was inspired by and colluded with Inkpaduta in the planning of the Sioux Uprising.

Despite these allegations it is unreasonable to argue that the Spirit Lake Massacre or the failure to capture Inkpaduta was a direct cause of the U.S. – Dakota War of 1862. Rather, it was the result of decades of mistreatment and mismanagement toward the Dakota Indians. No single event or incident resulted directly in the great Uprising, but it was rather the culmination of events brought on by an Indian System that was corrupt and ineffective.[8] The reasons and results of the Spirit Lake Massacre is just one example of the Indian situation along the frontier throughout the 1850s and 1860s. Furthermore, if one were to assert a direct cause of the U.S. – Dakota War of 1862, it was more likely because the Indians were poor and starving and therefore they did what they believed that had to do to survive.

Mrs. Abbie Gardner Sharp lived a long life while often dedicated to the remembrance and memorialization of the Spirit Lake Massacre. She had two sons and one daughter, though her daughter lived to be only eighteen months old. Her youngest son she named Albert in honor of her beloved nephew who was torn from her arms and murdered. She lived most of her life in Iowa while also spending a few years in Missouri and Kansas. Unfortunately for Abbie, she never truly recovered from her affliction and captivity. Her tragic experience undermined her health and left her an invalid for fourteen years, often confined to her room. As she stated she was "perfectly helpless."[9] Nonetheless she managed

---

7 Wingerd, *North Country,* 272.

8 According to Historian David Nichols, corruption was integral to the Indian System. David A. Nichols, *Lincoln and the Indians: Civil War Policy and Politics,* (Columbia: University of Missouri Press, 1978), 7-8.

9 Gardner, *History of the Spirit Lake Massacre,* 289.

to record her first-hand account of the Spirit Lake Massacre and her captivity many years after the incident. She also succeeded in officially commemorating the Massacre and creating a place for those who were killed to be remembered.

Since the time immediately following the Massacre, Abbie had always hoped to buy her father's cabin and the plot of land on which it stood. However, this plot of land was bought up as early as April, 1857, by a frontiersman named J.S. Prescott. In 1883 Abbie returned to Spirit Lake. Upon her return she was astounded by the changes and growth to the region. No longer was it an isolated wilderness replete with danger from potential Indian attack, but was a modern summer resort teeming with all the advantages and conveniences of advanced civilization. By 1883 Spirit Lake had become the county seat of Dickinson County and was a major crossroads of the Burlington, Cedar Rapids and Northern, Chicago, Milwaukee, and St. Paul railroads, connecting it directly with the great centers of population and trade. Years later, in 1891, when the original Gardner claim went up for sale, Abbie immediately bought up the land. The cabin, which was nearly in ruins, was redone and made to look like a museum to the Massacre. Oil paintings of the tragedy were hung on the walls while Indian relics or mementos pertaining to the history were placed inside. Once Abbie refurbished the cabin, she began to lobby the legislature of Iowa for the funds necessary to erect a monument to the memory of those early pioneers as well as permanently mark the spot where the tragedy occurred. In this Abbie succeeded and in March 1894, the Assembly of Iowa appropriated five thousand dollars to erect a commemorative monument. The monument was erected just a few feet from the Gardner cabin and burial plot. It was officially commemorated on July 26, 1895, in front of an assembly of seven thousand people. Many special speeches were made to dedicate the event which included speakers such as Charles E. Flandrau, Chetanmaza of the Devil's Lake reservation, and Marpiyahdinape of the Sisseton reservation.

Following the commemoration, Abbie settled and lived just alongside the memorial at Pillsbury Point on West Okoboji Lake. She spent the rest of her days giving tours and telling her story to tourists during the summer months. She died on January 21, 1921, and was buried along with her family and the other victims of the Spirit Lake Massacre. In 1943 the Gardner Log Cabin at Pillsbury Point, Arnolds Park became a state historical site. It is still open and well maintained today.

As for Antoine Joseph Campbell, not much is known because he left few firsthand accounts of his life. He did continue to work as an interpreter for the Upper and Lower Sioux Agencies following the events of 1857. In fact, he played a pivotal role throughout the U.S. – Dakota War of 1862. During the War he and his family were protected because of their kinship ties with the Dakota Indians, but Joseph was forced to drive Little Crow by carriage to battles and act as his secretary for correspondence with Colonel Sibley.[10] After the Battle of Wood Lake, Joseph persuaded Little Crow to give him forty-six white captives, whom Joseph immediately surrendered to Colonel Sibley at Camp Release. In the years to follow Joseph continued to work for the U.S. Government serving as a scout on the Sibley expedition into Dakota Territory in 1863. He then lived with his family in St. Paul until 1870 when they moved to the Santee Reservation in Nebraska. By 1908 he moved to Montevideo, Minnesota where he lived with his daughter, Cecilia Campbell Stay, until his death on January 9, 1913.

> "Thus departed - - In the glory of the sunset, in the purple mists of evening, to the regions of the home-wind." –Abbie Gardner memorial

---

10 Gary Clayton Anderson, *Through Dakota Eyes: Narrative Accounts of the Minnesota Indian War of 1862,* (St. Paul: Minnesota Historical Society Press, 1988), 287.

BIBLIOGRAPHY

House Executive Documents. 1st Session, 35th Congress, Volume 2, Part 1.

"The Spirit Lake Massacre." *Roster and Record of Iowa Soldiers.* Vol. 6. (1911): 885-937.

"Typed Document on File at Hampton City Hall – 1951." Accessed on July 24, 2013. http://www.hamptonia.us/publicdocs/files/1951__Hampton_History_document_on_file.pdf.

Anderson, Gary Clayton, and Alan R. Woolworth, eds. *Through Dakota Eyes Narrative Accounts of the Minnesota Indian War of 1862.* St. Paul: Minnesota Historical Society Press, 1988.

Atkins, Annette. *Creating Minnesota: A History from the Inside Out.* St. Paul: Minnesota Historical Society, 2007.

Bakeman, Mary Hawker, ed. *Legends, Letters and Lies: Readings about Inkpaduta and the Spirit Lake Massacre.* Rosville, MN: Park Genealogical Books, 2001.

Beck, Paul. *Inkpaduta: Dakota Leader.* Norman, OK: University of Oklahoma Press, 2008.

Clodfelter, Michael. *The Dakota War: The United States Army Versus the Sioux, 1862-1865.* Jefferson, NC: McFarland and Company, 1998.

Daniels, Jared. "Jared Daniels Reminiscences." Daniels Papers. Minnesota Historical Society.

Duncombe, John F. "Mr. Duncombe's Address." *Annals of Iowa.* Vol. 3, No. 1. (April, 1897): 491-508.

Eastman, Charles Alexander. *Indian Boyhood.* Garden City, NY: Doubleday, Page and Company, 1915.

Flandrau, Charles E. "The Inkpaduta Massacre of 1857." *Collections of the Minnesota Historical Society.* Vol. 3. St. Paul: Minnesota Historical Society, 1880: 386-407.

Flickinger, Robert Elliott. *The Pioneer History of Pocahontas County, Iowa: From the Time of its Earliest Settlement to the Present Time.* Fonda, Iowa: The Times Print, 1904.

Folwell, William Watts. "Rescuing the Captives." In *A History of Minnesota.* Vol. 2. St. Paul: Minnesota Historical Society, 1924.

Gardner-Sharp, Abbie. *History of the Spirit Lake Massacre and Captivity of Miss Abbie Gardner.* Okoboji Lakes, Iowa: Abbie Gardner-Sharp, 1885.

Holmgren, David. "Sharp, Abigail Gardner." *The Biographical Dictionary of Iowa.* Iowa City: University of Iowa Press, 2009.

Hoover, Harris. "The Tragedy of Okoboji." *Annals of Iowa.* Vol. 5, No. 1. (April, 1901): 14-26.

Howe, Orlando C. "The Discovery of the Spirit Lake Massacre." *Annals of Iowa.* Vol. 6, No. 1. (April, 1913): 408-423.

Hughes, Thomas. "Causes and Results of the Spirit Lake Massacre." *Collections of the Minnesota Historical Society.* Vol. 12. St. Paul: Minnesota Historical Society, 1908: 263-282.

Keenan, Jerry. *The Great Sioux Uprising: Rebellion on the Plains August – September 1862.* Cambridge, MA: Da Capo Press, 2003.

L.P. Lee. *History of the Spirit Lake Massacre!* Fairfield, WA: Ye Galleon Press, 1857.

Lethert Wingerd, Mary. *North Country: The Making of Minnesota.* Minneapolis: University of Minnesota Press, 2010.

Natte, Roger. "Williams, William." *The Biographical Dictionary of Iowa.* Iowa City: University of Iowa Press, 2009.

Nichols, David A. *Lincoln and the Indians: Civil War Policy and Politics.* Columbia, MO: University of Missouri Press, 1978.

Oneroad, Amos and Alanson B. Skinner. *Being Dakota: Tales and Traditions of the Sisseton and Wahpeton.* Ed. Laura L. Anderson. St. Paul: Minnesota Historical Society Press, 2003.

Richards, Charles B. "The Address of Capt. Charles B. Richards." *Annals of Iowa.* Vol. 3, No. 1. (April, 1897): 508-524.

Riggs, Stephen R. "Dakota Portraits." *Minnesota History Bulletin.* Vol. 2. (1917-1918): 481-568.

Schenck, Theresa M. *William E. Warren: The Life, Letters, and Times of an Ojibwe Leader.* Lincoln: University of Nebraska Press, 2007.

Smith, R.A. "A Risk that Cost Two Lives." *Annals of Iowa.* Vol. 6, No. 1. (April, 1913): 424-428.

Smith, Roderick A. *A History of Dickinson County, Iowa.* Des Moines: The Kenyon Printing & Mfg. Co., 1902.

Teakle, Thomas. *The Spirit Lake Massacre.* Iowa City: The State Historical Society of Iowa, 1918.

United States, Office of Indian Affairs. *Northern Superintendency in the Annual Report of the Commissioner of Indian Affairs, for the year 1857.* Washington: William A. Harris, printer, 1858.

Wells, Philip F. "Ninety-Six Years Among the Indians of the Northwest: Adventures and Reminiscences of an Indian Scout and Interpreter in the Dakotas." *North Dakota History.* Vol. 15, No. 2. (April, 1948): 85-133; 169-215; 265-312.